# A
# Clean
# Death

## ADRIAAN VERHEUL

About *A Clean Death:*
Driven by fate, three men of very different ilk meet in the jungle. Oliver, a junior banker, is seeking answers about the death of his father, Johan. Captain Christmas leads a murderous community of armed men, women, and children, hiding from justice and looking for dignity in the forest. Young Davey is unemployed, fanatical about guns and sees a worldwide conspiracy in the disarmament of Christmas' group, which Johan had organized in an attempt to balance peace and justice. On a dare, Davey travels overseas to stop the disarmament. Their meeting, moral struggles, and the surrounding events cause each of them to lose something of consequence: illusion, conviction, or life itself.

ISBN: 978-0692047699

Cover photo by the author, taken at Maï-Pili,
Republic of Congo.

This is a work of fiction. Any similarity to places, situations, institutions, persons or events is entirely coincidental.

To those who lost or found a life on mission.

# ACKNOWLEDGMENTS

I am very grateful to friends and family who were so kind to read early drafts of this novel and provide me with their critical views on the book, its plot, and its characters: Mark Dalton, Nicole Edmison, Bernard Harborne, Jamie Metzl, Julie Maher, Fabrice Rousselot, Isabelle Sharman, Jo Walker-Sagar, and Tante Dee. Your feedback was tremendously helpful, especially when you disagreed without knowing it. Finally, I would not have been able to write this novel without the love and support of my wife, Mandy Sagar. Thank you, my love, for helping me realize an old dream and improve a Dutchman's English.

A.

# Part I
# Johan

ADRIAAN VERHEUL

# Chapter 1

## GETTING DAD

Oliver woke from his slumber with a dry mouth and a distant headache. He hated flying. Aircraft were crammed and always uncomfortable. Even his business class seat had a hard spot that no doubt would give him a backache as well. It was his first time flying business class, which suited his six-foot, three-inch frame rather well. However, he had taken too much of the alcohol offered by the flight attendant, and he now had to suffer the consequences. Groggy, he fumbled with the seat controls and arrived at a more comfortable position, half-leaning, half-lying. He opened the window shade and was surprised to find it was totally dark outside, except for a few stars, maybe a planet, and bright orange-yellow clusters of light below some towns or villages, he supposed, who knew where.

"You should go get Dad," his sister had told him. "You're better at this kind of stuff than we are, and we have kids at home in their last year at school." Or whatever her excuse was.

In any event, Mom wanted him to go, and that should be enough of a reason, no? His father, Johan, was dead, killed in

1

some faraway land that few of Oliver's friends would know how to find on a map. He had to look it up himself, again.

Dad's body was at the morgue of some City by the Water. Nobody knew exactly what happened. His mother, Charlotte, had received a phone call and then an official e-mail from Johan's employer, Gavels and Ploughshares International, or GAPI, stating in formal language that it was with the utmost regret, our heartfelt condolences, most unfortunate incident, official investigation under way, our prayers are with you et cetera, et cetera. Well meant, but vague, too; everybody agreed. The e-mail also asked for the next of kin to travel and sign for his body and personal effects. The flight from Connecticut to the City by the Water was paid for—business class, of course.

Mom was terribly upset upon receiving the news. She fell to the floor and could not bring out a single word for an hour. When the sobs subsided, she started asking questions. "I knew it, I knew it," she cried every five minutes or so. "One day he was going to get killed. I asked him so many times not to go—what did he do? What happened to him? I knew it, I knew it." Once she found a moment of composure, she turned to the business at hand. "Do I need to go myself to get him, or could one of you do it?" she said, looking at Oliver and his sister and the in-laws, wiping a tear from her left cheek. They had all rushed to Mom's home in shock, held her and then one another, offering help. Anything we can do, Mom. Really. Anything, Mom.

But all their faces showed hints that this shouldn't include taking a week or so off from work to travel halfway around the world to come back with the corpse and clothes and shoes of their dead father. Oliver could see it coming.

"Perhaps you should go, Oliver. You're good with paperwork and official stuff. We'll stay here with Mom," said his sister Louise. So there he was, flying over God knows where, looking for the bottle of water hidden somewhere in his seat.

Good with paperwork he was, indeed. One of three bankers at the local suburban branch of the third biggest bank in the country, he enjoyed the order he could bring to peoples' lives by helping them fill out the right forms in the right order. A mortgage, investment accounts, business or car loans—all easily achieved by responding to the prepared questions, page by page. It was the same with life, really. Do things in the right order, stick to the truth, and you should be in good shape. He felt he was in good shape, physically and financially. He had gotten good grades at school. Weren't exams just forms with a different label?

His wife, Mary, was a little messier. She was an elementary school arts and crafts teacher and seemed to be fond of a measure of chaos wherever she went. She was back at their home, in their country of green grass, family homes, and two-car garages, looking after their two young kids. He considered himself happy. They had a good life, and he thought he'd done well asking her to marry him—another prepared question and easy answer: yes. Of course, they had the occasional argument, like the one just a few weeks ago about the color of paint to put on the walls in the spare room. She wanted some bright shade of violet, but he couldn't possibly imagine his parents, especially Dad, wanting to stay there. That was all academic now. Oliver liked his life to follow a path he could anticipate, with no surprises—or at least as few as possible. In that sense, he clearly didn't take after his dad. Dad seemed to love to do things in a much less predictable way.

Oliver had brought with him the clipping from a national newspaper that mentioned the incident that had caused Dad's death. Oliver lifted it from his breast pocket and read it again, for the tenth time: "Disarmament specialist killed in City by the Water." The article was a collection of "yet to be confirmed facts" and speculation about what might have happened. According to the article, Dad had been found by the side of the road with "multiple gunshot wounds to the chest," assailants unknown, and no clear motive, although the article mentioned that Dad had been working to "take the guns away" from some rebel group that was hiding in the forest and was guilty of awful crimes.

Well, it wasn't really *taking* the guns. More like a voluntary surrender program with certain rewards, like goods and cash for anyone who brought in a gun, as Oliver understood it. Maybe some "local misunderstanding involving a rebel leader who named himself Captain Christmas" had led to the tragic incident, which seemed to have been planned in advance, not the "common opportunity robbery by local thugs."

Investigations were under way. Mom and Louise cried every time they read it but kept reading it nevertheless. Louise had taken a pair of scissors and, without saying a word, cut it from the newspaper, folded it neatly, and given it to Oliver. It might help you over there, she said later at the airport amid teary goodbyes, tapping his chest where the clipping was stashed in his shirt pocket.

He found the bottle of water, which had slipped into the space between the seat and the plane's cabin panels. He took a sip of water and then another. He rubbed his forehead and said to himself, almost aloud, what the fuck was he doing here, traveling across the ocean to a place he didn't know to fetch the body of a man he didn't know, either, to be honest? Sometimes, it had felt that his dad was not his father, at least not in the way Oliver himself tried to be a father to his kids, always there, watching them grow up every day, driving them to school, play dates, and doctor's visits, putting them to bed in a playful routine, pretending to be an elephant, a lion, or some other animal.

His own dad had never been there. It was always Mom who did the driving and the talking and the soothing and the bedtime stories. Oliver remembered going with the whole family in the old station wagon to the airport to pick up Dad from some long overseas mission.

In the beginning, he used to look forward to those trips. Dad always brought candy and presents. Most of the presents were supposedly educational—something cultural from some faraway tribe, a carving with barely recognizable figures of people and animals, or a weird hat with embroidered symbols that Dad tried to explain to them. "This funny hat will keep evil spirits away," or "the amulet will keep you dry if it rains."

Of course, the gifts never delivered on Dad's promises, and ever since the class bully had made fun of Oliver, relentlessly, when he brought a wooden carving to school for show and tell, he left all the artifacts in a cardboard box in his closet, hidden under a pile of soccer shirts. The candy was always good, though.

It was never clear to Oliver what his Dad really did for a living. When asked at school, he always repeated what Mom told them. "My dad is helping poor kids in the countries overseas," Oliver used to say, with a face that he hoped showed some pride. But the reality was that he'd rather have his dad at home to help him with school projects or play soccer, like the other kids' dads. But maybe he simply wasn't poor enough for Dad to care.

As a teenager, Oliver hated going to the airport to pick up Dad. It always got in the way of homework or something he'd set up with his friends or, worse, potential girlfriends. So, he got away with waiting at home, supposedly doing his homework. Dad's arrival at home would be announced by the noise of suitcases bumping into doorways and stair rails, footsteps on the stairs, and then Dad's head sticking through the doorway.

"Hey, Oliver. How are you, Son? Give me a big hug!"

Oliver used to get up from his bed where he was faking studying, give his dad an awkwardly quick hug (he could smell the stale air of airplanes and the sweat on his shirt), and say that he'd talk to him later. He had some homework to finish first. This suited Dad just fine. He was jetlagged most of the time and used to go straight to bed, with Mom, who would always emerge half an hour later with her hair wet, combed back, and in an off-center bun.

The cabin crew had sat down and strapped in, obeying the captain of the plane, who had just announced that landing was imminent. Oliver could see that for himself, looking through the window at the ever-closer green hills in the early daylight. The forest was dotted with patches of orange and yellow with red roads streaking through villages of clay huts and thatched roofs. He could see streaks of smoke where burning lines of fire were leaving the earth a messy charcoal gray.

The plane banked left, leaving him nothing but sky and tall clouds to look at. Through the windows on the opposite side of the cabin, he saw light reflecting off the waves on the water. The plane leveled, and as it descended, buildings started to streak by, a bit too close for comfort, he thought. He gripped his armrest, trying to make it look casual, hoping the pilots knew what they were doing. He was landing at the City by the Water, and he had no idea what was waiting for him.

# Chapter 2

## OFFICIAL FEES

Even though he had been close to the door, Oliver was still surprised at how quickly he was out of the plane's cabin. You spent half a day immobile in one place and leave it behind in seconds. He set foot on the metal platform outside the plane leading to a flight of stairs down to a group of uniformed people on the tarmac. Both the intense light and the strong heat of a tropical morning almost made him stumble. He reached for the rail and carefully made his way down, struggling to hold onto his luggage. He felt relieved to feel the hot tarmac under his heels.

At the bottom of the stairs, he saw a woman wearing one of the bright yellow vests of the kind traffic workers and airport personnel wear, with light-reflecting tape across the back and chest. She was dark-haired and broad-hipped and carried a fixed, warm smile as well as a sign that said, "GAPI welcomes Mr. Oliver."

As he walked up to her, he noticed various other people with signs like hers. They all carried some token of officialdom, either a collection of photo IDs, insignias sewn on a blazer, or a simple baseball cap with the logo of the organization they represented.

They all started to shout names and tried to make eye contact with him, hoping that he was their man. He shook his head and made his way to the big lady, giving her a nod.

"Mr. Oliver, sir?"

"Yes." He nodded again, trying to match her smile.

"Welcome to the City by the Water, sir. So sorry about your father, sir, please follow me."

She grabbed the handle of his carry-on luggage and walked resolutely to a collection of vehicles that apparently were picking up passengers. Looking around, he spotted several gatherings of people in various degrees of official garb, shaking hands with heels tight together, as if standing at attention.

"Welcome back, Your Excellency," he heard someone say, "I hope you had a most fruitful mission, Excellency."

Whoever the Excellency was did not respond. Oliver had never heard anyone called "Excellency" before, but he guessed from the body language on display that someone of high authority was about to step into a black Range Rover with tinted windows. Oliver caught a glimpse of the man. He quickly recognized him from the flight they'd just shared. He had been sitting two rows in front of Oliver. He was tall, wore a flowing light-blue robe and a big, gold watch. He had round cheeks and stern, dark eyes above a mouth that seemed frozen in a scornful laugh.

"Please step in the car, Mr. Oliver, sir," the broad lady said.

She held the door open for him. It was a boxy type of SUV with large tires and mud streaks on the side panels. He climbed into the rear seat, which was burning hot despite the car's air conditioning going at full blast. The driver nodded a greeting to the reflection of Oliver's sweaty forehead in the rearview mirror.

The woman turned to Oliver. "Mr. Oliver, sir, we will go to customs and immigration office. You stay in car. I will take care. Did you bring dollars?" A slight raising of her eyebrows accompanied that last phrase, as if it was almost unnecessary to ask.

"Well, yes. Why?"

"Official fees for officials. If you have a few twenties and a handful of singles, that would help. Also, passport and luggage stub, please, sir."

Oliver opened the zipper of his inner jacket pocket, which he had had tailor-made to make sure he didn't lose any cash, or worse, get ripped off by some pickpocket. He took out fifty dollars—two twenties and ten singles. He found the baggage stub stuck to the back of his passport and handed everything over to the GAPI woman, who put it in a pocket of her vest, which seemed to be there for just that purpose.

"Will I get a receipt?" he asked, all businesslike.

"No, sir. You will get passport stamped and suitcase back."

Oliver wondered about this arrangement. GAPI said they'd handle all costs, presumably including the costs of what began to smell of corruption. He was annoyed. Plus, the door was still open, keeping the car uncomfortably hot.

"Excuse me, Ma'am," he told her, as she was about to leave. "How come GAPI isn't covering this? They promised that—"

"It's the Resolution, sir," she interrupted, nicely but firmly, with a tone that should make it perfectly clear to Oliver that he had asked the eternal question that she had heard a thousand times before.

"GAPI Senior Council Resolution say write down all financial transactions and stay away from business that not give us receipt, like official fees," she stated matter-of-factly and shrugged her shoulders almost imperceptibly.

Oliver noticed it, though, and concluded he must have arrived in a world where the rules he knew no longer applied. His dad's world. He wished he could've asked him how to handle this.

The woman closed the car door and disappeared with his passport, baggage stub, and cash into a crowd of similar-looking people in a disorderly queue in front of a door, above which a sign said in yellow and red letters, "Welcome to the City by the Water."

Oliver sighed. Good thing the air conditioning was working. He was sweating through his trousers and felt his back stick to the seat, which had seen cleaner days. God knows what caused these stains.

He looked out the window. They were still on the airport's tarmac, and he could see the runway with some really old, if not antique, aircraft parked on both sides. Some planes had engines missing, and one of them, an old DC-3 or something, had laundry hanging from its wings, an assortment of ragged T-shirts, and shorts. Kids were playing under the fuselage, and a goat was tied to the rear landing gear, looking quite relaxed as it grazed in the long grass that grew next to the runway and in cracks in the tarmac.

Oliver noticed that the driver was staring at him in the mirror—had been looking at him all that time, probably. The driver smiled at him, a shy grin barely showing teeth. Oliver smiled back to the image in the mirror and said, "Hello." The driver turned and extended both hands through the opening between the front seats, with his left hand resting on the wrist of the right hand, which he extended for a handshake.

"My name is Henri, Sir," he said in a low voice. "I drive your father all the time. Nice man. Very nice man."

"You know, I mean, knew my father?" Oliver asked superfluously and shook the driver's hand. The drive held on a bit too long for comfort, even if comfort was intended.

"Yes, Sir, I drive him many times. Very nice man. So sorry, Sir. The Good Lord take care of him now. No need for drivers in heaven."

Oliver held his breath for a few seconds and looked back at the window to rest his eyes on the grazing goat by the plane. He did not need this reminder of why he was here, not right now. He needed to find his bearings before he could start thinking about getting Dad out of here.

"Sir? What was your name again?" It was rare for Oliver to forget names. As a banker, he prided himself on remembering his clients' names. He must be tired.

"Henri, Sir. Are you all right, Sir?"

"I'm tired, Henri. When do you think we can get to the hotel?"

"We go to GAPI HQ first. Bags and passports almost ready, then we go."

Oliver looked back at the building from which people were beginning to emerge, holding pieces of paper, accompanied by young and old porters on bare feet, carrying luggage. He spotted the broad lady in her yellow vest clutching what must be his passport and a white sheet of paper. She moved fast; the porter behind him carrying his bags (thank God, they made it!) was barely keeping up. The rear doors opened, and the heat and noise of the airport entered the vehicle at the same time as his bags.

Finally, they could leave the airport! The broad lady gave a folded piece of paper to a soldier on duty, who carried a weapon Oliver had heard about often but had never seen up close. A Kalashnikov—an AK-47—the metal shiny with age, its wooden stock unvarnished and scratched. The soldier glanced at Oliver, frowned, and then removed a dollar bill (his dollar bill!) from the folded paper, which he gave back to the lady. Without making any unnecessary move, the soldier slowly opened the gate. He smiled at Oliver, saying something to the other soldier at the gate, who smiled at Oliver too, as the car drove onto the road leading to town.

# Chapter 3

# THE PROGRAM

"Welcome! Welcome to the City by the Water GAPI headquarters, Mr. Oliver, I am Bruno, GAPI country director. Did you have a good flight? Please accept our most sincere condolences on the passing of your father. He was well liked, you know, indeed, well-liked by all. He was my friend, of course."

"Yes, yes..." mumbled Oliver, still shaking Bruno's hand.

Bruno was tall, lightly tanned, and in his fifties, or maybe late forties. Must be from some country on Mediterranean shores. He was wearing an impossibly white shirt with sleeves rolled up to make the dark hairs on his arms look even darker. He looked like the kind of guy who would play the lead character in the sentimental romantic movies Oliver's mother-in-law was fond of watching—a handsome and charming man, perhaps a little flawed in some dark way. Talked too much, perhaps.

Bruno had been waiting for Oliver on the steps leading into Headquarters, a dirty, green building with air-conditioning fans humming at every window and large antennas piercing the sky. Electrical wires hung across the compound, which was surrounded by a concrete cinder-block wall with dull shards of glass cemented along the upper edge, which had long lost any ability to harm a possible trespasser.

"Please follow me," said Bruno, taking a step up while making some sort of wavy gesture with his hand toward the long corridor that was visible beyond the door. One of the office doors was taped shut.

"Terrible, terrible, what happened to your father. That one with the tape is, I mean *was*, of course, his office. Such a nice man. I'm glad you could come. And so quickly. How is your mother holding up?" Without waiting for a reply, Bruno went on. "It must have been a terrible shock for her, of course, losing her husband like that, so out of the blue and so..."

Oliver had had enough. "Sorry, Sir. Losing him like that. Like what? What happened, exactly? It was not very clear from your end." It came out much sharper than he intended, but then, this Bruno chap could have been a little more forthcoming and not talked so fast.

"Ah yes, of course, of course. All will become clear later, later. Please step inside, Oliver, so we can discuss your program here. Everything has been arranged."

Bruno opened a leather-clad door into a well-lit and spacious office. Large, white leather chairs were arranged around a glass coffee table covered in piles of glossy magazines, newspapers, and various bound documents. A large mahogany desk was at the left. A smaller desk stood beside it with two large computer screens. The walls featured colorful paintings of bright yellows, reds, and blues, more than one of them showing women with naked breasts. Bookshelves held pictures of Bruno shaking hands or embracing various dignitaries, ministers, bishops, or diplomats, Oliver guessed. I don't want my picture to end up there, Oliver thought. Before he could check if Dad was among the smiling, handshaking crowd, Bruno guided Oliver into a chair while handing him a light blue folder labeled "Mr. Oliver's Program," with the dates underneath.

"As you can see, Oliver—can I call you Oliver?—your father was a good friend. He spoke about you often. Feels like I know you. Well, as you can see, Oliver," Bruno spoke in rapid-fire English, "we have a good program for you on the occasion of your visit, which I wish had not been necessary. Such a sad incident. But you are very welcome here, of course, of course."

"Thank you, Bruno." Oliver reciprocated the informality even though Bruno was much older. From his demeanor and that of Bruno's colleagues, Oliver could guess that he wanted to be looked upon as a senior official, due all necessary respect, *of course*. "But maybe you can tell me now what exactly happened to Johan, to my father. And why it happened. My mother is very anxious to find out. She always feared that something like this would happen."

Bruno leaned forward in his chair, drew in air through his teeth, cupped the fist of his right hand in his left hand, and tapped his chin with his crossed thumbs. "Well, we are, of course, conducting an official investigation, together with the local police chief, who is on your program for tomorrow. Can we go over your program first?"

Without waiting, Bruno flipped open the folder and rattled off the neatly entered program items in a casual manner. "Meeting with country director—that is now and me, of course—some paperwork at the office next door for your dad's personal effects and your temporary ID card, transport to your hotel for rest and meals—of course, GAPI will cover all costs, except beers, wine, or liquor, of course—then tomorrow we will visit the morgue for a formal identification and a quick meeting with the local police chief—a courtesy thing, you know. Then day after tomorrow, GAPI will hold a memorial service. I will speak, of course, and we hope you can say a few words on behalf of the family. Followed by a reception, hosted by us. There will be many who would want to pay their respects. You see, your father was really liked."

"I could say a few words, I think," Oliver said quickly while Bruno drew in another breath of air through his teeth, getting ready for another burst of words.

"Ah, that's wonderful, thank you so much. Then the day after the reception, our driver—your Dad's old driver, Henri—will take you to his apartment to help you prepare his personal effects for shipment overseas. If all goes well, your father's human remains will be ready for repatriation as well, and we can wrap up your program by the end of the week." Bruno unlocked his hands and gently clapped twice.

"Sounds good, Bruno, but are you sure that this will give us enough time for all the formalities?" Something in Bruno's words gave Oliver the impression that he was not as welcome as they said he was. Or did he always speak that fast? Still, he could understand it if they wanted him gone as soon as possible. Suited him fine. He was exhausted and not looking forward to any of the program points, except going to the hotel now for a rest.

"Yes, yes, plenty of time, of course, of course," Bruno said, moving forward to the edge of his seat, placing one hand on the armrest with his elbow pointed up, signaling he was ready to stand up. As he got up, he gently put his other hand on Oliver's arm as if to assure him of how well his program had been thought through. "Speaking of formalities, come with me next door. We have paperwork for you. Flora?" he called out to one of the women in the office next to his through the open door.

"Yes, Bruno, I have the file ready," said a pleasant voice from within the office next door.

Oliver could hear a chair scraping on the floor and the sharp tap, tap of high heels approaching on the hardwood floors. In the doorway appeared a striking woman. Flora was in her mid-fifties, or older perhaps—hard to tell. She was short, clearly overweight, but held herself as if she were a ballroom dancer at the top of her game. She wore a long, tight dress in yellow and orange tones, with some sort of flower pattern printed or woven all around. Oliver could not help but notice a tattoo on her right breast, the lines of which in faded red and blue were partly visible above the top of her dress. Another flower, guessed Oliver. She gave him a motherly smile as she guided him through the door. Oliver suddenly felt a bit embarrassed, as if he was some teenage kid needing some guidance in life. Actually, he did—at least in this place.

"Mr. Oliver, if you care to take a seat in our office, we can go over the paperwork." She closed the door behind Oliver, who had wanted to ask some more questions or at least say goodbye to Bruno, who had walked toward his desk with a determined look. Some other urgent or definitely more important business was demanding his attention now, and he waved a distracted goodbye to Oliver, nodding his head as if everything would be all right.

Once Bruno was out of sight, Flora turned to Oliver and threw her arms around him, pulled him down slightly to her height, and gave him four kisses, two on each cheek. Oliver could smell her perfume, mixed with the sweat of half a day's work. Where he grew up, strangers did not give people hugs and kisses like that, but he was in no position to protest. Different rules applied here, apparently.

Flora let him go, but held on to his fingers with both hands. "Poor Johan, poor Mr. Oliver, so sad, so sad. Please accept our heartfelt condolences. We will miss him so much. I'm sure your family will miss him too, very much, but you know, you can be very, *very* proud of him. He was such a nice man and so wise."

Flora's smile was turning into a grimace as she was trying to hold back tears. Oliver did not know what to say and mumbled a barely audible thank you. Flora did not let go of his hands as she looked at him for a response.

"Yes, yes, of course, of course," Oliver replied, unintentionally imitating Bruno. "It was a shock to our whole family, and we will miss him a lot," he said while wringing his hands free of Flora's affection. "I'm a bit tired and would like to go to the hotel and rest a bit, please. This is all a bit much, you know."

"I'm sorry, Mr. Oliver. Henri will take you to your hotel in a few minutes, but first you need to sign a few papers. The paperwork is here in this folder. Let me explain. Please sit down, please." Flora pointed to an empty chair by her desk.

Flora opened a large manila envelope and took out a cell phone and a bunch of papers. There was a temporary ID card, a disclaimer saying that Oliver could not sue GAPI for whatever reason "while under its care or using official GAPI transport," a three-page form to claim expenses, and a letter to the government saying that he, Oliver, would be signing for his dad's human remains and personal effects. There was also a letter, signed by Bruno, to the local bank where Johan kept his account, to inform them that Mr. Johan had passed away "in a tragic incident," and could they please freeze the account "effective today" and assist his son, Oliver, who would come to the branch to handle the balance. Oliver's banking instincts kicked in immediately. What balance? Dad was not very good with money, and Oliver was not prepared or even willing to pay for any large debts he may have left behind.

"The cell phone is for your local use, so we can reach you. The number is on the back," Flora continued. "Also, here is a list of safety precautions you should take around here. Unfortunately, our security team leader, Tom Jenkins, is out in the field at the moment, but as soon as he comes back, he should give you a briefing about the overall security situation. For now, you are OK. This part of town and your hotel are safe. So, are you ready to go to your hotel now, take a nap maybe?"

Flora leaned toward him, again with that motherly smile. Oliver got up from his chair and caught a glimpse of the flower tattoo as he looked down to answer Flora.

"Now *that* would be a good idea. Should I go out front to meet up with Henri?"

It was a short drive to the hotel. Oliver was looking out the window, but did not really have much of a chance to get an idea of what this town was like. They passed green trees and dirty streets, small, one-woman stands selling vegetables and bottles with a pink liquid in them, and endless streams of seemingly reckless two-stroke motorcycles with helmeted drivers and passengers, leaving a gray-blue mist over the road as they passed and avoiding skinny dogs roaming for scraps. Lots of people walking too, some on bare feet. Oliver felt people looking back at him as he looked at them.

"Henri, there are a lot of motorcycles on the road here. What are they? Some kind of taxi?"

"Yes, Sir, like taxis, but drive like crazies. If you need transportation, you can get one, but not safe."

"Well, I better stick with you, then," Oliver said as they drove into a walled compound that was hiding a complex building with several oddly sized towers and balconies.

The hotel looked nice. It was right on the water and offered an impressive view of the mountains in the distance. Henri carried his luggage into the hotel lobby, which was filled with discolored chairs in fake yellow leather and abstract statuettes in dark, polished wood.

Nearly all the chairs had people in them, all men. A few businessmen were talking on their cell phones, and there was a fat man in uniform, a high-ranking officer it would appear from the colorful markings scattered on the shoulders, chest, and arms of his uniform. He looked bored, as did the rest of the crowd. Some were sleeping. Henri said something to the lady at the front desk in a local dialect.

"Ah yes, Mr. Oliver, welcome to our hotel!" the lady said a bit loudly.

Several heads in the lobby turned toward him. The fat officer turned his head, looked Oliver up and down, then got up and left the hotel, after kicking one of the sleeping men awake. The man jumped up, pulled a key from his pockets, and ran to the camouflaged jeep in the hotel's courtyard, followed by the officer in slow motion.

Oliver felt uncomfortable, but could not think about it much since he had his hands full with filling out a guest registration card, writing down the code for the Wi-Fi Internet connection, and handing over his passport to be copied. He would ask Henri what was going on tomorrow.

The room smelled of mildew, but Oliver couldn't see any. The shower was OK, but the towels were small and thin. He looked at himself in the small mirror, standing naked in the middle of the bathroom. He determined that he did not look *that* tired. He'd been putting on a bit of weight the last six months, but not quite enough to affect his tall, athletic frame. Still looking good, he thought.

Oliver wrapped a towel around his waist and opened the windows. He had a corner room with two windows, one looking over the water reflecting the tall clouds above the mountains, the other with a city view of red metal roofs and green tree canopies. About a mile away, there was a smoke column rising above the trees—burning garbage, probably. Overall, not bad a view, he told himself. He pulled out his laptop and entered the code for the Wi-Fi connection. It worked.

# Chapter 4

## TWO YEARS EARLIER

The plane that took Oliver to the City by the Water had been flying that route for years, its schedule unchanged, coming and going once a week, one of maybe four planes that serviced that location. You could not quite set the clock by it, but its approach let people know that it was time to go to work, school, or church, or wherever their daily routine took them. Before the plane reached the city, it descended over the mountains and the forest. Most of the people that lived there, in small, seemingly unorganized clusters of thatched huts with walls of sticks and clay or cow dung, had gotten used to it passing overhead. But there were always a few dreamers who saw themselves on that plane, coming back from a place faraway where they would make their fortunes and then come back to show off and share some of their wealth with the village, maybe marry the pretty daughter of the village chief. Once the plane had gone from sight, the dream passed, too. Back to working the land or clearing the forest.

One day, about two years before Oliver would sit in that plane and look down on the forest, Captain Christmas could hear the plane before he saw it, the rush of air over the wings combined with the high-pitched roar of the turbine engines. On that day, the plane's noise reminded him that it was time for his weekly sermon to his followers, to boost their morale or keep them in line. He had been giving these sermons since they left their country, *their* country. Forced to run before the guns of the others, who now as before ruled the country that God had given to *them*, promised to *them*. The revolution had failed, but their time would come.

Christmas walked slowly to the clearing between the huts. The floor was dry, the compacted earth swept clean this morning. Shredded plastic bags and tree leaves were burning slowly on a pile that held the ashes of the previous day's dirt and of the days before. He was accompanied by his lieutenants, Mirage and V-6. Christmas was the smallest of the three and clearly the oldest. His hair had turned gray, and the strength of his youth had long gone. His eyes were bloodshot and tinged yellow, but his stare could still compel respect among his people. *His* people.

As he entered the clearing, he saw that the soldiers stood in formation and came to attention, as expected. The sergeant major, his old friend—neighbor, in fact, from well before the exodus—gave the command. His troops executed well. Few had shoes, and their shirts, bleached in the sun of a thousand afternoons on the march, were full of holes. But there was still pride in the way they brought their salute, their right fist raised high and their heads turned down and to the left, rendering their necks vulnerable to a blow by a club or machete.

Power and submission. Keep it that way, boys, said Christmas to himself. Some of his younger soldiers had been born after the exodus and had never seen their land. They were among his most fanatical believers. Maybe it was easier to believe in something you had never seen.

Mirage and V-6 came to attention. Christmas walked on, alone, toward the middle of the clearing. He stopped, facing his troops in front of him. To his right were the women, girls, and those boys not old enough to fight. All were silent, waiting for him to speak. They knew more or less what he was going to say, but there was always something new. Christmas knew well that you had to keep things fresh, surprise your people from time to time, even shock them if you had to, to keep them on their toes. Today, he would start like always.

"What is our fight?" he shouted.

"For our land and our freedom!" Everybody shouted loud enough.

Good, because the other day, Christmas caught a young woman who was nursing her baby and not even moving her lips. He did not want to have to repeat what he did then, but obviously, it was still having an effect.

"Where is our land?" he asked.

"Where the clouds climb the mountains and the sun shines on us!" Everybody was pointing at the sun, which at that precise moment was hiding behind a cloud.

"Who gave our land to us?"

"The good and powerful Lord!"

"Who took it away from us?"

"The others!" They all booed and looked angry. Even the toddlers joined with pouting lips in imitation of their parents.

"Will we return?"

"Yes, we will! Yes, we will! Yes, we will!" Everybody fell silent. Mothers hushed their babies and children.

"At ease, soldiers. Let us pray," Christmas said, folding his hands and looking at the sun with eyes closed. He could hear his troops bring down their arms from their raised salute and fold them behind their backs.

"Dear Lord," he began quietly in his usual timid fashion. He wondered sometimes if his followers knew he faked it. They must at least wonder about it sometimes, but would never dare to say anything.

"Dear Lord, please look upon my children with mercy. Show us the way to the land you promised us in response to our prayers. Be kind to your soldiers. Give them courage and strength. Stop the bullets fired at us in midair. Please guide us on our righteous path to a life of peace—peace in our hearts, peace in our land. Our land, dear Lord, which is occupied by the others who do not fear you like we do. The others, who won't listen to a mortal's plea, do not worship you the way we do. Dear Lord, send them hardship and pain to make them see the truth. Their land belongs to us. Let them leave quietly, or if they stay, teach them respect for our peaceful reign over the mountains and fields that are ours to tend to. Amen."

"Amen. Peaceful reign!" his followers chanted.

Christmas knew how to pause for effect. This time, he would give his speech a little twist.

"How long have we been at this camp?" he asked softly.

Without waiting for a response, he answered himself. "Almost three years now. This is too long. Yes, we're surviving off the gold we dig up from the mud, from the hills and rivers—the gold we sell on the market, so we can buy guns and ammunition, a few cell phones, and clothes. Yes, we grow some food for ourselves. But is it enough? Some of you shiver with malaria, because we have no medicine. Some of our babies die of disease. There is poison in the air. See my eyes—they are burning from the poison in the air."

"Yes, we suffer. We suffer for our land. We miss our land. But we're not getting any closer to our land. Does anyone outside even know we're even here? Is our struggle respected? The *others* have managed to persuade the world, many other countries, and international organizations to be against us. Everybody is against us. They say we have committed crimes—in our land and in this land. They say that you and I will be arrested when they catch us and put us in jail or worse. They will kill us and feed us to the wolves or sacrifice us to the evil spirits in the water. They will take our children and fill their heads with their lies."

"We shouldn't allow people to forget us. They should know us and remember us, so they will understand us and support us. We need to be. Our struggle needs to be on people's minds. But we have no TV stations, no transmitters, no stories for newspapers to write. Shall we give them a story to write?"

Christmas paused again. He looked around the crowd, which looked right back, waiting for the next line.

"Shall we give them a story to write?"

"Yes!" The crowd came back, but it sounded hesitant.

"Indeed we shall, indeed." Christmas sighed and turned to face his soldiers. "Soldiers, tonight, I shall order you to leave on a mission. You will venture out and bring us back new hope. Change our future to look like our glorious past. Remember, we have nothing but enemies. They are all against us, all of them. They are all to blame for our misery. Anyone who stands in our way does not believe in our holy mission, and you should strike them down. Strike them down and give them mercy. Strike quickly, and do not waste your bullets. We need bullets for when the army comes, and come they will. Come they will, my brothers and sisters. Be ready. Mirage and V-6 will issue instructions."

The session ended after the usual declarations of loyalty by the followers, professing their admiration for the leader, describing the land they missed in lyrical terms, or giving prayers for the heroic soldiers. Christmas did not really like this part, but he needed to keep up the notion that theirs was a democratic movement, unlike the others. Plus, this way, he could measure how much they liked him still. Or maybe "liked" was too nice a word. Frankly, he did not give a damn if they liked him. Respect would be nice. Fear would be good, at a minimum. He knew that they all remembered what he did to the nursing woman. He could tell from their looks, but they never said anything about it.

That night, Christmas and his lieutenants led their troops in a single column on the path they had used a few times already in preparation, occasionally cutting down a branch or some tall grass that had grown to obstruct their road to their target, a village about a six-hour march away. This would be the first time they would target this particular village.

Christmas often wondered how the army had never been able to find them. They had tried, though. They flew helicopters over the forest—that is, if they could pay for fuel—and sent out patrols to find their base. But the forest had become their ally. And the rains too, he thought. The rains were on their side and would dissolve their fighters' footsteps and the tread marks of motorbikes. The rain would also feed the forest to grow moss, grass, thistles, young trees, and vines to cover their tracks, hide their huts, and provide cover for their purpose. That, or the army must be horribly inept. Or corrupt. Or both, thought Christmas, smiling to himself.

The soldiers marched on, his officers' bare feet in rubber boots, the foot soldiers wearing flip-flops. Christmas was always scared that one day somebody would lose a flip-flop heavily impregnated with a scent that could give the army dogs a trail to follow to their camp. He therefore made his troop account for their flip-flops after every excursion. If one was lost, the offender was beaten and given no food for a week.

The village was asleep. Some fires in front of the huts were still smoldering, the embers emitting pinpoints of orange lights. The fighters had come to a rest just outside the village on the edge of the forest. V-6 would give the command soon, before the village awoke in the light that would stream in straight blasts through the trees.

Their mission had three simple goals: steal as much as you could—food, goats, chicken, clothes, tools, and guns (if they could find any); kill all the men and older boys who could give chase; and for any fighter who wanted to, rape the women and girls as a reward. Any villagers who resisted at any stage would have their skulls split by a dull machete or be forced to eat their own intestines or those of their children. Most fighters had inflicted horrors before or at least seen them inflicted. Yet some young ones were still nervous and stood ready with wide-open eyes, breathing through their dry mouths with lower jaws extended. Those on their first excursion were fidgeting, nervously looking at their commanders and peers for clues on what to expect, one clasping the grip on his weapon and then letting go, as if milking a goat.

They would do what was needed, Christmas knew. They had no other way to deal with their anger or find some respect in the eyes of their peers. If they did not participate, they knew he would deal with them himself.

Christmas saw the first signs of dawn on the horizon, a hue of blue and orange visible above the canopies of the forest. Somebody stirred inside a hut, and a chicken made its way to the remains of a fire, pecking the soil for bits of food.

He nodded at V-6, who raised his fists and yelled, "For our land! Against all who stand in our way!"

He fired a couple of rounds from his weapon into the huts of the village. The shots ended the troops' nervousness, and they fanned out, running and shouting, with weapons pointing at the huts. Their shouts were answered by anxious screams and angry cries coming from within the huts. Christmas' fighters forced everyone out of the huts and made them kneel in a line in the open space that was in the center of the village. Some resisted and were quickly killed, their blood blacker than red in the early light—a young man, a girl, an older woman, a father who held onto a toddler, the toddler, too. A few escaped from the huts on the edge of the village by running into the forest. Christmas did not mind; if the wild animals did not eat them, they would come back and serve as witnesses for their cause.

The villagers were forced on their knees, and Christmas moved forward to face them. It always amazed him how few people fought back and how the majority actually obeyed his orders when the alternative was immediate death, even if death would come in the end anyway. What were they thinking? Obedience would buy them time at best, nothing else. He despised them. A large woman near the end of the line started to plead with them, her hands raised to the nearest attacker, asking for mercy at least for the children, please, please.

Christmas gestured to Mirage, who in turn pointed to one of his junior troops. "You. Cut off her lips." The young man leaped forward, threw the woman on the ground, and with the help of two of his fellow fighters pinned her down. He pulled his knife.

# Chapter 5

## THE REPORT

The massacre made headlines, tentative at first because information was scarce, but for one week now, the local newspapers reported on any latest snippet of information, every day displaying the same photo of a police official looking down on the murdered villagers laid down in a row, covered with colored sheets and frayed plastic tarps to shield the reader from the cruelest of sights. It was still pretty bad.

Bruno skimmed the headlines as usual. He needed to know what was going on in the local media and what folks on the street might be thinking. For details, he preferred to wait for GAPI's own report on the investigation. Not the "official" police report, which would be full of unwarranted accusations, usually had the numbers wrong, and always made an appeal for more equipment, vehicles, and money, so they could finally punish and prevent these terrible inhumanities in the future.

Since nobody wanted to talk to the police anyway, Bruno had sent his own people to investigate. Some of his best local staff members, with always at least one woman, had gone undercover and talked to survivors, visited the site itself, and shopped and gossiped at the nearest market. He liked these people, especially the oldest, a gentleman named Ibrahim, who appeared to know everybody and everything. In spite of Ibrahim's past that, some people said, might be just a tad darker than shady, Bruno had learned to trust him and never had a reason to regret his trust.

Flora knocked on the open door. "Bruno, Ibrahim and his team are back. They're working on the report. It's almost done, but they just wanted to talk to you about something. Something they said you need to know." Flora was not smiling.

The team came in, Ibrahim first, then another man and a woman whose names Bruno could not recall that quickly. Ah yes, her name was Aisha. As they walked in, slowly and modestly, their expressions were sober and sad. They sat down on the seats around the coffee table and recounted their story. This one was bad, boss—much worse than the other attacks. The killers had used knives and axes, instead of bullets, and had eviscerated all the victims, tied them together with their entrails, and bludgeoned their faces to a pulp. They had raped the girls and had left the pretty ones alive and intact, saying they would be back for more, laughing. One pregnant woman had her fetus replaced by the head of her husband, using sharp sticks to hold it all together.

Bruno inhaled sharply and was going to say something, but couldn't. He felt sick to his stomach and looked away from his visitors, out the window, to look for comfort in the blue sky. His mind was racing with thoughts of disgust, anger, and revenge. What is wrong with these people? Fuck these bastards. Find them, and shoot the motherfuckers on sight, no questions asked. No, cut off their dicks, their balls too, and let them bleed to death. Fuck. Shit. Damn.

Bruno drew another breath, slowly this time, and forced this train of thought to stop. Human as his gut reaction might be, this was not what GAPI stood for; this was not what *he* stood for. Hold on a second. Count to ten. Think of the victims. Think of the physical and psychological trauma these beasts had inflicted on the living, who probably wished they had died with the rest. Their pain and anguish must be unbearable. This poor country. These poor people. In the end, he was here for them, he reminded himself.

"There is one more thing, Boss," the woman said softly, with a face tired from empathy, pity, and suppressed anger.

Bruno, his eyes closed, nodded for Aisha to continue. She touched his arm and explained that, this time, the news of the massacre was more likely to spill across the borders and get international attention. Christmas had killed a foreigner, a Polish aid worker who had come to see what the village needed, maybe a school or a pharmacy. The aid worker had stayed in the village overnight and was raped and killed with the rest. Some survivors said it was Christmas himself who had done it, leaving her face intact to be recognized. Apparently, he had called her a "spy for the others," her death "a message to the world." It was not clear if Christmas knew beforehand if she was in the village.

Although Bruno didn't know the aid worker in person, he knew the organization she worked for. Shit, this one hit close to home. It could have been one of his own people. The team left his office after he thanked them deeply with handshakes and hugs. When death is near, touching the living gives comfort.

He closed the door, sat down again, and allowed himself a few minutes with his head in his hands. Then he opened the door again and asked Flora to come to take notes for the preliminary report he had to send to his headquarters, which had been asking for it impatiently for days now with increasingly haughty language, as if the massacre had happened for them exclusively.

# Chapter 6

## BACK TO ROOT CAUSES

During this whole episode of the massacre, about two years before his death, two years before his son Oliver would be looking for the bottle of water in his business class seat, Johan had been back home on leave. He had heard of the massacre through the media and mentioned it to his family over a dinner at Oliver's house.

"Jesus, Dad," Oliver had said. "Do you *have* to bring this up? And over dinner too, in front of the kids?"

To emphasize Oliver's point, Charlotte had kicked him under the table. Johan got the message and apologized quickly.

"By the way, Oliver," he said. "Do you need any help cleaning up the garden—you know, getting rid of these leaves and branches in the back, so the kids can run around a bit?"

With an inaudible and invisible sigh of relief, everybody agreed that this was indeed the right thing to do.

Johan had long ago learned that his family preferred not to talk about his job. That was OK with him most days, but it meant that, by the time his leave was up, he really looked forward to going back to his colleagues and friends out there in the field. They spoke his language and could read his mind. He was going to go soon.

Johan got back to his office a few days after he cleaned out Oliver's garden in a light drizzle. It had given him a cold that caused him some discomfort in the dry air of the plane taking him back to his place of work. He would miss his family for sure, but he was happy to be back in the heat, back to his office, back to his mission. He drove his rusty 4x4 into GAPI's compound and parked it in the spot that had been assigned to him, three cars away from Bruno's shiny luxury SUV, which was closest to the building's official entrance. Nice way to remind him of the pecking order at work, he thought. It was time to get another parking spot soon and move closer to the entrance.

His office was pretty much the way he had left it. He greeted the pictures on the wall, mostly GAPI public relations posters of happy women in well-tended fields or children in school uniforms writing their ABCs. He wiped the dust off his chair and sat down behind his desk. His computer would be filling up after startup with e-mails and reminders that would keep him busy before he could return to running his programs.

At this moment, he was running a really nice program that involved the promotion of the private sector. Money from abroad had helped him set up a project that helped local farmers export their crop of small thistles. The thistles grew abundantly in the red soil, provided no standing water could accumulate, requiring a system of ditches and canals to manage the flow of water coming down from the sky every so often. The thistles had no value here. You couldn't eat them. In fact, they were called "serpent heads" in the local language, good for chopping off only.

Fortunately for the locals, some businessman abroad had started a story, backed by "independent research," that a tea made of its flowers could stop baldness, even grow back hair.

True or not, the story generated enough of a demand to allow the poor farmers here to earn a decent living off the silly pride of gullible foreigners who had the luxury of not having to worry about more existential things.

Johan had pulled together a cooperative to finance and build a central factory to receive the thistles, remove and dry the flowers from the thistles, package them with a fancy label, and ship them off to balding men around the world. Based on this success, he was now trying to sell an extract of the leftover product as an aphrodisiac pill. Hey, if it can grow hair, who knows what else it can help grow? Besides, "serpent heads" had a nice phallic ring to it.

The project had done well, providing employment in an area that had been plagued by crime and roving bands of murderers and robbers, not to mention Captain Christmas. With the money earned from the serpent heads, the villagers could now afford to pay for protection. Private security guards with decent weapons patrolled the fields and villages, and even the police had shown an interest in actually doing their job, in exchange for money for fuel (or booze). The project was now running itself, so it was time to move on to something new.

Flora stuck her head around the doorpost. "Hi, stranger!" she said with her usual warm smile. "How was your leave?"

Johan got up and gave her a big hug. He really liked Flora. She never failed to make everybody feel at home. They chatted a bit about family and work. Johan caught up on local gossip, which was dominated by speculation about the massacre that was still fresh on people's mind. Apparently, military intelligence had sent a big shot down here from the capital because of the foreigner that was killed.

Flora went back to her office but was back within two minutes, looking quite serious. "Bruno wants you to drop everything and come to his office. Now!"

Johan got up, grabbed a notebook and pencil from his desk, straightened his hair, and marched determinedly down the corridor to Bruno's office. He knocked on the open door and stepped in without waiting.

"Ah, Johan, there you are. Welcome back," Bruno said from his chair, gesturing for Johan to come forward.

To the right of him sat an elegantly overdressed gentleman, wearing a lightweight suit with a silk tie. He was in his fifties, thin hair impeccably combed over a balding head, with dark and penetrating eyes that were sizing up Johan in a manner that betrayed a high level of self-confidence.

"Let me introduce to you Ambassador Zamorski of Poland." Bruno waved his arm toward his guest in a gesture that would fit in a classical ballet.

Johan shook hands with the ambassador, who did not bother getting up, forcing Johan to make a bow. Bruno went on to explain to Johan the purpose of his visit.

"His Excellency has honored us with his presence today to convey his government's great dismay, if not disgust, with the recent massacre committed by Captain Christmas and his gang, which as you may know, Johan—who is just back from leave, Excellency—involved the very tragic death of one of the ambassador's compatriots. The ambassador knows that we have a good presence on the ground, of course, and has come to discuss how his government can help to deal with Christmas. Of course, GAPI has worked with Poland before in other countries, successfully I might add, Mr. Ambassador."

Bruno leaned back in his chair, making another theatrical gesture to indicate that he would now leave the stage for his visitor to continue. The ambassador acknowledged the gesture with a nod. Turning to Johan, he started to speak in a deliberate and emphatic manner.

"Nice to meet you, Johan. Let me assure you that my government is not going to let this slip. Our parliament has raised all sorts of hell and is bent on seeking justice for our victim and all the other victims of Christmas. Our minister of foreign affairs *himself* has made public statements to the effect that our patience has run out. We cannot stand these atrocities anymore."

At this point, Zamorski showed a bit of indignation in his face but then continued with a professional, neutral expression.

"The local government *has* to take this more seriously. We have made various *démarches*, at the highest level, I can assure you, and we have offered to pay for training and equipment for the police and the army. As you know, we were already involved in human rights training, but this time, and I do not need to tell you how exceptional this is for my government, we have even agreed to provide *lethal* equipment, including ammunition."

At this point, Zamorski raised his eyebrows, tapped his armrest with his fingertips, and looked around to gauge his audience's reaction.

Johan nodded, very seriously, he hoped. His first thought was that the police would probably sell their allotment of ammunition on the black market to supplement their salaries, since they rarely got paid. Prices would drop, and more scum criminals would be able to buy ammo to feed their AK-47s.

Zamorski raised his shoulders and spread his hands before him before he continued. "But that's not all. It's the desire of my government to see that justice be done. We have always been keen supporters of the fight against impunity, as you may be aware. In this case, too, we would like to see Christmas and his followers prosecuted and punished in accordance with the severity of their crimes. Now, my government is willing to put some funds aside, about twenty-five million dollars, for some sort of program that would help achieve that goal *and* bring stability to this country. It has suffered long enough, don't you think?"

Johan quickly glanced at Bruno when Zamorski mentioned the twenty-five million. GAPI's offices overseas were rated by headquarters by how much money they raised, and Bruno could not help but produce a badly hidden smile at this opportunity. Twenty-five million was no small change.

"Of course, of course, very sad indeed," Bruno followed up with a serious look. "It has gone on much too long, and GAPI is ready to help where we can, of course, in *full* coordination with donor governments such as yours and, of course, with the local government. Johan here has broad experience in working with vulnerable communities and would be our point person for any sort of program that would meet our common objectives. Have you by any chance heard of our serpent heads program? Very successful, sustained impact, totally green, community involvement, et cetera, et cetera..."

The ambassador had actually never heard of the program but was not about to show his ignorance.

"Yes, I must have heard it mentioned once or twice. Please refresh my memory. What exactly was it about?"

Bruno waved his hand at Johan, who knew it was his turn to speak, but was not quite sure at first how to explain the success of a fake anti-balding herbal remedy to the obviously balding diplomat. Soon, he found his usual groove.

"Gap in the market abroad for certain cosmetics, chemicals only found in thistles growing in this area, organizing local farmers, building on local expertise, work with local authorities, and engagement with women groups in a conflict-sensitive approach."

You could never know in advance which phrase or concept would trigger a potential donor's interest, so Johan and Bruno, like most other GAPI officials, had developed a habit of providing a broad range of slogans and then guessing from bodily or spoken language which one seemed to carry the most appeal.

So far, no phrase seemed to have made an impact on Zamorski, who was listening with an interest that appeared as genuine as it was neutral, no doubt the product of thousands of hours of diplomatic meetings with a premium on not displaying any emotion that could be read the wrong way.

"Very impressive, very impressive," Zamorski said without any apparent conviction, turning his head from Johan to Bruno. "I've no doubt that something like that will be required, but we're really more interested in justice for Christmas. Get him out of the bush into jail, with his fighters. Render him harmless. Take his guns away or something."

"Well, sir, that sounds very much like something we would be able to pull together," Bruno said with a smile. "Johan, what do you think? Would that work?"

"Yes, I think so. With the right mix of incentives, we may be able to get some of these guys out of the bush, with their guns, too."

Zamorski perked up. He may have liked the mention of the right mix. Johan, encouraged, continued his argument.

"You see, Sir, there is a bit of a problem with the idea of putting them in jail. That only works if you can find them and arrest them, which will require military capabilities that do not exist for the time being, not in this country. First, to find them, we need intelligence that you can only get from drones or satellites, with high-definition cameras and infrared night vision—things like that. They are well hidden, these criminals. To find them will cost more than fifteen million or so. GAPI doesn't really do that kind of stuff; nor does the army. And if and when you should find them, they're likely to put up a stiff fight against an army that's not quite willing or prepared. Or they could flee deeper into the bush or across an international border. Nobody wants that. So, we need a well *calibrated* mix of positive and negative incentives to get them out of the bush as peacefully as possible."

Bruno, smelling success, jumped in. "If I may add, Mr. Ambassador, and sorry to interrupt you, Johan, it will also be extremely important, of course, to address the root causes of violence in this country. You see, our solution will have to be *sustainable* so our investment—I mean *your* potential investment—is not going to waste, but will instead make a lasting contribution that will show your country in a positive light for years to come. This may require some additional projects, of course."

"Of course," Ambassador Zamorski said with polite enthusiasm. "That sounds very good and constructive. What do you propose as a next step?"

The next step to add twenty-five million to my portfolio, thought Bruno, may also be a next step to a promotion out of here to a nice, senior-level post at headquarters. "Well, usually we prepare a draft *non-paper* for a potential donor, you know, like an unofficial proposal with some preliminary terms of reference and costing, and see if that's more or less in the direction of where your government would like to go with this twenty-five million. Johan here will start working on such a paper right away, Sir, so you can have that in a few days for consultations with your capital."

"Excellent!" said Zamorski, shifting forward in his seat and putting both hands on his knees, ready to push his body up to a standing position to indicate that the meeting was over and that he had other important matters to attend to.

"We will look forward to receiving your draft in the next few days," he said. Looking at Johan first, then nodding at Bruno, he did get up quickly, shook hands, and left Bruno and Johan behind to ponder the next steps.

Johan looked at Bruno, who had gone back behind his desk. "I'll get right to it, Boss. Looks like a great opportunity for us—interesting challenge and all of that stuff. Great money, too. I'm just not sure if we can do something about those root causes you mentioned."

"Yeah, yeah, I know. But we need to *say* something about it, don't we? Maybe for a follow-up project or something. In any event, when you do the costing, make sure you end up around the thirty million mark. Now, off to work. About six pages of narrative should do, a one-page costing. Can I have your draft by close of business tomorrow?"

# Chapter 7

# THE RIGHT MIX

Justice for Christmas. Sounded like a wonderful idea. Easier said than done, if ever it could be done at all. And what the fuck was GAPI going to do about root causes here with twenty-five million in cash, maybe thirty? In this country, to fix root causes, you'd need billions and billions, as well as a complete overhaul of the government and the economy, if not history itself, Johan thought while typing away on his keyboard.

The words on his screen were not quite as cynical as his thoughts—quite the contrary. The draft non-paper was shaping up rather nicely, he thought, hitting a concerned yet optimistic tone. It was all there: solid objectives, well-crafted implementation mechanisms, an inclusive consultative framework, involvement of central and local government, but essentially GAPI in charge. Or to be more precise, Johan himself in charge. This was a big deal. Maybe he could be in a different parking spot in a few months, closer to the entrance. He wrapped the draft up that same day, but decided to sleep on it and look at it again tomorrow morning, review the whole thing, and write a *killer* executive summary for the first page. He drove back to his apartment, opened the windows, and poured himself a glass of the expensive scotch in his fridge to toast the sunset over the water and the mountains in the distance.

The following day, he wrapped up the draft at his desk and looked over the executive summary once more:

    Disarmament and Stabilization Program (or
    DSP)

    Costs 32.5 million dollars, implemented by
    GAPI with Government support.

    Program objectives include the peaceful
    disarmament of Christmas' fighters through the
    provision of positive incentives, including a
    "citizen kit," comprising essential household
    items for each functioning firearm
    surrendered, and a custom-designed
    reintegration package to enable former
    fighters (FF) to find durable employment based
    on existing skills or preferences. FF will
    need to subject to screening to determine
    their eligibility for forgiveness and for
    various integration alternatives.

    DSP runs parallel to and in complementarity
    with enhanced military pressure on Christmas'
    militia as a negative incentive. Those found
    to have committed the gravest crimes will not
    be forgiven and will be prosecuted.

"Exactly!" Johan said aloud to his computer. "This is it: give up your gun and get a bag of goodies and a job *or* stay in the bush and get killed. Unless you deserve it, like Christmas! It's all about the right mix. What say you, assholes?" he asked his screen, as if the "FF" were hiding behind it.

    DSP is intended to contribute to local and
    national stability by removing the threat
    posed by Christmas and by a smooth transition
    of FF from a life of violence to making a
    peaceful contribution to society.

"Hmm, that sounds a bit bland. How about..."

```
    from a life of violence to a dignified
existence as a free citizen in a peaceful
society.
```

A bit pompous but sounds better. Now for the root causes, he thought.

```
    The DSP is expected to be integrated into a
comprehensive country strategy to address root
causes of conflict through additional program
components for which additional funding will
be sought in due course.
```

That should do it, Johan thought. He sent the draft to Bruno and, just to make sure, decided to walk down the corridor, poke his head around the corner, and announce the arrival of the draft in Bruno's e-mail inbox.

"Hmm, non-paper, I hear. Very good. So, more projects for Johan soon?" Flora said to him in a teasing voice.

Johan laughed, shrugged his shoulders and without giving any response walked back to his office. He might as well start work on the larger project document that would lay out all the details and budget requirements. He made a mental note to include some extra 4x4 vehicles for program management. And spare tires. His car was showing signs of aging, especially the shocks, and the last thing he wanted was for it to break down, especially in this town.

# Chapter 8

## DUCK BILL

Bruno came off the phone with Zamorski. The non-paper had been a great success, a smash hit, he concluded. Although Bruno had padded the budget with another 2.5 million in program components for a total budget of thirty-five million, Zamorski's bosses back at the foreign ministry in Warsaw basically took it all, hook, line, and sinker, for a contribution of thirty million, promising to work with other donors to find the remaining five million, subject to a complete project document and additional talks.

"Holy crap! That's utterly brilliant," Johan exclaimed after Bruno briefed him on his phone conversation with Zamorski. "Now what?"

Bruno smiled and pointed at Johan. "*You* are going on a field trip, my friend."

"OK, and where is it I'd be going?" asked Johan, moving to one of the chairs to sit down. This could be a long conversation.

"You'll take Ibrahim and Aisha, as well as our security guy, Tom Jenkins, to visit Christmas in the bush. Unless we have some kind of understanding with Christmas, or at a minimum keep him informed of what's going on, we will get nowhere, of course. We can't just show up one day and say, hey, we need your guns, and in exchange, we have some really nice benefits for you."

"Wait a minute," Johan interjected nervously, realizing that this was different from drafting a non-paper from behind his desk. "You want us to go talk to that murderer, at his base, with his people? Jesus, Bruno, they just killed one of us."

"I know, I know. And trust me, I feel the same way you do, Johan. But we've got to be serious about this, especially for this amount of money."

"Can't the government people do this? I mean, isn't it their job to deal with Christmas? This is what I had in mind with this 'inclusive consultative framework' in the non-paper. Remember that phrase?"

"Look, if the government had wanted to do something about Christmas, they would have done it by now. I'm also not sure, but don't quote me on this, that you can trust these guys to deal with Christmas, or deal with us for that matter, in one hundred percent good faith. We need our own channel of communications to Christmas. So, get your gear, and talk to your team. Ibrahim has already made some preliminary contacts. Flora has all the paperwork, of course. Go, go."

Johan admitted to himself that this one was not going to be like the serpent heads program, where meetings with the thistle farmers were always jovial—more like family gatherings than formal business meetings. In fact, the DSP could be dangerous to everyone involved.

As Johan stepped out of Bruno's office to collect the travel authorization and other papers from Flora, he made another mental note to put in more money—this time in the "miscellaneous" budget line—for additional security guards.

To get to Christmas, you had to travel in two stages. Although you could do it in one day, Johan preferred to arrive well rested and had pleaded for a stopover. First, they would go upriver on a boat, spend the night at the town by the foot of the mountains, then leave early in the morning in a convoy of 4x4s to a spot where they would change to motorcycles to navigate a narrow path through the tall grass. Henri, Johan's driver, and one other driver had already gone ahead by road with the 4x4s and would meet them at the dock.

For this occasion, they decided not to take the usually overcrowded public ferry. It took too long, especially if the current ran fast, which it always did, so the ferry had to hug the shoreline to make progress, often causing it to run aground.

Flora had booked them on the "VVVIP Express," a fiberglass speedboat that was once the property of the son of the former head of state (more properly remembered as the decadent son of a crazy despot). Outfitted with a shiny new outboard, the vessel had been baptized Prayer for Prosperity and was captained by a skinny gentleman who called himself Skipper Boutique.

Boutique had plied these waters for a dozen years or so. He knew the river well, with its shifting sandbanks and treacherous eddies. Johan looked at him closely as they sped over the water toward their evening destination. Boutique appeared intensely focused on the water and the shorelines and hadn't said a word to them during the whole trip. Every now and then, he would reach a flat stretch of water and push a lever forward to let the boat accelerate. Only at that point would he look around briefly at his guests to size them up. They were all fitted with faded, orange life vests, as if sinking was imminent. This was GAPI policy after Boutique had hit a submerged tree trunk a few years back and one of Johan's colleagues, who could not swim, had fallen out of the boat while taking a picture of the landscape. He almost drowned trying to keep his expensive camera out of the water. Johan hated wearing a life vest. It made them look helpless.

Ibrahim gestured at Johan to come closer. "Boutique doesn't say much," shouted Ibrahim over the whine of the engine and the whoosh of the water. "But he remembers every single person he had in his boat and when. Sometimes he would remember the *why*, too. He's a friend of mine. A good one to have in these times."

Johan could barely hear it, but he got the message and gave Ibrahim a thumbs up to let him know he understood and approved. He was wondering if he should tip Boutique and decided that he would take Ibrahim's cue. GAPI would be paying Boutique a small fortune anyway if this new program were going to take off.

They made it to the town dock well before sunset. Henri stood there waiting for them and helped them offload their luggage. Their hotel, a bright, pink-colored building with large panels of smoked glass, was a few hundred yards away. After checking in and changing clothes, they met for drinks and dinner to go over the program for the following day. Henri was invited to join them, but he chose to stay with a family member instead, cashing in on the daily mission allowance meant to offset the cost of staying at a hotel. Nobody blamed him for that.

While Johan was formally in charge of the mission, it was Tom Jenkins and Ibrahim who did most of the talking over dinner. Tom insisted on going through a whole range of scenarios on what could go wrong, from hostage-taking to celebratory gunfire. He was ex-military and was fond of quoting his former drill sergeant, "Duck Bill," whom he credited with saving his life on multiple occasions through applying the wisdom Duck Bill had shared with his soldiers. Johan never really understood any of Duck Bill's sayings, but he was happy to humor Tom whenever he brought it up.

"As Duck Bill would say, 'Better prepared than pretty,'" Tom said. "Now, let's go through the protocol for using these radios to check in with call sign Hotel Quebec one more time."

The team complied since GAPI was strict on applying security protocols, if only because they wouldn't pay out any insurance or pension if you happened to die on a mission and had not followed protocol.

Ibrahim had more interesting things to tell. Speaking in a low voice in the half-filled restaurant, head bent forward, looking from Aisha to Tom to Johan and back again, he explained what they could expect. He tapped on his three smartphones laid out on the table next to his plate.

"I spoke to a few people, first military intelligence, who will be very interested to hear from us after the mission. The local battalion commander has been warned, and they shouldn't mistake us for Christmas' guys and shoot at us, as long as we wear GAPI hats, right?" He looked around twice to make sure.

"Good. Now don't ask me how, but I reached out to Christmas' people. In fact, he has a few liaison officers undercover here in town, and Boutique, our friend from the VVVIP Express, set up a contact for me. So, the good news is that they've agreed to meet us. The bad news is that we have to travel blindfolded for the last hour on the back of a motorcycle driven by people that Christmas trusts."

"Shit," said Tom. Johan put a hand on his arm to stop him from going into another Duck Bill story about the obvious dangers of driving blind.

"It is what it is," continued Ibrahim pragmatically. "Better for a first meeting to give in to their requests. We can always ask for something else down the road. Now, I tried to explain what this meeting was about, but they seemed more interested in finding out how *senior* Johan actually is. They haven't had an official visitor in a very long time, and they were worried about getting the protocol right. Plus, they want a case of Chivas Regal Scotch and six bottles of Ubamolak Cream Liqueur."

"Oh dear," said Johan, looking at his watch, "we better get to a liquor store before it gets completely dark. Or better maybe get up early tomorrow morning. And, *of course*, I'll have to pay for this out of my own pocket." Another thing to hide under *miscellaneous* in the project budget, since he suspected that any future meeting with Christmas would require heavy alcoholic lubrication. Sometimes, he wished GAPI's financial rules against bribes were not so strict. Imagine the things you could get done.

Ibrahim had more to add. "And could we please—they actually said 'please'—bring mosquito nets, some antibiotics, aspirin, two soccer balls, and"—he picked up one of his phones and tapped on the screen to read a note or an e-mail—"a box of generic sildenafil?"

"OK, we can do the nets and the medicines. Soccer balls are fine too, pretty harmless. We're keeping the press out of this, but just in case anyone asks, we can now obviously pretend that we're on a humanitarian mission. Perfect. But then we need to go shopping tomorrow early, before we leave. What was that generic thing you mentioned again?"

"Sildenafil."

There was a pause where Ibrahim appeared to be uncomfortable, apparently looking for the right definition. Not a very long pause, though, because Aisha surprised everybody with a sudden, low-pitched giggle as she explained: "Apparently, our friend Christmas has difficulties charming the ladies. He wants us to bring him the cheap local version of Viagra."

"Ah," chuckled Tom. "Christmas can't get his tree up anymore!"

They all laughed, a bit too loud perhaps, as a few heads turned at nearby tables.

"In any event," concluded Johan, "this is a great opportunity for GAPI, and perhaps for Christmas and this country as well. Tomorrow we go shopping, and then we meet Christmas in the bush. Now, who is in for a *digestif*—Ubamolak on the rocks, perhaps?"

# Chapter 9

## MEETING CHRISTMAS

The trip to Christmas' HQ camp was grueling. The initial part by car wasn't so bad—just the usual bumps and potholes. They stopped at a turn in the road on a steep hill slope with an impressive view of the tree-covered mountains ahead with a tall, blue sky overhead and large thunderstorms barely visible at the horizon.

They were met by several motorcycles and their drivers, two of them armed with pistols. A logistical hiccup delayed their departure, because they had not counted on having to transport the cases of booze, the two soccer balls, the box with mosquito nets, and the bag with medication.

Ibrahim worked his usual magic on the phone, and after a half-hour wait, during which Aisha was chatting and laughing with the "motos," two other motorcycles appeared. They tied down the cases of booze while Johan watched carefully. God forbid the bottles got broken under way. That wouldn't be a good start; it might even be a deal breaker.

The team was carefully blindfolded underneath their GAPI hats, while Henri—who would stay there to wait for their return—looked on. They took their seats on the back of the bikes and took off, holding onto the frame of the bike or the driver's shirt as best they could.

Johan was terrified. He had absolutely no control and felt the bike turning, trying to keep his upper body in line with the bike's vertical position. There was no way to anticipate the turns or bumps in the road. One particular downward slope seemed to last forever. The driver kept gaining speed, swerving to pick the best path among the rocks and the holes in the dry mud. Johan feared that at the end of the slope there would be nothing to stop them, a ravine into which he would be launched in total darkness, suddenly free of the rattles and shocks, floating free to a death he could not anticipate.

Once the convoy turned uphill again and slowed down a little, Johan was able to relax a bit, allowing him to think ahead. He needed to be better prepared for this meeting than he actually was. So many things could go wrong. Little misunderstandings could have big consequences.

He knew few details about Christmas other than what he had read in the papers and in Tom's intelligence briefs. A man with blood on his hands, for sure, to whom he would have to be polite. There was speculation—rumors, actually—about his wealth derived from the gold his people dug up, as well as about alleged cash transfers to government officials. A charismatic and brutal leader to his people, who called him Christmas apparently because he believed—or at least made his people believe—that he was an incarnation of Jesus Christ and that only under his leadership would they receive the gift of freedom in their own land, the promised land.

Until such time, he bestowed little gifts on his people every now and then, while keeping them poor and deprived. Of course! The mosquito nets, the booze, the soccer balls, and the medicine. Fuck. Johan had fallen into this trap with his eyes wide open. GAPI was bringing them their rewards for murder. No, Johan *himself* was bringing the gifts. He bought them with his own cash. Shit. At the end of the day, though,

GAPI was going to bring them the bigger gift of a better life—or so Johan justified to himself.

Johan could hear the village through the din and rattle of the engines—a goat bleating, the sound of utensils on a metal pot, and the cheers of little children. He could feel them touch his legs as they drove by. He quickly checked if the pocket with his wallet in it was still buttoned up. It was.

Finally, the motos slowed down and stopped. Their blindfolds were removed, and gingerly they dismounted, stretching their legs and backs while squinting in the bright light. The motos took off, with the case of whiskey and the bag holding the rest. Tom made an idle gesture to stop them. They had arrived in the middle of a small clearing in the forest. Tom scanned around to see where they had come from, but the edge of the forest didn't seem to have a visible opening or path.

In a circle around them stood a large crowd of women and children, staring at them intensely. Some were smiling, but most had a stern expression on their faces. Johan noticed that their clothes were old and ragged. A boy of about twelve was holding a ball made of strung-together plastic bags. About half of the crowd was on bare feet; the other half was wearing worn-out flip-flops. One did not need to be a doctor to see that this was not a healthy community, Johan noted. There were nasty coughs, weeping eyes, and open sores on dry and dirty skin. Involuntarily, he reached down to scratch his legs.

A command rang out, and the circle parted to Johan's right. In the opening appeared a group of armed men in military formation, marching toward GAPI's team to the tune of a rhythmic song belted out by a group of young women behind the troops. Johan had no idea what they were singing about and looked at Aisha, who knew several local dialects, for a clue, but Aisha didn't reveal any emotion. Another command rang out, and the troops halted their march and came to attention in front of the team, which had adopted a somewhat formal stance themselves, not knowing what to expect.

The camp fell eerily silent, except for the rustle of goats and chickens outside the human circle. "Present arms," a man on the left of the troops shouted. The men presented their weapons, holding them stiffly in front of them. Tom watched carefully and started making an inventory in his head: thirteen AK-47s, four G3s, one RPG launcher, two Q13s (how did they get here?), no uniforms, some bayonets, a few pistols—Makarovs from the look of them—and one light machine gun. Jesus, that kid holding it couldn't be older than thirteen. Before he could finish his list, he heard the lieutenant or sergeant, Tom couldn't tell what rank, shout again:

"Please, all rise for the arrival of His Excellency, president of our movement and supreme commander, Captain Christmas."

The command was superfluous. Everybody was standing already, most with their eyes on Johan, Aisha, Ibrahim, and Tom, who had a hard time standing still.

The crowd opened across from the troops at attention to make way for a small man with bloodshot eyes in a clean camouflage uniform without any rank insignia. Johan and the team had to turn to face him. Christmas walked up to Johan, extended his hand, and smiled.

"Welcome!" he exclaimed. "Welcome, senior program director of Gavels and Plowshares International, the esteemed Mr. Johan and distinguished members of his team. Welcome, welcome."

Christmas shook hands with everybody, except Aisha, who made a very modest bow instead. "Please, Mr. Johan, my honor guard is ready for your inspection." Christmas stepped aside and gestured Johan toward the neatly aligned troops.

Johan looked at Tom, mildly panicked, and whispered: "What do I do now?"

Tom maneuvered himself next to Johan. "Walk past them, look straight past the first line, and above all, look serious, man," he said in a low, soft voice. "Pretend you are a general, or Bruno, and when you're done, give them all a stern nod."

"Tom is my military adviser, Captain Christmas, Sir," Johan explained while he followed Christmas to the troops.

Christmas pointed to a straight line drawn in the dust, apparently expecting Johan to follow it, which he did. Johan followed Tom's instructions as best as he could. He could feel the eyes of the crowd on him. The fighters themselves looked straight past him, with shoulders straight and nostrils flared. Johan tried not to think of what he was actually looking at. Murderers. Rapists. What have these knives done? *Keep your mind on the mission.*

At the end of the line, he turned sharply to face the troops and gave them a firm nod in acknowledgement that they passed his inspection. Even so, he had the distinct feeling that it was, rather, he who was subject to their scrutiny. Christmas gestured to his lieutenant, V-6, who ordered the troops to stand at ease.

"Mr. Johan, Sir, would you be so kind as to address my people and explain, just a few words perhaps, who you are and what you have come to discuss with me. You see, I believe in transparency. My people have a right to know who is in their midst. I'll speak to my children after our private meeting. We will go there." Christmas pointed to an improvised tent, from where emerged sounds of bottles and glasses clinking. A large pot was steaming over a charcoal fire outside. "But first, you speak."

Johan feared that his lack of preparation would now become evident. What was he going to tell these people? That everybody on the globe thought that they were scum and that we've come with a plan to render them harmless? Better keep it neutral and hope and pray that his words would not come out too awkwardly, he thought.

"Good morning," he started, even though he did not know if time had moved beyond noon already. "I have come, with my colleagues here, to discuss with your leadership if there is any way we can help you, and your children, improve your lives. You have lived in the forest for a long time. And it's probably fair to say that your presence here has caused a problem for the government and some members of the international community. We, Gavels and Plowshares International, are here to help you solve that problem."

He looked around to gauge the response of his audience. There appeared to be little acceptance or even understanding of what he just said. Expressions hadn't changed much from their earlier neutral curiosity. He could see an older woman with missing front teeth shake her head. Was he on the wrong track? What had he said? Did they even understand his language? Maybe they never heard of GAPI. Better explain.

"GAPI is present in over one hundred countries, helping people who are poor to have some income and fend for themselves, especially farmers. Sometimes, we even buy them plowshares to work their land. We also help countries to build institutions, like courts and parliaments, so we give people the means to govern themselves. That's why we have the *gavel* in our organization's name, to help people make good decisions through good organizations."

Still no reaction. The old woman had stopped shaking her head and was now looking up to the sky. He saw a teenager look at him with vacant eyes and poke his nose. He was losing them. If he ever had them. Hell, these folks wouldn't know what a gavel was, anyway. Better wrap up quickly.

"I look forward to a productive and constructive meeting with your leader and, hopefully, go back to my leadership with the good news that we will be working together toward a fair and prosperous future. I thank you."

No applause. No changes in expression, either. That fair and prosperous bit was taken directly from a GAPI brochure, which he thought was pretty good. But not good enough here, apparently. He turned toward Christmas, who offered a wry smile and gestured him toward the improvised tent, made of wood, plastic sheets, and old curtains. It was open on three sides.

Inside the tent was a throne-like wooden structure with a picture of Jesus Christ behind it. The likeness had an exaggerated aura around it in all the colors of the rainbow, placed in such a way that, when Christmas was seated in front of the picture, it would—with a minimum of imagination—appear as if the aura was his.

The seat to the right of Christmas was a size smaller than the throne and reserved for Johan, then Tom, Ibrahim, and Aisha on three plastic chairs in faded red. To the left of Christmas were his lieutenants, Mirage and V-6, as well as two elderly gentlemen who were introduced as village elders. They were wearing—with great pride and poise—dirty three-piece suits that were several sizes too big, with a string for a belt and a stained polyester necktie. Tom would mention later that he thought that the suits could have been his old man's, since his father had given his entire formal wardrobe away to charity after retirement a couple of years back, and who knew where the charity had shipped them off to. Outside the tent, the members of the honor guard (not the most appropriate name in any circumstance, Johan realized) had spread out to form a security perimeter.

"First, refreshments!" exclaimed Christmas. The table in the middle of the semicircle was filled with glasses, bottled water, and the bottles of Ubamolak, now graciously presented with the compliments of the host.

The visitors asked to be served bottles of water, carried to them by identically clad young girls, who presented them with two hands, like a sommelier bringing a priceless bottle of Burgundy wine. Christmas was brought a whole bottle of Ubamolak for himself, while his subordinates were served a glass of the creamy liquor with a bottle of water on the side.

"Now," Christmas said in a serious tone, after taking a swig of Ubamolak straight from the bottle, "what can I do for you?"

"Well," Johan answered, "this is also about what you can do for *your* people."

Johan ventured into a long story that involved the hopelessness of the poor people here, a limited outlook for the children, no education or healthcare, how patience was running out on the part of the local government and the international community, and the recent massacre was not exactly helpful...

"Wait a minute!" Christmas interrupted angrily. "You have come here to accuse me of murder? What is this? I'm the leader of a peaceful political movement. These people here are refugees, hiding from political persecution. Where is your proof?"

He banged his bottle of booze on the armrest and looked around triumphantly, garnering murmurs and looks of approval from his assistants and the audience beyond the tent. The two elderly gentlemen smiled a toothless smile.

"Are you the police? Have you come to arrest me? Ha!"

The GAPI team was quiet. Aisha was biting her tongue and held a handkerchief to her forehead. Ibrahim sat there listening with a neutral expression; he'd heard these claims before and appeared not surprised. Tom got increasingly nervous and was slowly turning his head to map out possible escape routes.

Johan was taken aback at first but managed to recover. "Let me assure you, Excellency, that we have most certainly not come here to arrest you or accuse you of anything. To be clear, we have money for you and your people."

"Money? How much?"

"Well, it all depends on how effectively we can cooperate. Here is how it would work. Your people can come to us, and we can give them some tools to work the land or repair clothes. Or, we can send them to a business or to a school to learn new skills. Maybe become a businessman and get rich. To be frank, Sir, your people are not going to get rich here."

"You are wrong. Maybe they will not get rich with lots of money, but they are rich right now. Yes. You see, they have a dream that's worth *billions*, a dream that will take them to their land, our land, and *I* will lead them there," Christmas stated emphatically. He leaned over to Johan for emphasis, revealing the likeness of Jesus behind him.

"But, just for the sake of argument, Mr. Johan, how would this all work?"

Johan explained the process in as simple terms as possible. He assumed that everybody outside and inside the tent was listening, which was correct.

"Well, as I said, everybody can come to us and join a program that can help you get a medical checkup and treatment, some land, and agricultural tools to become a farmer, grow thistles, or learn some other trade, like selling scratch cards for cell phones or driving a moto. Now, we will pay for all of that in the beginning, but then anyone who joins the program now will be on their own later, making money and no longer be poor. Maybe they can buy a house or even a car down the road. The kids can go to school and learn to read and write."

So far, so good, Johan felt. Everybody was listening now. He moved to the sensitive part.

"For your soldiers, we have the same program and something else. And to get that something else, they will have to hand in their guns."

Christmas didn't show any reaction and took a lazy swig from his bottle, which was now half-empty. Mirage and V-6 instinctively put their hands on the pistols in their belt and looked at Johan with suspicion.

"So, when you hand in your weapon, it has to be able to shoot, of course—machetes and knives don't count—then you'll get a 'citizen's kit' in return. A bag with all sorts of items that will help you start a life as a civilian, like clothes, kitchen utensils, cooking oil, a broom, even a box of condoms. Yes. And most of them won't be arrested when they leave the bush. They will need to go through some sort of forgiveness screening, so any crimes they *may* have committed can be forgiven. The guns will be destroyed further down the road. Now, for this to work, we'll need your cooperation and support. There's potentially a lot of money available for this program," Johan closed optimistically.

Christmas had begun to look bored and tired. He put up his hand to indicate that he was going to speak now. Leaving everyone in suspense, he first finished the bottle of Ubamolak. He waved at one of the serving girls, who quickly came with another bottle.

He looked around the crowd slowly from left to right, resting a cynical gaze on everyone for a few seconds and ended with Johan, who was subject to Christmas' bloodshot stare for at least ten seconds. Johan noticed drops of Ubamolak trickling down his chin.

"Great. Just great." Christmas took another pause, then a deep breath. "This is bribery. You are buying my people, so they all leave from here and leave me defenseless, without my loyal troops. You want me to get arrested by the army. You are taking away their dream of going home, instead giving them plowshares and gavels and bicycles and automobiles and cell phones and whatever else you have in that citizen kit of yours. Very nice. *Very* nice. But let me ask you this, *Mr.* Johan from Gavels and Plowshares International, what do you have in your bag for me, for the president and spiritual leader? You want these people to go elsewhere, they will do so. But only if they follow me, their general, first. They will go when *I* give the order to go. So, what do *you* have in your bag for *me*, Mr. Johan, Sir?"

Johan knew immediately he had no real answer to this challenge. His non-paper did not cover this; nor had he thought about it much. The whole idea was to get rid of Christmas, not to reward him. Perhaps it *was* bribery. He needed to stall.

"Well, Mr. Christmas, that's still being discussed informally, and many options are on the table. For now, it's important that we establish contact and have a dialogue, so we can prepare a good program *with* the input of the beneficiaries—the people here, I mean, including yourself, of course."

"Very well, then," Christmas said, leaning forward and putting his hands together as if he was going to start a prayer. Indeed, he continued with eyes closed and in a raised voice, almost singing, in a sharp baritone: "Sometimes, I go deep into the forest by myself, and I pray to the Lord. And the Lord listens to me. The Lord hears my prayers; he hears those of my children. The Lord has promised me that they will return to our land and that they will find riches there and fortune. The Lord has given me command, and He trusts me, and only me, to lead my people to the Promised Land. To lead them to freedom. Amen."

"Amen," it came back as a whisper from inside and outside the tent.

Christmas stood up and announced that the meeting was over. Johan and the others came to their feet too, taken aback by this sudden move. Christmas went around to shake hands with the GAPI team, including Aisha this time, without saying a word and then left the tent abruptly, holding on to his bottle.

The GAPI team stepped outside the tent toward the clearing. The moto drivers were already there, gunning their engines and filling the air with the gray-blue smoke of worn-out, two-stroke engines. Somebody must have warned them to get ready. Johan looked around to find Ibrahim. He needed his perspective. Or that could come later. For now, at least, a quick acknowledgement that it went OK, because he wasn't so sure himself. He spotted Ibrahim still standing by the tent, talking to Mirage and V-6. They were having a businesslike discussion, with Ibrahim taking a few quick notes. Ibrahim looked up and saw that Johan was looking at him. He said goodbye to the two lieutenants and walked over to Johan.

"It's OK, Boss," Ibrahim said with a smile. "Christmas will play along, but he has a few conditions that he didn't want to say in a public forum like that in front of everybody. Let's get out of here first, and we'll talk about it tonight."

The trip back from Christmas' camp was a lot easier than the way in. For some reason, somebody had forgotten to give the order that they be blindfolded, but even with eyes wide open it would've been impossible to get precise bearings or even a rough indication of either position or heading. They were driving through tall grass and ten-foot high foliage with many turns and changes in elevation.

At one point, they encountered a group of men covered in mud carrying large plastic bags, escorted by an armed fighter, going in the opposite direction. Once they were out of earshot, Johan's moto driver turned to face him, letting go of the handlebar to point over his shoulder.

"Gold!" he shouted above the rattle of his engine.

Once they got to the cars, Ibrahim gave an account of his side meeting with Mirage and V-6. It was pretty simple:

Christmas must appear to be in command under any circumstance. He wants international recognition as a leader of his movement and assurances that he won't be prosecuted, anywhere. A global amnesty for himself and for his senior commanders. He also wants a senior military rank, brigadier at a minimum, and a decent pension back in his country, a house with strict security, with enough rooms for his wives and bodyguards, and a bulletproof car. He was fine with starting a "small pilot" program, not too far away from his camp, as long as the weapons were not destroyed and kept under lock and key, for the time being, and the army stayed at a safe distance. Ibrahim would talk to the army about that. He thought that they might just go along in exchange for a bit of intelligence.

"Dang!" said Tom, "and here I was thinking the geezer was drunk or crazy. Or both. Seems he's a few steps ahead of us."

Henri was happy to see them come back from the bush. While he drove them home, Johan was quiet and mostly looked out the window, watching the landscape go by in the setting sun. He realized this was not a slam dunk by any means. There was a lot of ground to cover, politically as well as operationally, before GAPI could meet the promises he had just made to Christmas and his followers. He wondered if Christmas would let his people go if they wanted to escape from their current reality against his orders. From what he had seen, if he was in their shoes and given the chance, he would. But then again, he was not among them.

What a trip this had been. His back ached from the moto ride. He felt dead tired.

# Chapter 10

## A STRONG SIGNAL

Johan got back to his apartment late in the evening. He took a shower and wrapped a cloth around his waist. The mosquitos were out in force, so he couldn't open the door to his balcony to enjoy the view over the water. He looked at his phone and saw that the signal was strong today, meaning he could have a decent Skype conversation with his wife, Charlotte. He hadn't heard her voice or seen her face in a while. After today, it would be really good to see her. He poured himself a large scotch and ice before he typed in her username.

"Hello? Johan?" He heard her voice before the video kicked in.

"Hello, my love." Now the video came online, and he could see her beautiful face smiling at him.

At first, they talked about how much they missed each other. Despite the distance, they had managed to keep their relationship deep and affectionate. She told him she was busy; the kids and the grandkids were OK. They were doing well at school. Johan hesitated to talk about his day, but did so anyway.

"Hey, guess who I met today? Captain Christmas, at his base camp, in the flesh."

"Oh my God, is that not the guy who committed that horrible, horrible massacre that was on the news the other day, when you were on leave? Were you safe? What was it about?"

"Well, I should tell you first the good news, that this is a big opportunity for GAPI and for myself, as well. There is this donor who wants to put in thirty million for a program to neutralize Christmas and get his fighters out of the bush. So, I had to go and start negotiations with Christmas. Today. I just got back. And, yes, I'm safe."

"But that's a totally repulsive man from what I read. Shouldn't you leave this to the military or police?"

"Well, yes, maybe, but darling, it's thirty million or more I'll likely get to manage. That's huge—maybe worth that promotion that you always said I deserved, maybe get a job at HQ so we can move to San Francisco and be together."

"Maybe so, love. But I don't like it at all—the idea that you'll be traipsing off deep into the jungle to meet with that man. He's a real killer. I'm going to be worried sick that you're going to get hurt."

"Don't worry about it, baby. It's going to be all right. I'll tell you more about it next time. Tom says it's going to be OK. You know Tom. So relax."

"Now, speaking of relaxation," Johan said in a mischievous voice, "let me show you...what I'm *not* wearing. But only if you show me yours first, you gorgeous woman."

# Chapter 11

# MORAL HAZARDS

The following weeks at the country office were rather hectic. Johan had to put together whole reams of documents. First, a so-called "goal pyramid," where actions formed the basis to create outcomes that support objectives toward the big goal at the top. It helped visualize the project for everyone, especially donors. At the top, he placed "peace" and "stability." Might as well have been "motherhood" and "apple pie," thought Johan.

What really mattered to him as a manager was the stuff that would allow him to make a name for himself, the lower rung of objectives and activities: "provide sustainable livelihoods for former fighters (FF)," or "remove weapons from groups and individuals posing risks to the population." Better still was the objective that read, "promote forgiveness and reconciliation," although Johan had to admit to himself that he had absolutely no idea how one could get a victim of Christmas' massacres to look the perpetrators in the eye, let alone forgive them.

Second, a detailed proposal for the Disarmament and Stabilization Program, with whole paragraphs lifted from previous project documents as far as some of the technical stuff was concerned, like procurement and financial management.

The hard part of the proposal was to describe the potential risks involved. The more he thought about it, the riskier it got. Were they not creating a reason for people to buy weapons and join Christmas' band to get the program benefits? Unemployment ran high, and people might be willing to make sacrifices to get ahead in life even a little bit, pick up some extra cash, and perhaps even get a job on the way out of misery.

What about the security of his own staff? They needed the local army or police involved. What if nobody qualified for forgiveness? They'd have to go to jail. But wouldn't they make a run for the bush first? And never come out? Dozens of other problems came up in his head, too many to write down in the proposal. Maybe too many to convince any potential donor that their money was in safe hands and would be well spent.

"Let's kick that particular can of worms down the road," he sighed. Then he started a paragraph called "Inclusive Implementation Management Committee," the body that would have to solve these problems later, and even better, share in the responsibility if things went south.

Finally, there was the budget itself, now swollen to fifty million. There was the original thirty million from Zamorski and then another twenty million in "Deep Stabilization" projects to tackle root causes, which were conceived so broadly that they could cover pretty much everything, from motorcycles for the local police to stationery supplies for the tax collector's office to medical supplies for the local maternity ward, the rental of an earthmover to dig the ponds for a fish farm, a herd of goats—anything you wanted, really, as long as it was processed through GAPI's office, of course. With Johan himself in charge, he smiled at his computer screen.

Bruno had told him that getting the extra twenty million would not be a problem. He had been to see Blomqvist at the national capital, and together they had made the rounds of the local embassies, as well as government offices. The DSP had caused quite a buzz. It was *the* big thing on the diplomatic circuit, and no embassy could afford to miss out on this opportunity to be *involved*, to do something.

Pledges of support were rapidly coming from all sides. The government was rather skeptical but in the end agreed to cooperate, provided that the Office of Military Intelligence could have a seat on the management committee, all their expenses paid, including a daily allowance for time spent on the committee. Bruno did not like this at all. The idea that the army would spy on their operations at GAPI expense was really not acceptable to him, but Zamorski had managed to persuade him to go along. Whatever way you look at it, he explained, you need those guys in uniform around, with their guns, in case things go wrong. Besides, he had said, rather undiplomatically, it's better to have them inside the tent pissing out than outside the tent pissing in.

The whole thing about a military rank and amnesty for Christmas was a complete nonstarter for the local embassies. They all wanted to see him in front of a judge, except for one diplomat from a country in the region, who simply wanted to see him dead, but did not want to be quoted. The government wasn't going to say anything at all about it. They were going to ignore the question of amnesty for now, probably as a way to test the waters, to see if Christmas would cooperate with the pilot program in surrendering his weapons and then take it from there.

The unmistaken signal that they would be sending him was that this was not *off* the table, just not *on* the table for now. GAPI headquarters had sent a lengthy instruction on this issue, full of convoluted legal considerations and warnings about "moral hazards involved in dealing with Christmas," which concluded with the rather self-evident observation that ultimately this was the government's call.

Good, Johan thought. He would copy and paste this instruction in full into the program document. That should make HQ happy. He was pretty sure they too preferred the funding opportunity and the potential for high visibility over any moral hazards. At the same time, he had no doubt that they would use this instruction later to occupy the moral high ground and blame him and Bruno for any shit that would undoubtedly hit the fan down the road.

# Chapter 12

## EMBERS OF PEACE

Once the documents were properly edited, approved by at least a dozen people, and finalized with glossy photos and fancy graphs, they went out to the printer. Johan could now turn his energy and this team's to organizing the official launch of the program. The launch would be symbolic, since nothing was quite ready yet. It wouldn't matter. Symbolism was what they needed now to generate momentum and donor interest. The launch would be a big event upstream, at the pink hotel in the town by the foot of the mountains. The ambassadors would all come. The minister would be there. Heads of other international organizations, and perhaps—Ibrahim was working on that—Christmas himself might show up to personally surrender the first batch of weapons and receive the first "Citizen Kit," which Aisha had gone out to put together from items on the local market, bought from GAPI petty cash, and put in a duffel bag with a GAPI logo sewn on. The actual kits for the fighters had to wait to go through the GAPI procurement office, and that might take a while, since the rules for procurement were rather demanding, especially for big contracts where goods had to go through customs.

The weapons that they would hopefully get from Christmas for the launch ceremony would have their firing pins and any ammunition removed first (Tom insisted on that) and then be burned in the center of an adjacent field, which would first have to be cleared from grazing livestock and their excrement. The pyre of guns would be set ablaze by a trio composed of the minister, Bruno, and Zamorski, the latter on behalf of the international community. Big photo opportunity for all, next to the "Embers of Peace." Then drinks and a nice meal for everyone afterward. Skipper Boutique had already been put on notice to get extra life jackets.

Johan and the team had set up shop in the pink hotel a few days before to make sure everything was organized and in its place when the guests arrived. On the day of the launch, the weather was perfect, with barely a cloud in sight. The field next to the hotel had been cleaned, and a hundred plastic chairs had been arranged in a U-shape facing a speaker's podium and a pyre that was awaiting its customers: the guns that would be turned into embers. At the bottom of the U were wooden fauteuils with faded yellow leather cushions, rented from the hotel for the occasion, to accommodate the VIPs. In front of them was a coffee table with bottles of water, biscuits, and nicely bound copies of the official DSP, covered by a cloth until the guests arrived.

There had been a lengthy exchange between the ministry and GAPI about where Christmas would sit, if and when he showed up. The Protocol Office had a fit. It was *unthinkable* that he would sit next to the minister, with the ambassadors or heads of organizations. At the same time, GAPI needed him on board and to cooperate with them on the program. Bruno came up with a compromise solution, setting up a low podium opposite the VIPs on the other side of the pyre, with his own fauteuil and low table. This way, nobody would have to mingle with Christmas, while he could participate in the ceremony and perceive "a level of respect, of course," as Bruno put it.

Tom had been working on security arrangements with the police and army. Having received top-level instructions to cooperate, the local commanders were very forthcoming with their support. Ibrahim had been in touch with Christmas' people to explain the ceremony and what was expected from them. They appeared rather blasé about the whole thing, as if they had done it a thousand times before. Aisha, however, thought that this attitude was to hide their anxiety about their future.

Dealing with the media was a cause for anxiety for Bruno. The local journalists were fine; the ministry and the army appeared to have a good grip on them. They would write what they were fed and dutifully publish the approved pictures. Bruno was worried that one of the international correspondents would show up. This was a hard-to-control crowd. Many of them were very critical, or even downright cynical, toward GAPI and its work, looking for scandals at every turn. Last year, one of them had done a piece on an independent audit of GAPI's management. The confidential report had leaked, and Bruno suddenly had to explain why the auditors had referred to "a management style that put status over substance" or "opaque recruiting criteria and messy accounting." The whole thing blew over, but since then, Bruno was always looking over his shoulder, figuratively speaking, to see if there was an international correspondent in his proximity. Today, fortunately, the air was clear. Boutique had told Ibrahim exactly who had been aboard the VVVIP Express, and international journalists had not been among his passengers.

At the agreed time, the official guests started to trickle in. The minister entered the field from the hotel with an entourage that included his office manager, then a briefcase carrier, who also had the minister's cell phones in his pockets, and two tall bodyguards with sunglasses and bulging black jackets.

Ambassador Zamorski made his entrance a bit more modestly, but he made sure that people noticed that he was there by his loud and jovial greeting of the minister. Bruno had been there early, wearing a dark blue suit with a silver plowshare lapel pin. He shook hands with every official guest and guided them to their assigned seats.

Johan was in the hotel lobby, chatting with Vashti, who ran a human rights program for a non-governmental outfit called Inherent. Vashti was an old friend of his. By coincidence, their deployments to various countries always seemed to overlap, and they shared memories of at least half a dozen countries. Johan liked her intelligence and determination to always put human rights at the center of her work and her life. Besides being smart and passionate, she was also very attractive. Johan believed he would never make a pass at her—he was happily married, and Vashti was much younger—but who doesn't like being around a person who is beautiful inside and out?

Bruno came over, carrying a concerned look to interrupt their chat. He offered a quick "hi" to Vashti and took Johan aside. Where the fuck was Christmas? he wanted to know. Johan immediately ran off to confer with Ibrahim, who had been standing behind Christmas' podium with two cell phones in his hand and one in the other hand pressed against his ear. Ibrahim gestured he was busy, could not talk right now. "Where X-mas????" Johan wrote on the back of the receipt for the hotel chairs  and showed it to Ibrahim.

Ibrahim nodded and pointed at the phone, all the while talking in a local dialect to someone on the other end that might hold the answer to this burning question.

Ibrahim took the phone off his ear and turned to Johan. "Bad news. Christmas isn't coming. Instead, V-6 will be joining us very briefly to drop off some weapons, but he doesn't want to take part in the ceremony or have his picture taken. He should be at the parking lot at the back of the hotel in five minutes."

"Thanks, Ibrahim. I'm guessing that these guys still have little confidence in what we're trying to do here. I'll get Tom, and then we'll go with you to help bring up the guns."

The two of them went to the back of the hotel. V-6 was hiding in the booth of the parking attendant and came out to greet Ibrahim and Johan. V-6 was a powerfully built man with an athletic stride. When he ran, he could outrun everybody in both speed and stamina, running on all cylinders as people said, hence the nickname. He carried about eight rifles in his arms and put them on the ground in front of Ibrahim and Johan.

"That's it," he said with an angry look on his face. "Where is my bag? You promised a bag of goods."

"That's right, Mr. V-6, but we'll need the bag for the ceremony and use it as a sample for the visitors, especially donors, so they'll have an idea what their money will be spent on. I hope that's OK. You'll get your citizen kit later, I promise."

"No." V-6 crossed his arms, causing his biceps to bulge menacingly. "No kit, no guns."

"Come on," Ibrahim tried, "this is just a first step. There will be many kits later."

"I said no," V-6 said. "We need proof that this program of yours actually works. No kit, no guns."

"All right, all right," Johan said, reaching for his wallet. "How about cash instead?"

V-6 unfolded his arms. The angry look left his face while he held out his hand. "How much?"

"One hundred."

"Two hundred. Dollars. Cash."

"OK, that's fine. The important thing is that we get this program going," Johan said with a sigh. He took the money out of his wallet to give to V-6. He was pretty sure he wouldn't get a receipt. More money lost for a good cause.

"Hold it. Not so fast," Tom interjected. He had been looking at the weapons on the floor. Looking V-6 in the eye, he said coolly: "This is a pile of crap. Look at it. Rusty old barrels, missing parts. There's even a steel pipe fixed to a wooden plank. We were talking about functioning and serviceable weapons. This junk won't shoot."

"It's fine, Tom. This is all a symbolic thing for now. Nobody will be able to tell the difference once they're on fire," Johan said soothingly to Tom while handing the cash to V-6.

V-6 quickly walked away without saying another word and stepped in a waiting car with peeling paint and tinted glass that drove off in a cloud of smoke and orange dust.

"Damn it, Johan," Tom said with obvious disappointment, "this is not a good start. You know, *we too* need to know if this program is going to work—V-6's own words, Johan!—also from *their* side. Duck Bill would call these weapons as useless as a one-legged dog trying to bury a bone on a frozen lake."

"Not funny, Tom. Let's get these guns on the pyre without someone else coming to the conclusion that we're burning plumbing supplies instead of guns. And let's get rid of the podium for Christmas. Make these protocol folks happy after all."

Bad and fake guns notwithstanding, the event was a great success. Bruno gave the first official speech and provided an account, straight out of GAPI public information material, of how well-placed GAPI was to help out, based on its vast experience with programs like these in this country and others. He also provided a sketch of the program, mentioned how they had reached out to Christmas and had secured his cooperation, ending with a pitch to donors for more money to tackle root causes. Vashti, who had heard Bruno's speeches before, was keeping a running count of how many times he said "of course." She was disappointed. Only six times today.

Zamorski was obviously happy about being in the spotlight. His speech was eloquent and philosophical. He quoted Machiavelli—"The prince who does not detect evils the moment they appear lacks in true wisdom." Then he went on to pay everybody present (which of course included himself) the big compliment of not only having detected evil, but also having the wisdom of doing something about it, with his government spearheading the effort.

Johan and Vashti looked at each other when Zamorski made this point, each thinking in their own way that nobody had detected any evils up to the point a foreigner was killed. Zamorski concluded by announcing his government's very significant donation and by paying tribute to the minister for his leadership.

The minister, for his part, gave a glowing speech about the need for everyone to work together to reach peace and prosperity and promote healing between victims and actors. He also went on a rant about the huge numbers of guns in circulation, pointing at the pyre, and alluding (without naming names) to a nefarious and evil conspiracy from across the border that was responsible for invading the minds of the young and poisoning peaceful communities through the spread of firearms. He thanked current and future donors for their generosity and closed by inviting Zamorski and Bruno to carry a torch to the pyre of weapons.

Tom had made sure that the thing would catch fire by stacking dry wood and straw soaked in diesel fuel underneath the guns. As a result, the whole thing whooshed aflame with a heat that made the dignitaries take a few steps back, lest their expensive suits be scorched. The official photo of the "Embers of Peace" made the headlines in the national press. It showed the minister and Zamorski smiling and shaking hands, while

Bruno was looking at the pyre with obvious apprehension. When asked about the photo a few days later, Bruno admitted that he was thinking of the people who were killed—those men, women, and children were killed with knives and farming tools, not with guns.

# Chapter 13

## A BAD REPORT CARD

At first, the DSP took off at a good clip. The first stages were all about procurement and logistics: buying cars (Johan got a brand-new 4x4 *and* a better parking spot), hiring international and local staff, setting up a satellite office in the town at the foot of the mountains, and renting steel containers for the safe storage of the collected weapons as well as of the citizen kits and other program supplies, if and when they would come in.

Skipper Boutique got a nice contract moving supplies and people back and forth. His boat was now flying the GAPI flag with the gavel and plowshare against a light green field. Ibrahim received a promotion and became the head of the satellite office to facilitate contact with Christmas and his lieutenants.

The start-up phase of the DSP was, as usual, the most expensive. Before a single gun had been collected, GAPI had already spent or earmarked fifteen million. Which was really all there was in the bank, anyway. Zamorski had only given a check for fifty percent of their pledge, while the other countries were processing their contributions through their respective bureaucracies, which they said could take up to a year and several "assessment" missions.

The first meeting of the Inclusive Implementation Management Committee under Johan's chairmanship was a minor success. The Office of Military Intelligence did show up in the form of a well-decorated and somewhat obese colonel by the name of Neptune, who took scant notes and kept taking phone calls on his mobile, causing him to dive under the table and explain that he was in a meeting and would call back later. Otherwise, he contributed nothing.

Donor representatives were enthusiastically micro-managing the program by referring at length to their own history and/or experience elsewhere and suggesting that GAPI adapt their best practices to fit into its projects. Johan noted that the diplomat who spoke the most represented a country that had promised the least amount of money, none of which had been transferred yet.

On the ground, things moved only very slowly. Getting the citizen kits together proved to be a nightmare, since every item required an individual procurement order, one for the pots and pans, another for the towels. Some items had to come from abroad and pass customs, which was another major hassle. The thing was, the kits were ready for distribution to the "Former Fighters" only when all the items could be packed in the bags so the whole thing was complete, meaning that the slowest item to procure dictated the pace of the whole program. No shortcuts existed, at least no official ones. In the meantime, salaries needed to be paid, vehicles needed to be fueled, and cases of Ubamolak needed to be shipped to Christmas' camp on schedule. The Disarmament and Stabilization Program, or DSP as it had become known, was running out of cash quickly.

And it had very little to show for it. The first fighters to hand in their weapons were the two village elders in their three-piece suits, each carrying a rusty World War I bolt-action rifle without any ammunition. They were very patient as the GAPI team took their names, dates of birth (which they could not provide, since they did not know precisely), took their photographs and fingerprints, and handed them their official DSP "Former Fighter ID" cards. They looked at them with obvious happiness.

Ibrahim, who was supervising the whole process, asked them why they looked so happy. They answered that this was the first document they had ever owned that showed who they were. They would carry it with them day and night. After their intake interview, where GAPI registered their interests for the future, the two left to go back to Christmas' camp in the bush with their heavy, still improvised citizen kits on the back of a donkey. Ibrahim looked at their forms. Under the heading "Preferred Occupation," it said, "village elder."

After these two, there was a trickle of old and sick "fighters," including a woman who looked terribly ill and had to be taken to a hospital with an acute case of cerebral malaria, which could be deadly if not treated quickly. When Christmas heard about this, he sent everybody who was sick through the program with the oldest weapons he could find. The hospital, in turn, started to charge five hundred dollars per patient, putting yet more strain on the budget. Their medical reports confirmed what Johan had seen during their visit. This was a very sick community. Malaria had taken its toll, certainly, but there were also cases of tuberculosis and a single case of leprosy. Johan took an extra-long shower the day he read that particular report.

Bruno and Johan put on a brave face to the donors and the government. It was early days, they said. They needed to build up the system and their implementing partners' capacity, as well as create trust with Christmas, who had been behaving rather well since the program started.

Internally, the strain was building. Their international headquarters, which was based at San Francisco, was sending reminders that the DSP would need to be accelerated to avoid loss of face, or worse, loss of donor confidence in GAPI, while warning them again that they should raise the amnesty issue in accordance with their legal analysis sent earlier.

In reality, it was Bruno and Johan who were losing confidence in the donors. Where the hell was their money? When would the checks come in to allow them to continue? The next phase of the program would be the job-creation process, which was expensive and required the activation of schools and businesses that were not about to accept a bunch of murderers without some solid financial compensation up front, cash in hand.

So far, the small number of FFs who had come forward to join the program had all taken their kits and had gone back to the camp in the bush. Some of the items in the kit had started to show up on the local markets in nearby villages, bartered for booze or cash. The villagers themselves were figuring out that Christmas' people were getting benefits of some kind and, according to Aisha and Ibrahim, had started to grumble. What about us? they said.

What hurt more was that Johan had also taken a beating from his friend Vashti. She had scolded him one night over dinner for what she perceived as his cynical disrespect for human rights. It was a pleasant dinner at first at The Floating Cloud, one of the restaurant barges on the river's edge where the expatriate crowd would hang out most evenings. As usual, Vashti's good looks drew a good number of stares from the men, but she completely ignored them. Halfway through the dinner, she put down her fork and looked him straight in the eye with a mildly disappointed yet stern look, like a mother to a child who had just brought home a bad report card.

"I need to say something, Johan." She held her breath for a second or two. "You know I like you, and you've done really good work here. But this DSP thing? Really, Johan, I'm sorry, but how could you reward these criminals with goods and jobs? How come you guys aren't investigating their crimes instead of giving them presents? Why aren't you handing them over to the police? What about the victims? Yeah, sure, Christmas' followers haven't killed anyone recently, but they haven't stopped digging for gold, either. I could go on like this for a while, but I need to tell you that it is *not looking good.* Not at all."

Johan listened carefully while he was using a toothpick to remove a piece of river lobster shell stuck between his teeth. Jesus, she's really angry at me, he thought. Or at least at the program. He had to admit that she had a point.

"Look, Vashti, I hear what you're saying, and you're right. As usual, I might add. But what do you expect me to do? Tell Zamorski to keep his money? Do nothing, and leave Christmas in the bush to carry out another massacre and continue to spread fear and terror? You know as well as I that the army and police won't act against him. They don't have the means, and even if they had the means, they probably wouldn't have the will. At least, the way I see it, we're doing some good taking some guns away and trying to keep these fighters busy so they stop killing and stealing and raping."

It was clear that nothing Johan had said would change her mind. Vashti was getting impatient and started to draw lines with her fork in the taffeta tablecloth.

"No, Johan, you're *not* doing any good. How can you be so naïve? Or so cynical, I don't know which. The guns are mostly useless. Your buddy, Tom, says so himself. The goods from your so-called citizen kits are being sold on the market. You've helped Christmas gain some status as a leader of a movement. I hope you didn't call him Excellency. There's even talk of an amnesty for him, for Christ's sake! And you've gone out to shake his hand and drink Ubamolak with him! How can you, Johan? The man has blood on his hands. And now you have, too."

She was on a roll now, and Johan knew better than to interrupt, even though he felt the last comment was unfair.

"Jesus, Johan, there are people out there who have lost everything, who wished they were dead instead of living with the trauma of rape and seeing their family's guts dragged through the dust. There are girls out there pregnant with your flipping FF's babies. What are you doing for them? And fuck Zamorski. Fuck him and his Machiavelli. Why couldn't he give the money to my human rights organization to work with the victims instead? You know Inherent would do a much better job. *I* would do a better job."

Here was an opening, and Johan took it.

"You know what? That's a great idea. Maybe we can sub-contract with Inherent in one of the 'Deep Stabilization' projects. Let me talk to Bruno about it. I'm pretty sure that at least one of the donors would be willing to put up the funds. I think some sort of fund for victims would be perfect, managed by GAPI, naturally."

The professional in Vashti saw an opportunity, and she temporarily put her activist passion aside.

"Ah, now you're talking, my dear. But I see no reason why the money shouldn't go to Inherent directly. Tell me what donor you had in mind."

Johan laughed, and the tension left the table. Vashti had put her fork down and raised her glass instead, still serious. Johan filled his glass from the bottle of chilled red wine and raised his glass as well. They toasted.

"Did you seriously think I was going to tell you that? No, my dear, you are going to work for *me*."

"In your dreams."

"Shall we have an Ubamolak to seal the deal?" Johan asked with a wink.

"No way in hell will I ever have even a sip of that vile stuff or even come close to it. It's the drink of the devil. And there is no deal," she said, winking back at him. "But I really appreciate you listening to me, Johan. There are few men around here who I can be so honest with. So, instead, let us toast to good friends. Even though I'm still mad at you."

# Chapter 14

## DESIGNER SAFARI SUITS

Bruno's worst fear had come true. A well-known journalist had written a very critical piece in an international weekly that was widely read in San Francisco, meaning that all of the donors' ambassadors as well as Bruno's bosses—on whom he depended for a promotion and a ticket out—would have read it. The piece described in detail what exactly the program had done and not done. At its center was an interview with the two village elders. Apparently, the journalist, who had won several awards for her work in war zones around the world, had taken the slow ferry upstream instead of the VVVIP Express and made her way to the periphery of Christmas' camp, where she met with the elders. The story was headlined "Money flows to murderers; Christmas comes early in the bush."

Bruno was especially pissed off at the parts where the journalist had asked questions about GAPI's management. Why didn't she come to him for comments, so he could set the record straight? He read it for a second time and highlighted the most critical passages.

> *...GAPI seems more interested in padding the salaries of its senior bureaucrats, who all received promotions, and asking donors for more and more money for brand-new SUVs, than*

*in solving the very serious humanitarian and security problems caused by Christmas and his gang of bloodthirsty fighters...*

*...according to a source close to the Disarmament and Stabilization Program (DSP)...*

Who the hell leaked from our side? Bruno asked himself angrily.

*...one diplomat, who spoke on condition of anonymity, said that the DSP was a critical component of the international community's response to the climate of impunity and that all previous efforts to deal with Christmas had failed.*

*"At least now we're giving them a chance to leave the jungle and look forward to a life that doesn't involve violence," he said...*

Thank you, Zamorski, nodded Bruno.

*...The mood in the village where the recent massacre took place was grim. Most people refused to talk to me, and those who did were bitter and traumatized. One woman spoke very softly of how she'll never have her husband and children back: "Why has GAPI not come to us? I have no money, no job, no family. Why do these animals get the money?" she said, as silent tears streamed down her face...*

"Inherent/Vashti!" he wrote and underlined in the margins, "our new fund will handle this!"

But the hardest-hitting part was where the two old guys were quoted.

*...I managed to reach the outskirts of Christmas' sprawling base, where I met with two men who were the first to come through the program. They were old, how old exactly they could not say, and were wearing surprisingly formal attire. They proudly showed me their DSP ID cards. "This has been very good. We hand in our old guns, the one my father had, I found it under my mother's bed, God rest her soul. We cannot get ammunition for it anymore, so it's useless, but thanks to DSP we got a bag of things that we sold on the market for*

*good money. Christmas has told us to round up the old guns and hand them in for more money. He's still afraid that the army will come, so he keeps all the good guns and the ammunition. None of the young fighters or gold-diggers are allowed to enter the program..."*

*..."GAPI promised us a job. But we have not heard or seen from them since we got our cards. They need to pay us. Why would we come out of the bush if they don't pay us? Captain Christmas takes better care of us than GAPI."*

"They misunderstand the program," Bruno scribbled angrily, then added: "Need better communication strategy."

He called to Flora. "Get Johan in here ASAP, please."

Johan knew what the meeting was going to be about. He'd read the article, too and didn't think it was too bad. There was no such thing as bad publicity unless they misspell your name, was there? He thought the article could very well be helpful in generating more attention and perhaps even more money, especially for the Inherent human rights organization and Vashti's fund for victims. Of course, Bruno was a bit paranoid because of his previous issues with the media. He'd be all over this, he anticipated as he stepped into Bruno's office.

"What the hell, Johan?" said Bruno, as he slammed the offending article on the table. "This is not helpful at all, to say the least. A bloody disaster, of course."

"I don't think it's so bad, boss."

"How so? I already had a dozen calls from San Francisco, asking me if this is all true, and what are we going to do about it. And what *are* we going to do about it, Johan?"

Johan had thought about it. The options were limited. If you started to offer explanations, you'd sound defensive—maybe give the impression you had something to hide. If you said nothing, then this nasty piece would define the program in the eyes of the public. Better come out swinging. Set a new narrative.

"Bruno?"

"Yes, any bright ideas, Johan?"

"Doesn't your sister know people in the theatre district of San Francisco?"

Bruno's sister had been a musical star when she was younger and now ran a dance, music, and acting studio for talented high school students in San Francisco's suburbs. Her fame had faded perhaps, but her network might come in handy.

"What does my sister have to do with this?"

"Well, here's what I was thinking. We need to counter bad publicity with good publicity. Dominate the narrative, right? Where does our funding come from? Money comes from donors, which comes from budgets, voted by parliamentarians, who need reelection. Right? And who votes for them? Not the folks who read this magazine." Johan pointed to the article on the table.

"Where are you going with this?"

"Hold on. The people who vote for politicians read what? The *celebrity* pages. Why not engage some star power? It's been done before. Remember the actor who took on the cause of that rebellion about five years back? Had his picture taken in designer safari suits every other week with victims, riding camels and petting goats. He made it very difficult for politicians to ignore the issue."

"I remember. Although he completely misunderstood the real issues further south. But yes, we had a good year fundraising back then because of the publicity. Aha. I see what you're getting at. Go on."

"How about we get a big star—singer, dancer, actor, doesn't matter, as long as he or she is against guns and for kids, motherhood, and apple pie—to lead some public event or ceremony at Headquarters? Publicity guaranteed! For example, we could get a bit of ground near the lawn at HQ and dedicate a—"

Bruno smiled and put up his hand, signaling that he got it now. "A Garden of Peace..." he said slowly and emphatically.

Johan was relieved. This would keep Bruno and headquarters happy and change the public's perception of the program. Zamorski would probably love it too. He might even use his taxpayers' money to pay for the costs if it meant having his picture taken with a beautiful celebrity. Had to be a woman.

"I think it has be a woman, Bruno."

"Right, right. I'll speak to my sister. Why don't you think about what this Garden of Peace should look like? As long as it doesn't involve growing your ugly serpent head thistles." Bruno laughed. "And by the way, please do find out who that leak, that source close to the program is, if it isn't you, of course."

"Not me, boss. But I'll ask around."

# Chapter 15

## GARDEN OF PEACE

The lawn by GAPI headquarters in San Francisco was filled with diplomats and journalists, some of whom were carrying cameras and microphones on long metal poles. The adjacent street was cordoned off, except to TV crews, police, and invitees. Johan was delighted. This was an even bigger deal than he had imagined. And it was *his* baby. Bruno had cancelled the trip overseas at the last moment and asked him, Johan, to lead the ceremony. He'd spent a few days at home in Connecticut and arrived the day before in San Francisco to oversee preparations.

Everything was going well. They had dug out an irregular oval about two feet deep and poured a base of concrete with stainless steel rods sticking out at regular intervals. Johan had organized twenty-four obsolete assault rifles—not the ones collected from Christmas' boys but obtained from a local weapons dealer who gave them away for free, as long as his name was *not* mentioned. Besides, it would've been an administrative nightmare to bring old guns, even if harmless, across several borders on board several flights.

The guns were mounted, each at a slightly different angle, on the steel rods and welded onto a metal frame. Another eight inches or so of concrete was poured over the frame to hold the weapons in place. On top of that, gardeners had placed a layer of soil that would hold the "seeds of peace," a mix of wild flowers and vines that would soon overgrow the weapons as a symbol of the power of growth over violence. Beautiful, wasn't it?

Johan was right about Zamorski making some funds available, but it wasn't quite what he'd hoped for. The only pot of money he had left at that moment was for "promotion of the arts." Not to worry, he said, I'll find something. And he did. His office had commissioned a modest work of art for a not-so-modest sum, which would be unveiled today as part of the Garden of Peace. It was an abstract rendering of a gavel, made of wood stripped from old guns, as well as an even more abstract version of a plowshare, welded together from gun metal. Johan thought the whole thing looked like a combination of a wooden calabash and a spaceship from the sci-fi movies his kids used to watch. There was a plaque, the same size as the statue itself, explaining that this work of art had been made possible through a generous donation from Zamorski's government and that he himself had been present at the ceremony.

But neither the guns nor the statue was the real attraction. All the buzz and excitement were about Geneva—movie star, singer, stage actress, and champion of many a lost cause. She was undoubtedly beautiful, with blond hair and blue-green eyes crowned by dark eyelashes.

It so happened that Geneva had started her career in a minor role in a play in which Bruno's sister played the main part. They had lost touch, but when Bruno's sister called, Geneva (or "Gin" as she liked to be called) remembered her fondly. "You were my role model for such a long time," Gin exclaimed.

It did not take long to persuade her. She was once married to a leftist senator whose term in office, as well as his marriage to Gin, was short-lived after he was caught having sex with an aide to a senator on the far right. However, the curtailed marriage had given her a taste of campaigning for social issues, and she loved it. She tried stray animals for a cause, anti-tobacco, preservation of coral reefs (after a snorkeling trip), and a few more. The media loved her. Although that relationship wasn't always reciprocated, she didn't mind using her celebrity status for a good cause. "Putting my best boob forward for the greater good," she was once quoted as saying.

When Johan came to see Geneva to discuss how she could help, he brought a few pictures of orphans, murdered villagers, and burned huts, explained how the presence of these rebels was effectively blocking economic growth and stopping the kids there from going to school and realizing their potential.

"There are so many potential artists among these kids, incredible dancers and singers, but we will never know because they will never get a chance, because guns are in their way," was Johan's best pitch, and it worked. Geneva was sold.

The media had a field day. They skipped through all the speeches by diplomats and focused exclusively on Geneva, who was wearing a tight, dark khaki pantsuit with a mint cream, low-cut blouse, as the press release indicated. She posed for pictures and gave a surprisingly passionate speech on how guns stand in the way of children's potential (Johan had given her a text, which was also in the press release). She planted the "seeds of love and peace" at the base of the guns with a serious expression. She also unveiled, next to a beaming Zamorski, the statue of the unrecognizable gavel and plowshare.

All in all, it was a great success. Johan's picture made the newspapers, smiling behind a serious and gorgeous Geneva. Bruno read the international clippings the following day and felt relieved. They had picked up Geneva's statement and quoted just the right lines. It had been on TV that day as well as the following day during all the morning shows. His organization looked good, his program looked good, and by extension, he looked good.

## Chapter 16

## CODE WORD

Davey woke up late that day. He woke up late pretty much every day, since he had no job that required him to get out of bed at any precise time. He sat up and looked out the window of the old Winnebago RV where he was living for the time being. The RV belonged to his uncle Bob, who had put up with him since his parents had split and left town. The transmission had given out a few years back, and it hadn't moved since. The originally sky-blue RV was slowly turning brown from rust, sticky tree sap, the pollen of many springs, and moss and rotting leaves from the many autumns on its roof. Someday, Davey would fix the transmission, clean the old RV, take off, and find some good job somewhere else. But not today.

The weather outside was going to be hot and humid; he could tell by the way the Blue Ridge Mountains looked in the distance. He looked up at the shelf over his bed with the two trophies he had won at the annual marksmanship competitions. One first prize for the under-eighteen division and one second prize in the adult division, his pride and joy. He couldn't help smiling as he took them off the shelf and polished the chrome with the corner of his bedsheet. Whatever happens, he said to himself as he'd done many times before, nobody can ever take that away from me. The best thing was, he had outshot his dad in the adult competition and for once shut up his old man, who was always complaining about his "good-for-nothing son."

He smelled his army-green T-shirt and decided it would do for another day. He put on khaki-colored working trousers, heavy boots, and his last pair of clean socks. He was ready to walk the hundred yards to Uncle Bob's Pawn, Gun, and Ammo shop, which included the Tennessee Freedom Fields of Fire Shooting Range. Davey helped out with cleaning the shop and range, making coffee, and some filing (he hated that), as payment for living in the Winnebago, some pocket money for food, beers at the Old Blind Bull, and an allowance of ammunition for Davey's Q13 sniper rifle.

He loved that weapon. When he bought it, it had a fiberglass stock and hand guard, but Davey managed to make replacements from a piece of old walnut wood that came from a tree next to the range. Sanded down, nicely varnished (six coats), and well maintained, the weapon looked like it came straight out of the factory, even though it was some fifty years old. Older than Uncle Bob, but shooting a lot straighter, he was fond of saying every time he hit a bull's-eye on the range.

Inside the store, he arranged some empty ammo boxes, cleaned the coffee table, and put out this week's editions of sports and gun magazines. He switched on the coffee machine and the small color TV that was tuned to the only news channel they liked, the one that brought them news about conservative stuff and gun rights and the good sports, too. This time, there was a reporter talking about some sort of event going on in San Francisco with a movie star.

"What the heck?" Davey mumbled.

"Hey, Uncle Bob, did you hear that? I mean, did you just see that?" he said a bit louder now.

"Guns stand in the way of kids? That's such bullshit! I mean, she's hot and all, but why did she have to say that?" Davey shook his head and poured himself a cup of coffee. These people, he was thinking, they have no idea what guns mean. Guns mean freedom. You give 'em up, and the government will come and run your life. Fuck no, over his dead body.

"I know, Davey. Here, it's in the newspapers too," Uncle Bob said from behind his cash register. He unfolded the newspaper and began to read, giving an occasional quotation.

"Movie star supports international effort to disarm rebels...Gavels and Plowshares seeking more funds to render a rebel group harmless...Schools instead of guns...They call it the 'Disarmament and Stability Program'...And listen to this one, Davey. She planted 'seeds of love and peace'...Nice piece of ass, though. I'd love to plant my seeds of love there anytime, if my wife ain't watching, of course," Bob said, laughing.

"I don't think that's funny at all, Uncle Bob. Don't you know what this means? I'll tell you what. Disarmament is *exactly* what it means, but *stability* is a code word, man—a code word for world domination. That's what these international organizations want. You always say that too, don't you? It's no big secret. It's all over the Internet."

Davey took another sip of coffee and went on, increasingly irritated at the news on TV.

"There are pictures on the web—look it up, man, if you want. I'm not kidding—pictures and videos of trucks with their logos on it riding on trains to secret locations all around the country. They want to take your guns away and set up a dictatorship, a world government. They're trying it over there first, and if they succeed, they will come here, and then you can kiss your guns goodbye. And they won't let you drive your pickup truck, either, 'cause it makes too much smoke, and that's not good for the trees."

Uncle Bob looked at him with an amused smile. "You really mean this, don't you? Seems like you been listening to me. I've been saying the same thing for a long, long time."

"Yeah, you bet I do. Goddamn, I hope these rebels over there stick to their guns, because if they don't, you and I'll be next. Now I gotta go. See you later."

Davey got up and walked over to the firing range. Today was a good day for firing his Q13, before the customers came and before it was all too late.

# Part II
# Oliver

# Chapter 17

## THE MOTO HOME

Oliver had logged into the Wi-Fi at his hotel. First, he sent e-mails to his wife and his mother to let them know that he was OK and that he would talk to them later. Then he decided that it was time to inform himself better. So far, Bruno had not volunteered a lot of information about his father's death or the context, so he'd have to find out some of it for himself.

In quick succession, he googled his father's name, then "DSP," and "Captain Christmas." He found a whole bunch of official documents on GAPI's website, none of which made him any wiser. He couldn't make much sense of the language in these documents. For example, what did "building resilience across communities in the context of comprehensive long-term recovery" mean? Some of this text must be his father's writing, he assumed. None of the sentences he read had the clarity of purpose and meaning that he was used to in his job, where every banking term had a precise and commonly understood meaning. How the hell was one supposed to measure, let alone account for "resilience across communities"? To Oliver, the most helpful source was the magazine article featuring two old guys who got some money and goods by trading in their vintage rifles.

So Dad had been in charge of the DSP, and from what Oliver read, the program was either a "promising example of what GAPI can contribute to violence-ridden areas" or "a cynical and failing attempt to throw money at an evil eyesore." Apparently, Dad had been in the bush to see Christmas more than a few times for "consultations on the DSP."

The web was rather generous with articles about Christmas. Oliver had heard about him earlier, but was still startled by some of the details, especially about the massacre that happened two years ago. Christmas had acquired a vast array of different labels, including mass murderer, failed revolutionary, missionary, prophet to his people, Jungle Jesus, gold-digging gangster, obstacle to peace, and booze-addicted madman. By all accounts, this was someone who would be capable of killing his father or, at least, ordering someone else to do it. But why? Dad hadn't done anything to harm Christmas. In fact, he had been supporting Christmas' people with goods and healthcare, had he not?

He folded the screen of his laptop down and picked up the safety and security instructions he had received from Flora. It contained a list of common-sense recommendations such as "do not open the door to strangers," "Beware of prostitutes," and "Don't wear any expensive jewelry or watches." Oliver looked at his watch, which he'd received from his wife for his thirtieth birthday. He couldn't say if it looked expensive or not. What *is* expensive in this country anyway? he wondered.

The most useful part of the instructions was a color-coded map. He found the hotel and GAPI offices, both in a green-shaded zone. Adjacent to the green zone were areas marked yellow (enter with caution, daylight only) and corridors along the major roads leading out of the city marked red (no go, permission required, special measures apply). There were also radio channels and call signs as well as a phone number to call 24/7 in case of any security problem. Oliver picked up his phone to enter these numbers and found that they had already been preprogrammed. Good, he thought. A sign of organization and efficiency.

Oliver yawned. He was tired and hungry now. What time was it? He looked at his watch and noticed that it was still on home time. He looked around his hotel room to find a clock. Nothing. He looked it up online and concluded that it was early evening. Time for a meal—and a drink. Maybe later a quick call home before bed. He missed his kids.

He made his way downstairs to the lobby. It wasn't immediately obvious where the bar and restaurant were. A small, carved, wooden sign to the left of the reception directed him through a narrow corridor, down a dark staircase, and onto an open terrace that featured chairs and tables under bright yellow parasols streaked with mildew stains. He found a table with a view over the water and ordered a local beer.

The terrace was empty except for a loud group of men two tables from Oliver. He looked at them and saw five middle-aged men with beer bellies under tight polo shirts around a table stacked with empty or half-empty brown bottles from which they poured themselves a creamy drink.

They must have something to celebrate, Oliver thought. Maybe they were contractors or businessmen from abroad who had finished up their contract on time and were turning their bonuses into booze. He couldn't understand what they were saying, but it must be pretty funny—to them, at least. They were very loud—so loud, in fact, that Oliver was thinking of moving to another table. He needed to think. At the same time, the view was soothing, so he was going to focus on that and on his beer and ignore the beer bellies.

It was a pretty sunset as the sun broke through the clouds over the mountains and reflected on the water to bathe the terrace in a sprinkle of dimmed light flashes. Oliver had another beer and nibbled on the peanuts that the waiter had brought him. Dad might have sat here at this same table, looking at the same sun, maybe with the same beer. He looked at the label but couldn't remember whether Dad had ever mentioned this brand, called Hyper Pro. Who did he come here with? What did he talk about? Would he have spoken of his family, of him? He could feel his chest hurt now. Must be the jet lag.

Oliver realized that he could have been here himself with Dad, if he had taken him up on the countless invitations Dad had extended to him. He was always too busy with his own life—study, marriage, the kids, work, moving in, moving out. But now these all sounded like lame excuses. Maybe it wasn't that he was too busy; maybe he just didn't want to be part of Dad's life here. It was too messy here, anyway. He took a sip of his beer and counted the peanuts that were left. Maybe he'd been afraid that he would have to forgive his dad for being away from home.

The beer bellies erupted in hollers. Oliver turned around and immediately saw why. Six women in high heels, short skirts, tight tops, and heavy makeup were coming down the staircase. They smiled invitingly at the beer bellies and at Oliver, as if they knew him, and sat down at the table next to the drinking men, one table away from Oliver, who immediately knew he should feign disinterest. The GAPI security brochure had warned against prostitutes. Plus, he was married and mourning on top of that. He beckoned the waiter and asked for the menu.

Oliver ordered a dish with chicken in a peanut plantain sauce and rice. It took a very long time before the meal made it to Oliver's table. Before his first bite, it had gone dark, and the restaurant had filled with new customers, mostly locals from the looks of it.

A DJ had appeared in a corner of the terrace. He set up large speakers and started to play some type of music that Oliver hadn't heard before—a fast kind of reggae with endless repetitions of a complex progression. The short-skirted ladies began to dance and were moving seductively around the beer bellies, who seemed to appreciate the action. Soon enough, the ladies were sitting on their laps after a bizarre round of musical chairs, since there were only five bellies and six short skirts.

Oliver saw the one left standing looking around the restaurant, and he quickly ducked behind his menu, pretending he might consider dessert. It didn't help. He stood out in this crowd as the naïve foreigner he was.

She moved over to his table, pulled out a chair, sat down, pushed his menu down with a long, red fingernail, and said, "May I join you this evening, since you are sitting here all alone? I thought you could use some company. What is your name?"

Oliver felt cornered. "I am so sorry," he tried. "I'm alone because I want to be."

"Why would you want to be alone, Mr....what's your name?"

"Oliver. My name is Oliver, and I want to be alone because I just got here, and my father just died."

Shit, he thought, was that a mistake he just made, giving his name and saying something about his father?

"My name is Fantata," she said and put her hand on his thigh. "I'm so sorry to hear about your father. You need some comforting? I'm really good at comfort."

Oliver looked at her closely in spite of himself. She wasn't attractive—too skinny for his taste. Maybe that was why she lost at the beer belly musical chairs. The other ladies were much heavier. Her face was nice, though, and her expression seemed genuinely concerned with his situation. But she was a professional, he thought, like him. He, too, could look very concerned with the fate of some of his clients who had run into bad financial luck. Showing empathy was good, his training taught him, and it didn't stop you from denying the loan in the end if the numbers didn't work out. He had to get rid of her.

"I'm sorry, Fantata, but I'm not in the mood for whatever comfort you had in mind."

"That's OK, sweetie." She smiled and took her hand off his thigh. "We can just talk a little bit. Will you buy me a drink, maybe?"

"All right then, one drink. But then I'll go."

Fantata called the waiter over and asked for a gin and tonic, no lemon, please.

"Is this your first visit to the City by the Water? I can tell, you know. How do you like it?"

"It is. It looks OK. Don't really know what to think of it. I haven't seen much of it yet."

Maybe this was a good opportunity to get some more information about the city, he thought. "Tell me, Fantata, is this a safe city? I mean, is there a lot of crime?"

"You've got to be very careful here, Oliver. It was Oliver, wasn't it? Just a week ago, they killed a foreigner who was working with one of these international organizations. People say it was like an execution, 'cause they didn't steal anything."

Could this be Dad she was talking about? Oliver wasn't sure if he really wanted to know more about his death at this point. He was tired and had enough to absorb for one day.

"Do you know his or her name, by any chance?"

"I think it was John or Johnny or something." Fantata moved her shoulders back and moved her chest forward, her breasts pointing in Oliver's direction. With her head cocked toward the group of dancing beer bellies and short skirts, she asked, "Are you sure you don't want to dance with me?"

"Hold on," Oliver gasped. "I think you're talking about my father. I've come here to pick him up—I mean his body."

Fantata's eyes opened wide, her shoulders hunched forward, and she put her hand on Oliver's arm. They were both silent for a while.

"My condolences to you and your family, Oliver. I'm so sorry. I didn't mean to..."

"It's all right, not your fault."

Oliver wiped away a tear. This was the first time he'd shed a tear over his father's death. He had been so collected and organized at home—he wanted to be strong for his mom—and now he was surprised and angry with himself for losing it in front of a total stranger, a prostitute, of all people. But she seemed nice. She was looking at him with real concern, all suggestions of a future sexual transaction gone from her body language, at least for now.

"I am fine. I'm fine, honestly. And thank you, thank you, Fantata."

"It's OK," she said, and stroked his arm.

"Do you know anything else about his death?"

He might as well ask her for more information. These people are on the street all the time, aren't they? She might have heard or seen something. Some facts that he could latch onto, to distract him from his feelings.

"Not much, my love. He was found next to his car, which was strange."

"Why?"

"Because a car like that, brand-new four-by-four, is worth enough money for someone to kill the driver and steal the car. But they didn't. We were talking about it just yesterday, my friends and I."

She pointed to the ladies in the short skirts, who were now being grabbed everywhere by the beer bellies, one of whom had his hand up his new girlfriend's skirt and was laughing out loud.

"Anyway, I figured that he was either killed by someone who is so rich that he doesn't need another four-by-four, or he was killed by someone or something who can't drive."

"What do you mean, something?"

"A spirit."

"Come on now, really? There are no spirits."

"Have you heard of Captain Christmas?"

"Yes, I have. My father was doing some kind of program with him."

Fantata closed her eyes, bent her head, and started humming. She shook her head for a while, looked up, and opened her eyes again. She let go of Oliver's hand.

"Your father must have angered an evil spirit that was set loose by Captain Christmas. He's an evil man and has done many evil things. Let me tell you, you listen now. One day, he killed a man, cut his head off, took the man's baby from his wife's womb, then put the head inside the wife, who died too."

"What?" stuttered Oliver, searching for words, "That is...that is..."

"I know, I know. This is horrible, but you listen now. Since then, since that murder, people in the villages all around here sometimes hear a baby cry at night, in the woods or in the streets. When they go look, there is nothing. But the next day, somebody dies in the village."

"I don't believe any of that," Oliver interrupted.

"Wait. It's true. Some people have seen them."

"Who?"

"The headless man who carries the baby and the wife who carries the man's head. At night, especially when it's raining, they come out and poison people, especially women who die when they give birth, and sometimes the baby dies, too."

"My father was shot. Spirits can't pull the trigger."

"Maybe they bewitched someone to do it for them, because he was a foreigner who might be resistant to their poison. Just ask if someone heard a baby cry the day before, near the place he was killed."

Oliver looked at Fantata, who had started humming again, this time with her eyes open. She appeared dead serious. To Oliver, this was all superstition. Babies are everywhere, and they cry at any time of the day or night. Women die in childbirth, maybe more so here than elsewhere for lack of medical care, and God knows what diseases were rampant around here. All good points, he thought, but something in Fantata's eyes stopped him from arguing with her. She stopped humming. A bottle fell and broke on the terrace floor to loud cheers from the beer bellies. Fantata looked up and resumed her flirtatious posture. She wasn't giving up. She needed to make some money.

"I think you shouldn't be alone tonight, handsome."

"No."

"Are you sure?"

She took his hand and placed it on her breasts. Oliver pulled his hand back quickly. He was not in the mood for this at all, not now, not ever, he told himself.

"I said no. I'm going now. Thank you for talking to me. Good night."

He got up abruptly and left. He would sign for the meal and drinks tomorrow. He just needed to get out of here quickly. He walked across the terrace and ran up the stairs to the lobby.

"Wait, Oliver!" he heard from the bottom of the stairs as he was walking down the corridor. He stopped and turned. Fantata stood at the bottom of the stairs, holding her high heels in her hand. She had run after him. The flirtatious look had made way for a strict, almost businesslike expression.

"How am I going to get home? I have no money. Give me ten for a moto."

Oliver didn't respond. If he turned, she might follow him to his room. Can't have that. Better deal with it here.

"Why would I do that?"

"It's dangerous to walk home. It's a long way. I need to feed my children. Come on. Give me ten."

Oliver reached in his pocket and found a twenty and threw it down the stairs. It fluttered and landed halfway down.

"Here. Now leave me alone. And next time, say please."

# Chapter 18

## DEATH

Henri was waiting for Oliver after breakfast in the lobby of the hotel. "Good morning, Mr. Oliver. Do you like our city? Did you have a good night?"

"Good morning to you, too, Henri. Yes, I like your city, although I haven't seen much of it. But no, I didn't sleep well. The air conditioning was very loud."

"Sorry to hear, sir. Shall we go?"

Oliver had dreaded this morning from the moment he saw it on his program, neatly printed with the time (9:30 a.m.), place (Department of Public Health, City Morgue), and purpose ('identification of human remains of late Mr. Johan). He was going to see his dead father. Last night, after Fantata had left, he made a quick call home to talk to Mary and the kids. He told Mary that he had no idea what to expect or how he'd react. She was very nice and tried to give him strength, which worked a bit last night. But now he couldn't feel any strength at all.

On the way there, Henri took it upon himself to be Oliver's tour guide and show him the town, occasionally going into historical detail. Oliver couldn't tell if Henri meant to distract him, but it was welcome nonetheless.

"See that rusty crane there? And the tower on the dock? That was built by the previous ruler, who believed that foreigners would pay thousands and thousands to go on a cruise ship and see the mountains and the animals. My uncle was going to work there, because he knew the waters around the city, but then the fighting started, and then the dictator was murdered. No cruise ship ever docked here. Well, maybe in future. Then, I'll drive rich tourists around, instead of you. Now, the tower is full of snakes. You know, the street kids catch them and sell them to food stands. Nice grilled."

As he was talking, Oliver looked out the window. The streets were filled with motorcycles again. He figured out that the liquid in the bottles sold by women behind the stands along the street was gasoline. Drivers, some of them smoking, were filling up their tanks from the bottles. People here seemed to have a different notion of risk.

"That there is the regional military headquarters," Henri pointed out. Oliver saw a large building with flags flying on every corner. Its courtyard was filled with 4x4s and light trucks, including one with a twin-barreled canon pointing to the sky. Soldiers were walking in and out of the compound. Nobody was saluting anyone, which Oliver thought was strange. Armies ran on discipline, didn't they?

Oliver swallowed hard as a long-repressed memory came to the surface. He had once saluted his father, standing straight and clicking his heels after an acrimonious row, in a bitter attempt to show sarcastic contempt for the authority of a man who was never there and then dared to tell him when he was there to get his grades up or else. It was not a happy thought, and he looked ahead to find a source of distraction. Henri turned the car off the road and into a courtyard.

"Look, Mr. Oliver. Flora is there already." Henri pointed with his chin to another GAPI vehicle parked outside a white building with a blue cross on the gable.

Flora stood on the steps leading to the front door with a folder in her hand. She had traded her usual smile for a strictly businesslike expression. Once Oliver got out of the car, she too asked him if he had slept well. He ignored the question and wished her a good morning instead. He had no intention of telling her that he had barely slept or that he kept thinking of crying babies and of his dad's features, or that he was trying to replay scenes in his head of when he last saw him.

Flora and Oliver walked down an unlit corridor, Henri staying behind with the car. Oliver wondered if this building had electricity at all. He sniffed the air, expecting to be hit by the stench of rotting bodies lying in an uncooled room. Nothing. The air felt normal, with faint traces of dust, sweat, and mildew.

At the end of the corridor stood a table with an old-fashioned ledger  on top. Behind the table sat a man of indeterminate age in a stained, yellow shirt and a necktie that was more knot than tie.

"Here," Flora said softly. "You need to write your name here, your father's name here, your relationship to him, and sign here."

Oliver filled in the required lines. The morgue clerk behind the desk got up and gestured them through a vast wooden door that opened into an office with a massive, varnished wood desk and chair with baroque ornaments. The door closed behind them, leaving Flora and Oliver behind in silence. They took the two heavy seats in front of the desk.

"Flora, what's going on?"

"I'm not sure. I think this is the office of the Director of Public Health. I don't know why; I guess he wants to see you. It's not every day a foreigner is here to see him. The last time was with that girl that was murdered by Captain Christmas, but we didn't handle that. Basically, all that you need to do is identify your father and sign for the human remains. At least, that's what I was told. And then GAPI will handle the actual repatriation."

The door opened. The man with the dirty shirt and big knot opened the door and with a stiff little bow announced the arrival of "the distinguished Mr. Lampuit, Director of the Department of Public Health and Chief Executive Officer of the Central Morgue of the City by the Water."

Flora and Oliver—not sure why—rose to their feet and looked at the open door, through which entered a massive, round man in an enormous dark suit and purple silk tie. He shook hands with Oliver, extended his "sincere condolences," and urged his guests to sit down as he deliberately stepped to his chair.

Oliver wondered whether he should've put on a suit himself and then how much this man actually weighed. Something like 350 pounds of officialdom. Lampuit sat down—or more accurately, allowed himself to fall slowly into his chair—and put on a pair of gold-rimmed reading glasses with both hands, in the process showing a diamond-encrusted, gold watch.

"Well then," he started slowly and officially, looking over his glasses to Flora, ignoring Oliver. "I understand you are here for Mr. Johan. You will see him momentarily. Unfortunately, we do not have the money or equipment to have you recognize him from a photo, so my colleague here will accompany you to the morgue."

"That's fine, Mr. Lampuit. I would like to see him, anyway," Oliver said, looking at Flora first, then directly at Lampuit.

"Right. I presume you're a direct relative? In fact, I can see the resemblance to the deceased, may God almighty rest his soul."

"I'm his son, and I'd like to know how my—"

"Please allow me to offer you my most sincere condolences, once again," Lampuit interrupted. "I know you must be anxious to find out, but I am one hundred percent positive that the *precise* circumstances and *full* details of his death will *all* be revealed in due course."

Lampuit waved to the man with the big knot, who had been standing behind him with a folder in hand. He took the folder and looked at it studiously through his reading glasses, then looked over the rim of his glasses to Oliver and then to Flora.

"I must not fail to let you know that there is of course some *minor* administrative issue that we need to resolve before we can release the remains to the custody of the family so he may receive a most proper and dignified burial. I have deemed it necessary that this issue be resolved before we enter the morgue and proceed with the identification and the handover."

He gave the folder to his subordinate, who walked around the huge desk to give it to Flora. She opened the folder and let out a barely audible gasp.

"You see," Lampuit started to explain, "given the *special* status of the deceased and the presumably extremely long distance the remains will have to travel, we will be required to apply a rather unique method for embalming, which regrettably requires significant financial resources much beyond our meager budget."

He paused and looked at Oliver, who had started to seriously dislike the man across the desk. What a pompous prick, he thought. Oliver held out his hand toward Flora and asked to see the folder. She passed it to him. In it was an invoice for twenty-five thousand dollars for "autopsy, conservation, and embalmment," plus a "contingency family fee" of five thousand and a footnote that said, "Human remains will be released upon payment."

The banker in him scanned the invoice twice. It had no letterhead. He turned it over to look at the back, which was blank. He rose halfway out of his seat and put the folder back on the desk.

"Excuse me, sir, but these amounts seem to be rather on the high side. I understand that you have to meet your expenses, but this, I don't understand. And what is this contingency family fee, precisely?"

Lampuit nodded and looked over his glasses directly at Oliver with an expression that aimed to convey great clarity with a hint of irritation.

"Let me be perfectly clear. I have explained these costs to you already and see no need to repeat myself. I will add, however, that this is in *full* conformity with our department's policies, and I'm in *no* position to diverge from these policies. As such, I'm afraid that I must insist on full payment before we can release the body."

"And what if we don't pay?"

"Unfortunately, I must admit that this does happen occasionally. This is a very poor area, after all. In such cases, we dispose of the body ourselves in the most cost-effective way possible."

"And, may I ask, what does that mean?"

"Well, we're close to the forest, so we allow nature to take its course. It's all very clean and hygienic."

Lampuit stared directly and assertively at Oliver, who was becoming increasingly angry. What a terrible place, and what a terrible man, he thought. It slowly dawned on him: this was extortion. Pay up, or we feed your dead relative to the animals. Just look at the man: how did he get so fat and pay for his big, golden watch? And the reference to Dad's "special" status probably meant that his family could afford to pay more, since they were foreigners. This man was disgusting, a vulture, feeding on the dead. Oliver's employer charged fees too, for all sorts of banking services, but not at this scale and not at the expense of mourning families. He was glad that he was here instead of his sister. She would have exploded and possibly strangled the guy with his own silk necktie.

He drew a deep breath. First things first. Oliver thought that he could match Lampuit's assertiveness. Looking tough and determined, or so he hoped, Oliver made his point.

"Very well, Mr. Lampuit. Certainly you have your policies, and I'm sure we can resolve this matter *in due course*. But the whole matter may be academic if the body you have in there turns out to be somebody else. So, if you don't mind, I'd like to move on and proceed with the identification."

Lampuit's expression didn't change. He had dealt with thousands of families before, and usually, he didn't compromise. But this was a potentially very big prize, and the boy in the chair before him had a point.

"Very well, then. My colleague here will show you the way. We'll be in touch again soon. Now, if you will excuse me..."

He picked up a document before him and, with a dismissive gesture, started to read. The man with the big knot led them outside the office and closed the big wooden doors. Oliver was fuming inside about the cynical abuse by this fat blob, selling corpses back to their families.

He would soon see the dead body of his father, and he was not ready, not now, to face the emotions he feared would come. He asked for a minute, leaned against the wall, and put his hands over his eyes. Cool down, Oliver, cool down. It's only money, after all. Soon you can forget about this fat monster. Flora came over to him and, without a word, stroked his shoulder. The voice of big knot interrupted him.

"Excuse me, lady and gentleman. My name is Sinamon. Allow me to escort you into the morgue. We have prepared your father's remains for viewing."

Oliver knew he would never be truly ready. Better get on with it, then. He nodded to Sinamon and took Flora's arm. He was glad she was there. Sinamon walked toward a metal door and threw a few switches just right of the door. Somewhere, a fan started running.

"You know," Sinamon started talking in a schoolmaster's tone, "we see death all the time here, and I must say that it comes in different shapes. I've thought about it often. In fact, you could say I've been so very fortunate to be so close to death to study it in great detail. You see, it can be ugly or swift, horrific or peaceful, unfair or deserved. Yes, all of these apply to death. I see it all the time. I keep a spreadsheet. In the end, though, death seems to be a good friend, really, to most people at least."

He opened the door and stood aside to allow his guests to enter the morgue. There were no windows. Against the walls were racks made of metal tubes standing on a tiled floor with a drain in the center of the room. Corpses, some with a shape that looked incomplete or twisted, were stacked three high, covered by dark green plastic sheets. These must be body bags, thought Oliver. The smell inside was awful—a mix of chemicals and decay. Both Flora and Oliver brought their hands to their mouths, suppressing the urge to gag and vomit. In the center of the room were three surgical tables, with a corpse on each of them covered by a stain-spotted, whitish sheet.

"These are the ones that we're working on now," said Sinamon with a hint of enthusiasm, as if he was a museum guide proudly commenting on the latest acquisitions of fine art.

"The one in the middle is your father." He pointed and proceeded to gently move the sheet to uncover the face.

No doubt this was Oliver's father. The skin was discolored, and the eyes were closed. But the nose and the mouth, the birthmark on the neck—*this* was Dad. Oliver thought Dad looked a bit sad, but then he realized that the dead have no feelings. Surprisingly calm, Oliver looked at Flora, who was crying, and nodded.

"Thank you, Mr. Sinamon. I can now confirm that this is the body of my father, Johan."

"You are quite welcome. I must say, you look like him, but a lot more handsome. Forgive me, but we don't get too many foreigners in here. If I may say so, your father died a good death. Of course, the investigation is not yet completed, but in my personal opinion, it was a *very* clean death. Two bullets right through the heart, like an instant sleep without dreams. Not like the other two we have here on the tables."

Oliver was actually relieved to hear that his father suffered little, if at all. He offered a timid smile to Sinamon, who took this as an encouragement to continue talking.

"You see, this one here," he said, lifting the sheet to take a peek. "This one died an ugly, horrific, but probably deserved death. Would you like to see?"

"No, thank you," Oliver and Flora said in unison.

"Good thing, too. She was beaten and tortured. Not much left to recognize her from. Some people die really badly, you know. And then the one on the other table, one side of him was run over by a truck going downhill without functioning brakes. Not so clean. And so unnecessary, too. Shall we go?"

They left the morgue as soon as they could. Once outside, Oliver made a few slow pirouettes in the wind with his eyes closed to cleanse himself from the smells. He felt calm. Somehow, the sight of his dead father and the confirmation that he was, indeed, dead gave him some peace of mind. He should call Mom and his wife soon and maybe not tell them about the extortionist Lampuit, big knot Sinamon and his half-baked, bizarre theories about death and dying, or the company Dad had been keeping these days.

# Chapter 19

## STANDARD STUFF

On the way back to the GAPI office, they were all quiet. Flora wiped away a few more tears, checked her text messages and applied her perfume. Oliver stared out the front windshield, deep in thought. Henri looked at the both of them and decided to keep his mouth shut and to just drive. Flora would tell him what had happened later, anyway.

Once they arrived at the office compound, Flora told Oliver that Bruno had sent her a text that he wanted to see him as soon as possible. Oliver felt tired, but he was here now. He might as well get it behind him.

Bruno beckoned him inside his office with a concerned smile. "Well, I heard you identified Johan's body. That's good. Sorry to hear, of course, about the treatment you received from this Lampuit character. Glad you didn't pay him up front. There've been some rumors going around for a while now about him running some sort of racket. Totally unacceptable, of course, but par for the course in this crazy country. Don't quote me on that, by the way."

Bruno looked as if he were about to wink, but then thought better not to. "You know, Oliver, sometimes you simply have no choice but to pay some debt, even if you're not responsible for it. Now, a few formalities to take care of. First, now that you've made the identification the authorities will issue a death certificate to the next of kin, meaning you, allowing you and us to move forward with the repatriation. We'll get a copy, as his employer. Second, there are just a few more things to wrap up with the formal autopsy and investigation, and then we're in the clear. You'll get a copy of the investigation report, of course—at least those parts that concern the family."

"Wait a minute, Bruno. Why would there be any parts that do *not* concern the family? I don't understand. Aren't we entitled to know what happened?"

"Of course, of course. There's just a lot of internal GAPI stuff, you know—administrative things that won't be of interest to you or your family. Now, finally, my third point. There are a few papers for you to sign—just routine matters regarding the passing of a GAPI employee. Standard stuff, you know. What can we do?"

Bruno had a look of contempt in his eyes, as if the papers Oliver was supposed to sign were really an unnecessary burden that no one should be expected to carry. Oliver gave Bruno a look of understanding.

"I understand, Bruno. In my line of work—I'm a banker, you know—we make our clients sign dozens of papers, some of which never see the light of day again. Corporate policy, just like yours, I suppose."

Bruno spread his hands and smiled in acknowledgement. Oliver shrugged, but made a mental note to himself that he was going to read every bit of small print on whatever papers GAPI was going to give him.

"I don't care about the papers, for now, at least," Oliver continued. "I'd like to know what happened to my father. What do you know? Is there anything you can share with me at this point?"

"Not much, I'm afraid. Look, this is out of our hands. The local police are investigating this. You will see the police today, right, just as a matter of courtesy, I think. Nothing of substance to discuss with them, really. We have our own people doing some checking in the background, all very discreet of course. Here's what we know: Johan was found dead early in the morning, on the ground next to his car, with two bullets through his heart, standard nine-millimeter pistol, we were told. Nothing was stolen or removed. The car key was in Johan's pocket, suggesting that he got out of the car maybe to talk to someone sometime during the night. No signs of a struggle, although I heard that, based on the tracks on the ground that somebody or somebodies may have tried to move his body. That's it. No suspects, no murder weapon, no motive."

"Yeah, what about a motive? Who could have wanted him dead? Could this Christmas fellow have had something to do with it?"

"We don't know, Oliver. But it seems to me that Christmas was benefiting from Johan's work, and they seemed to get along, as far as I know. I see no motive there. Anyway, I have some work to do. You have some forms to fill out and sign. By the way, are you ready for tomorrow afternoon? The memorial service?"

"I guess so. Could you please let me know if you find out something more about the murder?"

Dissatisfied, Oliver left Bruno's office, collected an envelope from Flora with the forms, and turned down the suggestion to sign them right there and then and get it all behind him. He was going to take the papers to the hotel and give them a thorough read.

For now, he had a "courtesy" meeting with the chief of police. The police station was not far away. In fact, it would have taken him less than five minutes to walk and less than five seconds to find. He could see a building with POLICE in bright yellow neon letters on an elevation in the middle of a walled compound.

Outside were small groups of armed policemen in blue uniforms and black combat boots hanging out, smoking, eating, or playing cards. They all carried military rifles, which struck Oliver as odd. A large truck was blocking the compound's entrance. It required Henri several times to explain that they had a meeting with the police chief. Only when he mentioned Johan's name did the driver of the truck pick up his radio to check and confirm. His orders came rapidly, and in a cloud of black diesel smoke, the truck roared forward to let GAPI's car in.

It took them another half-hour and three desks where they had to sign in and be escorted to the next desk before they were sitting in a waiting room with old burgundy plush sofas that probably hadn't been cleaned in a decade. They had to wait another forty-five minutes before an officer came in to tell them that the chief was ready to see them. So much for courtesy, thought Oliver.

Henri stayed behind, while Oliver was led into a large room that was dominated by a ten-yard-long conference table. At the chairman's end, there was a large rectangular desk that was completely empty except for a single sheet of paper and a large handgun with an ivory handle. Behind the desk was a large, muscular man in a blue uniform, his sleeves rolled up, looking at Oliver above the rim of his reading glasses. He didn't bother to get up and gestured Oliver into the seat to his left. As Oliver sat down, he felt himself sink a level below the police chief and felt horribly inadequate.

"Mr. Oliver? Courtesy visit, hmm?"

"Yes indeed, Sir," Oliver dared not address the chief by rank, as he was unsure what the insignia on the man's shoulder meant.

"First, allow me to assure you that my department, all my men and women and myself, are fully committed to find out what happened in this case, apprehend the culprit, and hand him over to the judicial authorities of this city so justice may be done. Second, I understand that you and your family have been struck with deep grief. Such a tragic loss. May the Good Lord rest your father's soul. Please accept my personal condolences for you and your family, Mr. Oliver."

"Thank you, Sir. We—that is, my mother, my sister, and I—are very interested to find out what actually happened to him. I just saw him at the morgue, you know."

"The investigation is ongoing. Until such time as the investigation is concluded, we can share very little information with you or anyone else. What we can tell you now, you probably know already."

"Is there nothing you can say? There are no suspects? No suspicions? What about the murder weapon?"

"Probably a standard nine-millimeter like this one here." The chief picked up the weapon on his desk with both hands to show to Oliver, then put it back again with a twist of his hand.

"However," the chief said, folding his hands and looking directly at Oliver with an inviting smile, "we can try to expedite the investigation with some help from your side."

"Any information you need. Anything at all. I'm ready. What can I do?"

"We could use some voluntary resources from your end for some enhanced forensic work."

Oliver was quiet. It was not quite déjà vu, but he had the uncomfortable feeling that this was going the same way as with the fat morgue director, Lampuit. Money. The chief wanted money. He knew it.

"Look, I'm an honest police officer. And I'll be honest with you. I would love nothing better than to find the crook who killed your father. But I also need to be realistic. We have no money for basic forensic equipment. My police officers do not get paid. How could they get paid if nobody pays their taxes here? Why do you think my men and women in uniform occasionally put parking and speeding fines in their own pockets? Communities or businesses that need protection, like banks, I need to charge them a fee for that service. Which is reasonable, no?"

"I understand," Oliver said, beginning to grasp once again that the rules back home did not apply here. "So, Chief, if I get this correctly, you are a public servant, but you need to rely on private money to do your work?"

"Well, yes. Some may call this corruption, to be honest, including perhaps yourself," the chief said with a desperate smile. He put his hands flat on the table and looked up to the ceiling, then back at Oliver. "I prefer to look at it as direct taxation, cutting out the middleman. How long have you been here?"

"One day, Sir," Oliver said. It felt more like a week already.

"Good. As you are driving around, you will come across some potholes in the road. There will be kids or sometimes adults there with a bucket to fill the potholes with dirt and rocks. They will stop you and ask for money for their repair of the road. It's a simple system, right? In your country you pay tax to a government who has some committee deciding which roads to repair, some other body to select a contractor, who will recruit and pay some guys to fill in the pothole. Much too complicated, don't you think?"

"Indeed," Oliver admitted.

Somewhere, in the back of his head, he felt that the chief's reasoning was not exactly watertight. Once the first vehicle had moved on, would the kids with the bucket not grab a shovel and restore the pothole to its previously unrepaired state so they could milk the next motorist for money? Oliver knew instinctively that he was going to lose this argument. Maybe it was good to get to the point and start negotiating.

"All right. How much do you need? And for what? I'm a banker, you see, and I'll have to insist on proper bookkeeping."

"But of course, Oliver. I like you. A man who gets to the point and who understands economics. You don't find too many of those around. Please, call me Frank Eugene." He stretched out his right arm to give Oliver a firm handshake, followed by a business card with gold letters.

"Call me anytime. Now, to get to the point. For starters, I would need a thousand dollars to pay the forensic lab. We have recovered the projectiles from your father's body and some artifacts around the crime scene, but have been unable to do detailed research on them. Then, another thousand for fuel and allowances and finally about five hundred to pay off informers. And if you want real results, you could post a reward for any information leading to the apprehension of the culprit. That would cost about five hundred for publicity, plus the actual reward, let's say ten thousand total."

Oliver was used to discussing numbers without giving even the slightest inclination what such numbers actually meant to him or the bank he worked for. He could keep a straight face anytime, even when obvious idiots would come to his bank with cockamamie plans to start some crazy business with a loan from his bank. Frank Eugene, chief of police, was no idiot, it seemed. Oliver was guessing it might be a good thing to be on a first-name basis with the local police chief in a strange town. But this was about money too, and Oliver needed to take charge. His face showed neither interest nor disapproval as he responded.

"So, we're talking three thousand for the investigation, plus a reward of ten thousand. Well then, Frank Eugene, let me think about it. I trust we will meet again soon. Thank you for your time."

Oliver pushed himself out of his low chair and shook hands again with the chief, who was caught by surprise by this sudden goodbye. Just before he left the room, he looked down over his shoulders to the legs of the chairs around the conference table. They had all been sawed off by about five inches.

Henri drove him to the hotel, looking at him in the rearview mirror every so often, as if he was waiting, hoping for Oliver to speak.

"Henri. You knew my father well, didn't you?"

"Yes, I drove him all the time, except after hours."

"I'm sorry. You must miss him too. But I need to know: do you have any idea who murdered him? Did he have any enemies?"

"No. No. He was doing business with many dangerous people here. Christmas, military intelligence, local businessmen who want payment for goods ordered by Johan. This is a very dangerous place, too. Sometimes people disappear or die for no reason. Sometimes, police make people disappear. Also, some people say angry spirits are around, especially near the water."

Oliver remembered what Fantata told him the night before, but decided to ignore Henri's comment about spirits. "Did my father have any friends he talked to a lot?"

"Oh, yes, Mr. Oliver, at the office he really liked Ibrahim. He's very good, Ibrahim. Knows a lot, talks to many people. He's easy to find. Just look for the man with many mobile phones in his hand."

Henri gave him a wide grin in the mirror. "And then there is Miss Vashti. She's a good friend. They have dinner together many times. Beautiful lady, like a queen or a princess. Very pretty."

Oliver had never heard Dad talk about either Ibrahim or Vashti at home and wondered why. Maybe he liked to keep things separate. Or maybe it was he, Oliver, and maybe Mom too, who liked to keep things separate, to keep Dad's work out of the family.

"Henri?"

"Yes, Sir?"

"When I arrived yesterday, I had the feeling that some of the people in the lobby, especially the fat military guy, had been waiting for me. What do you think?"

"I think maybe so. You see, Johan's program is very famous here. Create many jobs. High hopes for peace. Maybe people want to see the son. Maybe you come to take over. That's what happens here. When father leave job not finish, his family is responsible to finish."

"No way. I already have a nice job, thank you very much."

They drove into the hotel car park. Henri said that he would pick Oliver up the next morning to go to the bank and visit Johan's apartment later. The memorial service would be in the afternoon. Oliver ordered himself a beer from the bar and took it upstairs to his room. He opened the windows and looked out at the water.

He had a lot on his mind. Seeing Dad dead. Everybody wanting money. No answers anywhere. For about five minutes, he just looked at the waves and the foam circling around eddies in the water. It calmed him down and allowed him to sift through his impressions of the day. But first things first. Maybe filling out forms would help clear his mind.

He opened the envelope and sorted the papers in front of him. He started reading and found the first set of papers to be rather routine—confirmation of next of kin, addresses, bank accounts for any remaining salary payment, beneficiaries of his pension (this would be Mom, of course), and similar stuff. He filled them all out and signed where needed, until he got to the last document.

At first glance, he thought it was a simple acknowledgement that the transfer of the human remains from the authorities to the next of kin had taken place on such and such date. But this was on GAPI letterhead and in small print, too. He started to read the paper with intense focus, underlining the most striking phrases. It was about "exoneration of guilt" and "limitation of liability" related to the "wrongful death" of a GAPI staff member, "due to circumstances shaped by the staff member himself," which were "outside the framework of approved security measures," leading to "loss of benefits in accordance with applicable internal regulations."

It had his name on the bottom. He was supposed to sign and acknowledge the above.

"What the fuck? Bastards!" he said to the open window. This was incredible. Basically, they wanted him to agree that the death of his father was his own bloody fault—how appropriate this expression was now. Moreover, his mom could lose her survivor's pension, and on top of that, his family could not sue GAPI if he signed off on this. He read the paper again, and it became crystal clear to him that this was GAPI trying to cover its ass at the expense of his family. No wonder they wanted him to sign this quickly.

No way in hell was he going to sign this.

He needed another beer and room to think. He closed the windows, took his laptop, and left his room. Down on the terrace, he found his table from yesterday free and sat down facing the water. Fortunately, the terrace had few guests, and there was no sign of yesterday's beer bellies. He ordered a beer and asked the waiter to bring him some of those nice peanuts. He pulled out the cell phone GAPI had given him and tried to call home. The call did not go through.

He opened his laptop and was relieved to see that the Wi-Fi was working well. There were a few e-mails in his inbox from his family, concerned about how he was doing. He wrote two e-mails, one to Mary and one to Mom. They were quite identical—essentially, a bland description of events and whom he met without any of the details that might upset or confuse them, including the bit about the paper he had just refused to sign. He wanted to sort this out himself first.

At the end, he sent them his love and asked for their ideas for the memorial service where he was supposed to speak, because he wanted to get it right. Because at this point, overwhelmed by the sight of death and the impressions of a new and strange place, he had no clue what to say.

# Chapter 20

## THE ACCOUNT

The following morning, Oliver woke somewhat refreshed. He opened the curtains and the windows. He could smell the water. It had a peculiar perfume of silt and decaying organic matter. He stretched and fell back onto the bed to read his e-mails. He was relieved to see that Mary and Mom, as well as his sister, Louise, both had come through with good suggestions on what to say at the memorial service. Some nice anecdotes about Dad, his sense of humor, how he felt about his job, things like that. His children had sent him a few drawings of how they remembered Granddad. He smiled at the drawings and missed his children.

He went for breakfast in jeans and a T-shirt and took some notes for his speech. Back in his room, he changed into the only suit he had brought for the trip, a navy-blue two-piece with a subtle gray pinstripe, a white starched shirt, and the silk blue tie his dad had given him for Christmas last year. "The banker in mourning," he said to himself in the mirror.

As promised, Henri was waiting for him in the lobby of the hotel. Oliver was happy to see a familiar face and greeted him enthusiastically despite himself.

"Wow, Boss. Nice suit. Busy day today. We go to bank first, OK, and then to apartment to check out personal belongings?"

It was a short drive to the bank, a square building with extensive metal grills on the windows and doors. There were two policemen outside, dozing in plastic chairs on either side of the door. The name of the bank itself was unknown to Oliver. He would have to check up on where it was based, who owned it, and what its capitalization was. Another policeman was sitting inside behind a desk, scrutinizing everyone coming in and handing out numbered tickets to incoming clients. Oliver took one look at the large crowd waiting to be served at the teller windows and decided to take a shortcut. He looked like a banker anyway, didn't he?

"Excuse me, I wish to speak to the branch director. I have an appointment, if you'd be so kind to escort me to his office?" Oliver bluffed with a tone of authority imitated from his own regional director, a man he admired.

The policeman looked at him for a few seconds and without a word pointed to a staircase leading up to offices upstairs. Oliver nodded his thanks and moved determinedly up the staircase. At the top of the stairs was a corridor. Assuming the branch manager was at the end of the corridor, he started toward a door at the end when he was interrupted by a gruff male voice to his left, asking him where he thought he was going.

He looked around and saw a man in shirt and tie sitting in a small office, looking over his computer screen at Oliver. Well, he explained, he'd come to close his father's bank account. Seeing that the man was shaking his head and getting ready to point him back downstairs, he quickly added that it was Mr. Johan's account, from GAPI.

The man's demeanor changed upon hearing the name, and he gestured Oliver inside with a welcoming smile. He introduced himself as the deputy branch manager.

"Nice to meet you, Mr. Oliver. Of course, we've heard about your father's untimely death. Please accept our condolences. Now, I understand you have come to close the accounts of your late father. Do you have the paperwork?"

Oliver pulled out the envelope Flora had prepared and handed it to the deputy branch manager, who studied its contents attentively. As a banker should, Oliver thought.

"You know, Sir, I'm a banker myself. Small branch of a big bank back home. Very interesting to see how you do business here. Not much different, I'd think."

"Really, so we're colleagues? Very good, then, let me pull up your father's account details." The manager typed in a few characters and studied the results on his screen.

"How would you like to settle the balance, Oliver?"

"Well, it depends," Oliver said. He was hoping that he could simply take the cash, if there was any, rather than do a wire transfer. The fees to do a transfer from this place must be punishing, and he didn't expect his dad to have a lot in the bank. "What exactly is the balance?"

"Let me see. Checking and savings combined, it would be 143,711 dollars and 92 cents."

Initially, Oliver could not believe what he'd heard. Did the man say 143,000 and change? Dad never had this much money in his accounts back home. Where did this come from? And what was he doing with it? Keeping a straight face, he asked the manager if he could perhaps see statements from the last six months, perhaps a year, if possible. The manager agreed, and soon the printer next to his computer, an old-fashioned dot-matrix model, started screaming.

While they waited for the printout, Oliver realized that he now might have a way out with Lampuit and the police chief, Frank Eugene. His dad's own money could help get his corpse out of the morgue and pay for an investigation into his own death. It was doubtful that GAPI, with their anticorruption policies, would be able to help with either. He would still have to try to negotiate the amounts down.

"Here you go, Mr. Oliver, printed statements for the last year. Is there anything else you require before we close the accounts?"

"Um, I think, maybe, could we do this tomorrow or in the next few days, please? It's a significant sum of money, after all, and I would need to make some arrangements and consult my mother, as well."

"Of course, we can handle this between bankers. Take your time. Your money isn't going anywhere. Here is my card, with my private cell number on the back."

Oliver assembled his papers and the account statements and left the bank looking straight ahead, ignoring the beggars outside. Henri opened the door for him and took off. He opened his mouth to say something but saw in the rearview mirror that his passenger was studying some paperwork and looking very serious.

The statements were actually pretty straightforward. Every month, GAPI transferred a small "subsistence allowance" to the checking account. Oliver knew that Dad's actual salary was sent to his bank account at home to pay for the mortgage and living expenses. Every three months, Dad made a payment to a Ms. Nicolette, apparently for the rent of his apartment—where they were going now. The last payment was a month ago, so the rent was paid for another two months. Other than that, there were regular cash withdrawals from the checking account, about once a week, that looked like living expenses.

The savings account statements were equally simple. Dad had been making cash deposits at no particular frequency and of varying amounts. Sometimes there was one a month, another time there were four deposits in a week. It was the same with cash withdrawals. There was no particular frequency or pattern. The overall balance had been steadily growing over the year, though. Oliver saw no sign of any other transactions—no wire transfers or check deposits—either coming in or going out. The last transaction must have been made three days before he was shot. It was a deposit for twenty-five thousand dollars in cash. Jesus. What had Dad been up to? Where did this money come from?

"Henri?"

"Yes, Sir?"

"Did my father go to the bank often?"

"Yes, he did. But sometimes I go for him to make deposit or withdrawal. He trust me. I never look inside envelope," he said proudly. "If there is anything I can do for you here, I'm happy to do—go shopping, go to bank, deliver mail—just like for your father. We're almost at the apartment."

# Chapter 21

## TOP FLOOR

Henri stopped in front of a rust-red-painted gate and honked twice. A tiny slide in the door at shoulder height opened and closed again. The gate opened fast, swung by a wiry young man without a shirt, who greeted Henri enthusiastically.

"He my nephew, Joseph," Henri explained while effortlessly driving the 4x4 through the gate with less than an inch to spare on either side.

They parked in a courtyard of hard, red mud and gravel, lined with trees and shrubs. Joseph greeted Oliver and escorted him through an opening in the trees to a large, three-story house, set on about half an acre, perfectly landscaped right on the water, with a bright green lawn, rock formations, and palm trees.

"Johan lived on the top floor. Very nice apartment, you will see. Police have searched it already, and they said it's OK to go in," said Henri, who had decided to come along.

The front door was protected by an iron grill cemented into the concrete and locked by a fist-sized padlock. Joseph unlocked the door, and they climbed up three floors of tiled stairs in a barely lit stairwell. Their footsteps echoed against the bare walls. Oliver noted that there were three numbered doors on each floor, one in the middle and two on each side. Quite the workout, Oliver thought when they arrived on the top floor, which had only one door. Joseph produced a key and opened it.

Oliver was expecting to have a sense of homecoming and recognition. After all, he knew how they lived back home with the furniture, curtains, and paintings that he had grown up with in their well-kept and orderly household.

But this was different. The apartment was light, with two large windows and a glass door that opened onto a balcony. The water and the mountains were the only things in sight. It had an open plan. The only closed-off spaces were the bathroom and a closet. It was right under the roof, which was supported by four concrete pillars, around which Johan had placed his furniture.

The room was a mess. Whoever had come to look for whatever had not bothered putting anything back in its place. The sofa, the bed, chairs, the desk in the corner, were covered by clothes or papers. All the drawers had been opened, their contents spilled onto the floor. The kitchen floor was littered with utensils and empty bottles. Oliver looked at Joseph, the question self-evident.

"The police came," Joseph said with an apologetic grin. "But they only took the booze, nothing else. I couldn't stop them."

"Of course, you couldn't." Oliver laid a hand on his shoulder. "It's OK. It's OK."

Oliver knew that he had to do something. Ship Dad's goods over to Mom's or sell them here, locally. He couldn't possibly clean this mess up now. He was wearing his fine suit, which he was not about to get dirty, and he needed to focus on his statement. He pulled out a twenty-dollar bill.

"Joseph, I have no idea where everything goes, and we need to clean this up. Maybe later make an inventory. Here, take this, and you can start cleaning the apartment. I'll come later when I have time."

"Oh no, Sir, oh no. I work for you already. No need for extra cash now, maybe later when I do an extra-good job. Besides, you live here now. Miss Nicolette told me to give you a key. You can live here. Rent was paid for next two months, anyway. Here." Joseph pulled out a key with a key ring that looked like a tiny hand grenade.

Oliver took the key. This was not a bad idea. He would save some money on the hotel and work on Dad's case surrounded by Dad's stuff. He caught himself. Was he working on Dad's case, trying to solve his murder? Not sure that this was his goal. He had come to wrap up Dad's affairs and bring him home. He needed to focus on that first.

"Joseph, would you mind? Cleaning things up here? Do you think I could move in here tonight?"

"No problem, Sir. Maybe Henri can collect your luggage from the hotel?"

Henri was nodding. "After memorial service, we go to the hotel, get luggage, and maybe do some shopping. You need bread, coffee, beer, maybe some scotch? Your father really like his scotch, but the police take it all away."

"Well, I guess they like scotch too. Good idea, thank you so much. You guys are really very helpful. Thank you."

Both Joseph and Henri put their hands over their hearts and laughed at each other, and then smiled at Oliver, who did not know what to think.

"What?"

"You don't understand, Boss. You are in our land now, and we take care of our guests as if they are family. You are family now." Joseph extended his hand and shook Oliver's softly.

# Chapter 22

## GREY SKIES

Oliver was told to wait in his father's office while the GAPI staff set up the courtyard for the memorial service. He looked around at the bare office, which was not like his dad's at all. Someone must have cleaned up and taken the files from the cabinets. He opened the desk drawer. Nothing special there— standard pencils, some paper clips, an eraser. Could've been his own desk at the bank, except for the chair. This was a really good chair, he thought, as he swiveled around. He looked over his notes again for his brief remarks. He was comfortable now. Funny how he wasn't missing Dad yet, not really. When would that come? Would it hit him hard, or not at all?

The service was held in the open air under gray skies with clouds that looked like they wanted to rain, but somehow couldn't. A wind blew from across the water, bounced off the building, and swirled around the parking lot, which no longer held any cars, just people in folding seats. It was a rather large crowd—about a hundred people.

Oliver was sitting in the front row, opposite a table with a white cloth on which stood a large photo of his father, decorated with flowers and a few candles that wouldn't stay alight in the wind. Was that some sort of symbol? Oliver was wondering while he half-listened to Bruno's speech, which, he explained at the outset, was on behalf of the organization. Bruno was paying tribute to Johan in glowing bureaucratic terms—a hard-working, dedicated official who always had the goals of our organization *and* the needs of the local population in mind, great track record behind him, bright future ahead that was arrested by a heinous crime. GAPI would work with local authorities, *of course*, to make sure that the culprit was brought to justice.

While he said this, Bruno waved his hand in recognition at the police chief, who was sitting in the front row too, a few seats removed from Oliver.

Flora spoke on behalf of the staff, looking at Oliver every other sentence. Johan was a special human being, she said, who cared for everyone, who always was positive and never looked down on anybody.

Oliver looked at Bruno. Maybe this was implied criticism, but Bruno didn't show any emotion other than official solemnity as he looked at Flora speaking. Toward the end of her speech, Flora choked up. She would miss him. They would all miss him, his jokes and mishaps. She told the story about the time he was dancing at an office party—he could *not* dance—and ended up head-first in the tub that held the beer and ice, but kept on dancing anyway.

There were giggles and sobs in the audience as she told the story that everybody, except Oliver, seemed to know. A few tears running down her face, spoiling her makeup, she explained how he had made them all proud by putting their work on the world stage through the Garden of Peace. Seeing Flora cry made Oliver clench his teeth. He wasn't ready. He couldn't afford to lose it now. He needed to get behind the microphone and speak in a composed manner. He looked down at the ground and started counting pebbles.

Oliver's talk on behalf of the family was short and boring, he admitted to himself later. In any event, he had managed to keep it dry. He included obligatory thanks to GAPI, to Bruno, Flora, and all those who had worked with Johan or had been a good friend to him. He told the crowd some stories from back home—yes, we *knew* he couldn't dance to save his life—about the pride Dad had shown in his work, how devoted he had been to his wife and family.

At the end, he just had to raise the question why. It felt necessary, especially after he caught both the police chief and Bruno studying their phones.

"Why was he killed? A man who had done no wrong? My family is waiting for the answers. Thank you."

Both men in the front row looked up immediately and, realizing that no answer was expected, at least not now, started clapping modestly. The crowd followed, which concluded the official part of the ceremony. Beginning with the first row, people started to get to their feet and make their way to the refreshments being served at a makeshift bar. Oliver needed a beer, if they had any, and started toward the bar, but never made it there. Almost everyone, or so it seemed to Oliver, had to come over and shake his hand, wish him well, or tell him a story about his father. A few of Dad's female colleagues gave him hugs. Flora, her makeup running, held him in a tight hug for what seemed like a full minute.

It was getting to be too much; he had to get out of there. Not knowing where to go, he just stepped back into the building and went to Johan's office. On the way there, he bumped into, or rather collided with, the chief of police coming out of Bruno's office. The chief held him in a bear hug to keep him from falling over.

"Oliver, my friend, that was a very nice speech," the chief said as he put Oliver back on stable footing. "This may not be a good time, but have you given any further thought to the matter we discussed yesterday?"

"Yes, thank you. Frank Eugene it was, right? Yes, I have. I think we can do what you suggested. I don't quite remember the amounts now, but I thought that it was OK. Can we talk later, perhaps? I'm a bit tired."

The police chief gave him a polite smile. "Of course. I understand. Tell you what. If you want, this evening, come to Little Tromp Tower. It's a bar. Everybody knows it. Your driver should know it. I'll buy you a drink. In memory of your father. Sound good?"

Oliver hummed in agreement and closed the door of his father's office behind him. He fell back in the chair and gave it a swivel around with his eyes closed. These people here, they all meant well, but he wished he was back home, with his children, in the arms of his wife, to say or think nothing, just be held. Or back at work, with predictable problems. He stopped the chair turning and opened his eyes. There was a knock on the door. Before he could say enter, a woman stepped in and extended both hands.

"Hi, Oliver, I am Vashti. Sorry to barge in. Can we talk a little bit?"

Oliver took her two hands and realized that she must be the woman that Henri had spoken about, the beautiful one. He looked at her and had to agree. Probably late thirties, hard to guess her ethnic origins, must be an interesting mix, maybe something European with something Middle Eastern. Tall, in great shape, moved like a ballerina, just not as skinny. She was wearing the boring clothing one would wear to a memorial service, but she carried them as if she were modeling them. Her eyes were something else. They were beautiful green eyes that glowed with empathy and intelligence, and they were now looking down at him, no, *through* him, with affectionate concern.

"Or would you rather be alone? I would completely understand."

"No, please, it's fine. I just needed a moment, and I think I just had it."

"Good. You know your father and I were really good friends, and we spent a lot of time together, not just here, but in lots of other places as well."

"Oh, I see," Oliver sputtered, not quite knowing what to think.

"No, no, not like that. Trust me," she said with a serious smile, "never any sex, but we really liked each other. We talked a lot, about anything. And I miss him terribly. You must miss him terribly too."

She took his hands in hers again and looked at him, his mouth, his nose and eyes. "You look like him."

Oliver was still sitting down. Holding hands with Vashti was, in a difficult sort of way, comforting, but he thought he needed to let go, which he did.

"I'm sorry. Want to take a seat? It's not very comfortable in here."

"I should go, really. But I'll give you my cell phone number. I'd like to talk to you before you go, maybe over dinner? Or drinks?"

Oliver felt that he shouldn't refuse. She was Dad's friend and probably knew him better than he did. They exchanged numbers and agreed to meet for dinner the next day. She knew just the place. She left the office, her heels clicking on the tiles in the corridor. Oliver could hear her greet someone. A frowning face appeared around the doorpost.

"Excuse me, Mr. Oliver, if I may..."

"Yes, why not?" Whatever peace he was looking for here had disappeared now, anyway. "Please, do come in. What is your name, please?"

"My name is Ibrahim, Sir. I worked for your father. He was my boss and a very good friend, a dear friend."

"Nice to meet you, Ibrahim. Won't you sit down?"

"Thank you. I wanted to give you my heartfelt condolences, also for your family. Your father was a special man, you know."

"I appreciate that, Ibrahim. I think my dad spoke about you a few times at home. The man with the phones, maybe?" Oliver inquired, raising his eyebrows.

Ibrahim chuckled. He was a big-framed individual, and his chest moved up and down as he laughed. He already had one cell phone in his left hand and produced two more from the chest pockets of a neatly starched cotton shirt.

"Guilty!" he said with a laugh. His laughter was contagious, and Oliver, despite his mood, had to laugh as well.

"Er, Mr. Oliver, we—that is, the staff who worked most closely with Johan, with your father—would like to invite you for a lunch or dinner, or maybe coffee, if you are busy."

Oliver was happily surprised. Two invitations in five minutes. These were all good opportunities to find out more about Dad and about his death.

"That sounds great. How can I reach you?"

"Just ask Henri; he has my numbers. And, if I'm correct, my numbers should also be among the contacts in the phone you got from GAPI. I'll leave you be now. Goodbye."

Oliver got up, now eager to move on. First, get out of this suit and tie, and away from this office. He went outside to find Henri, but was intercepted by a dozen of his father's local colleagues, who were enjoying the refreshments. They all wanted to shake hands, hug him, and tell him something about Johan.

One of them, a nice lady named Aisha, asked him if he would be staying a bit longer, perhaps, maybe coming back to join GAPI. He said he didn't know, probably not, and moved along, with a consciously tired look that hopefully would tell people to leave him alone.

When he got to his father's apartment, after checking out at the hotel and getting some supplies, all with the diligent help of Henri, he was pleasantly surprised to see that Joseph had cleaned up the place and made up the bed. The windows and balcony doors were open, offering a great view of the water and the distant mountains—a view that had begun to feel familiar by now. The light and the air coming through the windows and doors gave the apartment an inviting sense of space.

Perhaps it was welcoming Oliver in its own way. It was indeed spacious, with each corner assigned its own function, whether it be sleep, work, reading a novel, cooking a meal, or having a drink. Every spot was furnished and decorated in a tasteful manner, a scattering of mostly local art, paintings, small statues, and rugs. There were photos of Oliver and his family—of his sister, Louise, a nice photo of Mom smiling, taken probably about ten years ago—placed together on the dresser near the bed.

Joseph had taken Oliver's suitcases and, without saying anything, started to unpack. He opened the door to a large walk-in closet, switched on the light, and moved some of Johan's clothes to make space for Oliver's stuff. After Joseph was done, and he and Henri had gone home for the night, Oliver opened the fridge and grinned when he saw that it held a six-pack of the local beer, Hyper Pro. What a name for a beer. He popped one open and walked through the apartment. He looked inside the closet and recognized some of his father's clothes. He would have to pack them for shipment back home. Or maybe it was better to leave them here, give them away. Probably cheaper that way. Should talk to Mom about that. And what on earth was he going to do with all the artwork? Box it and ship it or give it away? He'd have to talk to Mom about this and other things.

The bathroom was tidy and clean, and a bit impersonal, like in a hotel where all evidence of previous occupation has been removed before the next guest arrives. Nevertheless, there was a half-empty tube of toothpaste and a used toothbrush.

He opened the drawers of the desk. Nothing out of the ordinary—pens, pencils, paperclips, notebooks. Well, maybe the latter could be interesting, so he put them aside on the desk to read later. He tried out the bed. The mattress was much too soft for his taste.

He sat down in the leather chair that faced the balcony. He took a swig of his Hyper Pro beer and whistled some tune he made up on the spot. He had to admit to himself that he was not making much progress. He knew about as much now as when he arrived.

Maybe he was also not making progress in grieving his father. Should he be sadder than he actually felt? Or feel guilty for not crying every other minute? Not much point in musing about this, either, he decided. He finished his beer, got up, took off his suit and tie, and changed into khakis and a short-sleeved shirt. He was going to Little Tromp Tower tonight and hang out with his new friend, the chief of police.

# Chapter 23

## VIP TREATMENT

Since Henri had taken off with his nephew and the official GAPI 4x4, Oliver had no transport for the evening. He stepped outside in the light of dusk to see if there were any taxis to be found. No taxis, but ample guys on motorcycles standing across the road, who almost as a team swerved to pull up beside him as if they had been waiting for him and him alone. None of them spoke. They all just nodded to the empty saddle behind them while revving their engines. Oliver took the sturdiest-looking bike he could see, some unknown make and model fitted out with extra headlights and brake lights and a large antenna, even though there was no radio to be seen on the bike's frame.

"Little Tromp Tower? How much?" he asked and mounted the rear saddle. Without a sign of acknowledgement or answer, the driver took off, leaving his competition behind in a cloud of dust and smoke. On the way to his destination, he drew quite a few looks from people who must have been wondering what this tall foreigner was doing on the back of a moto on the streets of their city.

It was impossible to miss. Oliver saw T R O M P in bold, brightly lit gold letters stacked vertically on top of a whitewashed concrete arch that spelled welcome to those who entered in five languages, only two of which Oliver recognized. The bar or restaurant, Oliver did not quite know what it was exactly, was popular. Cars were parked on either side of the street, blocking traffic. Small kids were giving directions to help people park their cars, some offering their services as guards for the evening or running up with buckets and rags to clean off the dirt. Opposite the entrance stood a tall blue pickup truck with about eight armed policemen, who were watching the goings on with a mix of boredom and mild amusement. Several of them seemed to recognize Oliver and waved at him in an obviously friendly manner when he got off the bike and paid the driver. Did they know him? He couldn't recall seeing these guys earlier. Or maybe Frank Eugene had told them he might be coming.

Little Tromp Tower was not exactly little; nor was there any tower in sight. Spread over about an acre were several small buildings adorned with colored Christmas lights, around a central square with a small fountain. Each building seemed to have a different purpose. Oliver could make out two bars—one marked VIP, the other just advertising Hyper Pro—a restaurant on two floors, a dance floor with disco lights, and a barbeque stand, all connected by red brick pathways across a pale grass yard.

Bats were flying overhead, visible as fluttering black dots against the dark blue sky. He stopped at the fountain. It was probably a safe bet to assume that, if the police chief was here, he would either be in the restaurant or in the VIP bar, since he was a VIP around here, wasn't he?

Oliver was stopped in his thoughts by a tap on his shoulders. He turned and saw a man of medium height in a police uniform. He had his cap under his arm and asked Oliver to follow him to the VIP bar.

Inside, the light was low. People looked up to see who had just stepped in. Oliver could see several men sitting on or, rather, *in* deep cream velvet sofas. Most of them looked overweight in dark suits and bulging shirts, of which the buttons could pop anytime. Oliver half-expected to see Lampuit among them. Tables in front of them were stacked with glasses and bottles. Women in short skirts, just like the ones who came to work the beer bellies two nights ago, were standing nearby, some swaying their hips to the rhythm of loud music. One of the men raised a muscular arm in recognition.

"Oliver! Glad you could make it, my friend. Come, come sit down. Have a drink, anything you want. You are my guest!"

Oliver asked for a cold Hyper Pro.

"Ah very good, you like local beer already! Tonight, we enjoy ourselves. No business. Can wait until tomorrow. Can *always* wait until tomorrow," Frank Eugene said with a gesture as if he was slowly slapping an imaginary suspect in front of him.

That was not exactly the way Oliver had hoped the evening would go. "I'm sorry, Frank Eugene, but there are a few things I'd like to discuss tonight. In private, maybe?"

The chief of police looked a bit disappointed, but declared that this was no problem at all. He put his drink down, raised himself out of his seat, and took Oliver by the arm to the fountain in the middle of the compound.

"So, what is it, Oliver?"

"Well, I wanted to confirm first of all that I'm ready to make a contribution to help you with the investigation into my father's death. Not as much as you asked, but let's say seventy-five percent, which should still give you enough to work with, right? I could, for example, make arrangements for a transfer tomorrow, after I go to the bank."

"Ah, but that's very good news, very good indeed. Seventy-five percent is a bit low, but let's do that," the police chief said, squeezing Oliver's arm.

"Then there are two things," Oliver said, wondering if these negotiations were going too easily.

"Anything, dear friend, anything. Number one?"

Frank Eugene was still holding Oliver's arm. Very softly, Oliver pulled away from the chief's grip.

"I want to see some solid accounting of the money. Who gets it, what it's used for—dates, receipts, et cetera."

"Absolutely no problem. I will task our finance folks to be in touch with you on what you want—receipts, audits, the works. Number two?"

"I would like to hear from you, *tonight*, who your suspect is and why my father was killed. I'll be on the phone with my mother and sister later, and I don't want to tell them that I met the chief of police and that I'm giving him some of Dad's money, without at least *some* sort of insight from your end. That would be reasonable, no?"

"Very reasonable—makes sense, makes sense. Here is what we're going to do. First, we have a few drinks. We get back to your beer, maybe have another one, talk to the ladies—if you want—and then we will sit down for dinner to discuss quietly, between the two of us. In this country, things are not always what they seem. Come."

He took Oliver by the arm again and brought him back into the VIP bar. He was introduced as Oliver, the son of Johan, who was running that disarmament program with Captain Christmas. Eyebrows went up in recognition. Oliver could not quite remember all the names and functions of the people in the bar, but it was clear that there was a pretty good cross-section of the movers and shakers in town. Aside from the police chief, there was a bank director (though not from Johan's bank), the chief of staff of the city's mayor, a businessman who was the sole distributor of diesel and aviation fuel, and some others, all men.

"Are you coming to take over from your father?" they all asked him after offering their condolences.

Oliver did not like the idea at all of being expected to "take over" from Dad, so he emphatically denied that there was any such plan on his part and that he would be going home soon. Whatever his father had left behind, GAPI would handle, not him.

His mood was not getting any better, and it must have shown, because none of the ladies around made any attempt to get to him. He made some small talk with the bank director about how they were doing business here. Apparently, the biggest challenge was keeping up with inflation and exchange rate fluctuations, but that didn't interest Oliver at this point. He put his beer down and tapped Frank Eugene on the hand. It was time for dinner and chat.

"Well, well, well, where to start, my friend?" Frank Eugene sighed after they had ordered their meals. "Let me start with what we know for sure, just to be on the same page. Two bullets, nine millimeters, fired from short range, shooter was facing the victim, must have been the last thing he saw. Nobody in the neighborhood heard anything. Even if they did, hearing gunshots during the night is pretty common around here. Nothing stolen, car left untouched. Body found around five-thirty a.m., just before dawn. From looking at the state of the body, my bet is your father was killed around midnight. People passing by may not have seen him because he was lying in the space between the car and a wall. We have impounded the car and could, with your kind support, do a full forensic exam on it, though I doubt we'll find anything."

"Why not? Maybe there are fingerprints or fibers or whatever?"

"See, from the way your father was shot, I think he was standing just by the driver's door, facing backward, with his back against the open door. He fell against the door, then hit the wall with his shoulder, and hit the ground knees first.

We're not sure, but it looked like someone may have turned him around to go through his pockets. I also think the victim—I mean your father—knew the killer and stopped to meet him on that road. So..."

"So, what?"

"We have no hard evidence pointing one way or the other. I forgot to mention, nine-millimeter pistols are everywhere, and we do not keep a registration of who is armed or not. You can buy one on the black market for a song. Ammunition is a bit more expensive. Soooo, next step is to look at possible motives. Who wanted your father dead?"

"Are you asking me?" Oliver said, with a tired expression.

"Yes, why not?" Frank Eugene looked at Oliver deliberately. "Anyone in your family with an interest in seeing him dead? Maybe over money? Or sex? What about you? You hate your dad?"

"Fuck you, Frank Eugene," Oliver bristled. "First, I wasn't here. Watertight alibi, like everyone else in our family. As for money, we're all fine. In fact, Mom will probably lose, long term. They had a good relationship, too. And I may not have liked him very much throughout the years, but I never thought of killing him. Shit, would I consider giving you cash to investigate myself? Do *not* bring my family into this. Ever again. Please."

"Relax, my friend," Frank Eugene said, breaking into a smile. "Standard procedure. We cannot exclude any possibility, you know, just *had* to ask, routine. Sorry if I have offended you. Aah, here comes the food. You will like it. This is a good restaurant."

The two men paused their conversation as the waiter put plates on the table. Oliver had ordered braised porcupine, a local delicacy, on the advice of the chief. It was indeed delicious and the taste of the meat and mildly spicy sauce immediately put him in a better mood. That and the chief's apology.

"You are right, I understand. I apologize too for my outburst. Uncalled for. By the way, this is delicious. We don't get this at home. What are you having? What kind of fish is that?"

"Called pilot perch," Frank Eugene said with his mouth full. "A local fish, tastes good, firm white flesh."

Frank Eugene took another bite and washed it down with a red wine of uncertain origin. He continued his story.

"Now for possible motives. Around here—and I imagine it's the same elsewhere—people shoot people because of self-defense, hate, or money. Now, self-defense, I doubt that. The shots were neatly placed, well aimed, probably fired with focus and good practice behind the trigger, no sign of panic. Also, your dad was known to be against guns. He was trying to take them away from the rebels, so he did not have anything on him to threaten the attacker. Next hate, love, or envy, or any other emotion, plus drunk or high, or both. I don't know enough about your father's private life, *yet*, to make a guess here, but he seemed to be very decent, liked by everybody. You could tell that from the way many people spoke about him at the memorial service, right?"

"I thought so too. Go on."

"I have seen him hang out a few times with a real beauty, absolutely gorgeous woman, but she doesn't strike me as the murderous kind. Too smart. So that, for now, leaves money." Frank Eugene stopped here. He nipped from his wineglass and looked at it.

"Money? I know Dad had a bit of money, but that was— still is—pretty inaccessible," Oliver responded with the slightest of hesitation. Frank Eugene look at him for a second, drew no apparent conclusion about whether Oliver was hiding something and resumed his analysis. "Did you know what your Dad was involved in here?"

"Not in detail. I know he was leading some sort of project to have rebels in the bush exchange their guns for jobs."

"Have you any idea why people ask you if you are going to take over from your father?"

"Apparently, it's the local custom here."

"When it comes to money, there are no customs. You see, people here in the city really liked what Johan was doing. It gave a bit of hope, because Christmas' gang was causing too much trouble, too much killing. Bad for business. No tourists ever come here. Beautiful place, pretty birds, nice mountains, good food—you have seen it—but Christmas ruins everything. So GAPI should continue working on this peace project, as far as these VIPs back in the bar are concerned, whether you do it or someone else. It would be good for business, especially if your family remained involved. Issue of trust, you know."

"What about Christmas? Could he have killed my father?"

"Not personally, no. He would never leave the bush and come here. Too risky."

"So, could he pay someone to do it? Or, and this sounds crazy I know, I heard a story from a woman at the hotel about some ghost baby going around with a ghost dad without a head."

"Heard that one before. People are superstitious here, because they don't know any better. They are poor and uneducated; what do you expect? They don't read, let their imagination run wild, start some gossip or rumor to keep themselves busy. Somebody has a heart attack or a stroke; they say it's invisible lightning or their neighbor's poison. But as a policeman I've seen enough shit to know that all crime is human. Forget it. *Now*, back to Christmas. Personally, I think he's totally crazy, a drunk, and a junkie, been in the bush for years, on the run for decades, has not seen a doctor ever, claims he talks to God, and his people believe him."

"Have you ever met him?"

"If I had, he would be in jail now. Or dead. No, he's the army's problem. They sometimes talk to him. Military Intelligence. They have been trying to negotiate a deal so they don't have to fight him and his lunatics. Fucking cowards—the army, I mean."

"Why can't they do their job?"

"Endless excuses. Never enough money to pay the soldiers, no equipment, terrain too hard, no attack helicopters, not enough fuel, wrong time of year, blah, blah, blah, blah."

"Sorry, Chief, but didn't you give me the same story one day ago? How you need cash from outside to do your job? My family's cash in particular."

Oliver hoped his remarks did not come out too harsh. It was important to keep this police chief on his side.

"I hear you. I hear you. But for the police, it's *totally* different, believe me. When it comes to money, the army is always first. They are always sucking on the government's biggest tit and will let no one near the other ones. Police comes second or third or fourth, *always*. Police here have to pay for their own uniforms, pistols, belts, pencils and paper, gas for patrol cars, spare parts, *everything!*"

The chief was getting irritated. The subjects of Christmas and the army had obviously hit a raw nerve, and he was spitting out his words like sour grapes. Frank Eugene was pouring himself another glass of wine, which finished the bottle. He waved at the waiter to bring another one.

"You want more wine, too?"

"No, thank you. Or maybe just one more." Oliver wanted to hear the rest of the story.

"So, let me get to the point. I'll run your investigation, as agreed. But if I were you, I would suggest you keep a low profile."

"Why?" Oliver's dread that this was no ordinary murder was turning real. What had Dad gotten into? he wondered. What had he gotten Oliver into?

"Christmas is dealing in gold. Everybody knows that. His fighters are only fighters during their days off or when they need to pillage a village. Yeah, it rhymes, but it isn't funny. Most of the time, these men and boys are deep in mud trying to filter out the gold dust that runs in the streams coming down the mountain. They say it's worth millions a year. And the army takes a neat percentage."

"In exchange for what?"

"Peace and quiet. Let him be, go about his business, turn a blind eye at the right time. Every now and then, Christmas reduces the bribe, so the army threatens to attack his camp, and they make a new deal. And thus, the price of peace is determined."

Frank Eugene sighed and took another gulp of his wine.

"Can you prove this?"

"No, most people would call this speculation or a rumor, but I'm sure of it. The sad thing is, even if I could prove it, there is no guarantee that the government would do anything about it. I've no idea who else higher up is getting gifts from Christmas. It's a lot of money, Oliver. A lot of people are involved or want to get involved, and it's best if you don't talk about it too much."

"You think that this is what got my father killed?"

"Maybe, maybe. We will see. Just keep your mouth shut, no more questions, and let me handle the local politics. I'll keep you posted, I promise. Now, how about we finish off this nice bottle of wine, and I'll get my boys to drive you home.

Personal escort. With the compliments of the chief. And then, tomorrow, you'll get me the money."

# Chapter 24

## BROTHER JOHAN

"Mom, can you hear me?"

"Yes, Darling, I can hear you. How's it going? Are you OK?"

"Yes, it's OK. How are you holding up?"

"I'm fine, Dear. Did you see Dad?"

"I did, Mom. It's true. He's dead."

Charlotte did not respond for a while. Oliver could hear her sobbing and fetching a tissue, probably from the kitchen.

"I'm sorry, Mom. There's no other way to say it, and you always want us to get to the point."

"I know, I know. It's just, it's just that I hadn't really accepted that he was dead yet—that maybe he was just missing or on a long mission and would just come home one day, like he always did. I'm still hoping. It's not your fault."

"I'm bringing his body home, Mom. He didn't suffer."

"Good."

The phone went quiet again for a moment.

"We'll say goodbye when he gets here. Will you tell me when he comes, so we can make arrangements?"

"I will, Mom. Things are fine otherwise. GAPI organized a really nice memorial service. I'll tell you about it when I get home. People here really liked Dad."

"I know. I think he liked them, too."

"I met the police chief. The investigation is under way, but they have no suspects yet. Also, Dad's bank accounts are OK. He has no debts, and after I settle his local bills here, there should be enough to cover any funeral expenses at your end and maybe a nice vacation with all of us when it's all done. What do you say?"

"Thank you for doing this, Darling. I know it must be tough."

Another pause. Oliver could hear his mother trying to breathe.

"I'll say goodbye now."

The phone went dead before Oliver could say anything. He felt that he might have overwhelmed her a bit, and it hurt him inside. There was little else he could do. He would talk to her again later, and maybe he could tell her a bit more then. Now it was time to call his wife.

"Hello, Mary, my love. How are you? Is this a good time?"

"Not really, Oliver. It's is nice to hear your voice, but I need to take the kids to soccer and ballet in a few minutes. The dryer isn't working, so I have the house full of wet clothes. It's a mess. When are you coming home?"

"I don't know yet. Things are a bit messy here too, and the bureaucracy is terrible—much worse than I expected. I'll do my best to come home as soon as I can. How are the kids?"

"They're fine. They miss you, as do I. Look, I really got to go now. Can we talk later? Are you OK?"

"Sure. I'm fine. Just took a shower and starting my day."

"OK, love you, bye."

Oliver looked at the phone. He had hoped for a longer conversation. He needed to share the crazy things he had seen and heard with someone who would listen. Maybe Mary wouldn't be able to understand, anyway. She was perhaps too grounded in her own reality, which now seemed so far away. The dryer had been sputtering for a few months now, and he should remind himself to give it a good cleaning when he got back, if it wasn't too late. It was his reality too, even though it didn't feel that way right now.

It was the second morning in his father's apartment. He had made some coffee and toast and was staring out the window, digesting the conversations he just had with Mom and Mary, when he heard someone knocking on the door. It was Henri, who had brought a box with some of Dad's personal belongings from the office and a manila folder. The box held a few framed photographs, including a rare one of Oliver and his father together. It was taken during a fishing trip. And in spite of the smiles, it had been a disaster. Oliver had blamed his father for his not catching any fish, while Johan had pulled out one fish after the other. Still, on the photo they looked as if they were the best of friends, probably for the benefit of Mom, who had taken the photograph.

Also in the box were some keys. Oliver recognized the key of the house back home. The most interesting items were the two cell phones with their accompanying chargers. He put them back in the box and faced Henri, who had been waiting with a piece of paper in his hand.

"What is it, Henri?"

"You need to sign this, please."

Henri pulled a form on GAPI letterhead from the folder with two "sign here" stickers attached. Based on previous experience, Oliver was going to give it a good read. This one, he noted quickly, was plain stupid. He'd have to sign for the receipt of the personal effects as well as for Johan, who was dead, to certify that he was handing over the goods to Oliver, his own son. He understood that this was the way GAPI was accounting for everything, but still. He scribbled something on the form and gave it back to Henri. Whatever.

Henri also held out a sealed envelope addressed to him, marked "confidential." It held a photocopy of an official cable from GAPI's overseas headquarters with a handwritten note from Bruno attached, which read, "So sorry, HQ will not allow to pay Lampuit. See legal excuses attached." Oliver wasn't surprised, and in fact, he was glad to be able to take things into his own hands rather than having to wait for GAPI's bureaucracy.

"Henri, do I have anything on the program today?"

"No, Mr. Oliver."

"No news from the morgue or the police—or from GAPI admin?"

Henri shook his head.

"Fine. Why don't you come back in an hour or so? I'd like to visit a few places. Would you mind? Unless you have other stuff to do."

That was fine with Henri. He left the apartment and closed the door behind him. Good man, Oliver thought, while he rummaged through the personal effects. He couldn't find anything suspicious or any hint that would explain what had happened to Dad. No passport. That was interesting. He assumed GAPI still had it—that this was needed for the transport of the body. He tried not to think of Dad, how his body was lying there in the morgue, with some stranger pumping embalming fluid into his veins.

He took out the two cell phones and turned them on. Both were low on battery power, so he plugged them in first. Both phones were also locked, showing the usual keypad requesting a PIN number. Somebody had tried to unlock the phones before. The screens on both said, "You have 3 attempts left before the system locks." Oliver racked his brains for memories of codes that Dad might have used. His father wasn't really a numbers man, so it had to be something he could've easily remembered, like a birthday or his first telephone number. But then again, anyone trying to open the phones might also have had access to Dad's personal records, with dates of birth and addresses and telephone numbers.

Wait. What was the code again Dad used for the garage door, before he changed it after his sister had smuggled in a boyfriend? Oliver could not suppress a smile at the memory of that episode. It wasn't a number, but a gesture—a physical movement, like drawing a symbol. A ribbon. That was it, like an AIDS ribbon or a pink ribbon against breast cancer—9 1 3 7, maybe. Oliver made the move in the air with his finger. Moving from right to left didn't feel right. He tried 7 3 1 9. That made a lot more sense.

Then it dawned on him. Before they had him, his parents lived for nine years in a small, one-bedroom apartment, number 137. They had shown it to him once when they had visited their old town. Perhaps that 9 1 3 7 code reminded Johan of happier days every time he opened his phone, days without the pain and joys of young kids—just him and Mom. He imagined Dad would be smiling at times as he punched in the code.

He tried it on the biggest phone of the two, but it failed to open. One attempt less left. He'd have to come to that later. The smaller phone was an old flip phone. Its metallic silver paint had come off to reveal the black plastic body in places where it must have rubbed against his father's trousers. He tried the ribbon code.

Yes! The screen switched to a home screen that showed missed calls, text messages, and even e-mails. Oliver leaned back in his chair and looked outside. This was, he must assume, the first time someone had looked at this screen since his father had died. This was empowering. Instead of a seeker of information, which had proven to be an exasperating experience, he now was going to hold some information himself, to be dispensed carefully and deliberately. This was a card he could play with Frank Eugene and Bruno. Maybe.

Oliver opened the call folder and saw a bunch of names and numbers. Some names he knew already: Vashti, Bruno, Ibrahim. Even Christmas was among the contacts. Christmas had a long number—a satellite phone, presumably. The last conversation had been with Bruno, at 7:38 p.m. on the day before Dad was killed. Since then, there had been only missed calls from the day after. Bruno again, Flora, Ibrahim, and some others. They must have tried reaching him when he hadn't shown up at the office. Someone named Zamorski was on the calls list, too. All outgoing calls, never incoming. The name sounded familiar somehow, but Oliver couldn't put his finger on it.

Next, he moved to the e-mail folder. It showed an e-mail address for his father that he didn't recognize: ShadowDSP@factts.com. He opened the inbox and immediately realized what it was. All of the incoming e-mail was from a single address, Dad's official GAPI e-mail address, and it contained both received and sent mail. Oliver cursed in silence. If he had done this at the bank back home—if the system administrators would even allow it—he would have been fired on the spot for breach of confidentiality. But apparently Dad got away with it. Or GAPI's electronic security was as leaky as a rusty sieve. Or both. He started reading, but realized quickly that there was too much to read for now. Most of it looked like administrative and organizational stuff, anyway. Not very exciting, and it revealed nothing.

He hoped that the text messages folder would yield more tantalizing information. It did. The last message on the day before the murder was a simple "yes" to a question from Bruno if dinner was still on. That made sense with the last phone call. Maybe Dad had called Bruno to say he was running late, or the other way around.

There were several messages from Vashti, mostly to suggest or confirm dinner or coffee dates. Here was an interesting one, from Captain Christmas: "BroJo, when kits? You promised. What about my uniform and cars? Bring some U!" The message was dated about a week before the killing. Oliver felt some unease creeping up. BroJo? So, this killer guy called his father Brother Johan? It suggested some level of familiarity—or maybe even complicity. Sure as hell this didn't mean he was going to call Christmas "Uncle," if ever he should meet him. And what was the deal with the uniform and cars? What was "U"?

Oliver now began to wonder if Dad had been making deals with this guy inside—or maybe also outside—this DSP program. What if those deals had gone sour? Dad did tend to overpromise, Oliver remembered, one year failing to buy him that air rifle he'd really wanted for his birthday, despite vague hints, smiles, and promises that he'd get it. Instead, he got a fancy fishing pole and reel, Dad grinning that this was more peaceful but still a hunting tool. It didn't matter now.

Oliver's reminiscing was interrupted by the distant sound of a diesel engine and tires grinding through the gravel in the parking lot. He looked at his watch and concluded that this must be Henri's 4x4, coming to pick him up. He put the two phones in his pocket, together with his own and the one GAPI gave him, and went downstairs with bulging pockets to greet his driver.

# Chapter 25

## DOPPIO DOPPIO

Henri pointed to the skies.

"Boss, it wants to rain today. Very soon. Very bad."

Oliver could feel the gusts of a warm wind on his skin and looked up to see heavy, dark skies. Better get going. This morning, he wanted to see the spot where Dad had died, on the ground, bleeding from two holes in his chest.

Henri was quiet on the way there. The town seemed in a hurry. Motorcycles and vehicles were impatiently trying to get to their destination before the rain came down, swerving and honking as they went. Oliver saw at least five near-accidents that all seemed to magically be avoided in that one millimeter of margin that, at the end of the day, suffices. The clouds, the busy roads, and his own destination depressed him to the point where he felt the need to cry, but he couldn't, like the clouds that wanted to rain.

The street where it happened was off a main thoroughfare. From the map Oliver had received from GAPI, this main thoroughfare connected all the international offices and the restaurants and bars deemed safe to go to. The side street was narrow, mostly walls and metal doors protecting the houses behind them in small compounds. It was an unpaved road, shaped in the mud by the tires of passing cars and trucks. Small patches of grass grew at the base of the wall, interspersed by heaps of garbage and plastic bags. Oliver could see a goat grazing at the side of the road.

"Here."

Henri parked the car and stopped the engine. He pointed to the wall on the other side of the road. Oliver got out and walked over. There was nothing to see, nothing at all. It could have been any other wall on this street. No blood stains, no police tape or other markers. Just dirt, plastic bags, and dusty grass. He could see a few fresh tire prints of cars that must have passed in the last hour.

"Are you sure it's here? I see nothing."

"Yes, Mr. Oliver, it's here. See the house number on the gate? Number seven. That's where Mr. Johan was found."

Oliver knelt and touched the soil. He caressed the grass and picked up a few pieces of dried mud. He looked at them to see if they would perhaps talk of that evening and then squeezed them to dust. He thought about bringing some home but then let the dust flow between his fingers. Maybe some of these particles had touched Dad when he was dying. Maybe the delicate brush of the grass against his hand was the last sensation he'd felt before the end—if he felt anything at all.

Maybe he was dead before he hit the ground, without feeling, hopeless. Oliver didn't believe in heaven or hell. Or in God, for that matter. But against his own convictions, he closed his eyes and in his head said a prayer to his father. It wasn't very long or eloquent, but he felt the need to tell Johan that he missed him, that he wanted to talk to him one more time, that he was sorry that Johan had to leave them here on this spot without color or comfort. Oliver put his hand against the wall and pushed himself up. He looked around and promised himself he would never come back to this spot again.

A sharp explosion and a blue-white flash of electricity nearby brought him to his senses. Henri had opened the door of the car and was signaling him to come inside as rain started to fall. First the patter of a few individual heavy drops, followed seconds later by a downpour that beat a steady drum on the metal roof of the car. Oliver got inside just in time. He looked through the window, through the water streaming down the glass outside to the scene he had just left.

This was a good thing, he thought. Let nature wash out this place and make it new again. Whatever blood Dad had spilled here was now taken down to the water and from there to the ocean, with an eternity to get there.

The rain caused Oliver some measure of comfort. He couldn't stay here anyway, but he had no firm plans. This was a good day perhaps to do some thinking, put things in order, look at Dad's e-mails again, make a mental spreadsheet, like he always did to solve problems—who, what, when, and why. Call Flora to ask where they stood with the preparations for the repatriation of remains. But first things first. Oliver asked Henri to drive to the bank to get the money for the morgue and the police.

The bank manager was very nice to Oliver and offered him small talk and coffee while a teller was getting the cash. He needed thirty thousand for the morgue and ten thousand for the police, plus another two thousand for himself, just in case, as well as ten thousand to take home, the maximum he could take with him in cash. That would save him and Mom a bit on transfer fees and pay for the funeral back home. The manager was chatting about the rain, saying something about the local folks believing that the spirits came out with the vapor rising from the warm ground after the rain had passed.

"The rain liberates them," he said. "But of course, people like us, like bank managers, who are from the real world don't believe in that nonsense, right?"

Oliver nodded and sipped his coffee. It was awful. In fact, he hadn't had a decent cup of coffee, or an espresso or macchiato, in a long time. He would ask Henri if there was a good place in town.

He was slightly nervous about riding around town with so much cash, which he kept in a plastic bag, since the four cell phones already occupied his pockets. Oliver paid visits to the morgue and the police station.

Mr. Lampuit, the fat extortionist, offered him coffee as well, which Oliver refused, while he sat behind his desk, slowly counting the bills and preparing a receipt. The receipt was on official letterhead and needed to be stamped three times: one stamp to accompany Lampuit's signature, one stamp for the date, and one stamp to say "paid," each stamp treated with equal precision and patience.

Once it was all done, Lampuit looked over the receipt with great care, almost affection, and handed it to Oliver, who thought the whole thing was bullshit. The receipt would only have meaning to him. It would go overseas and never come back for an audit of the books, which did not exist anyway, since Lampuit did not make a copy or enter anything in a ledger. He put the money in his office drawer and announced, with a deliberate pomposity that Oliver had begun to loathe, that the embalming process was nearly done and that Mr. Johan's remains would be able to return in full dignity to his loved ones on schedule within a few days, no problem.

The visit to the police station was a little more satisfying. Frank Eugene greeted him in a courteous manner—not overly friendly, perhaps a bit distracted, as if he had something important on his mind—and sent him to the finance office. Oliver gave them two thousand for now, got a real receipt with a copy kept by the finance officer, and signed what looked like standard contracts for his payment and the reward money. No stamps this time.

The next stop was the GAPI office, where he wanted to park his cash in a safe. The office was rather empty. Flora was alone, holding down the fort, she said, while everybody had gone out to a big donor meeting, chaired by Ambassador Zamorski. Of course, she could safely store the cash. There was a safe in Johan's office he could use, and she had the keys and combination for him. Oliver felt relieved. She also gave him a printout of his itinerary for his trip home and some paperwork for the accompanying coffin. Things were on track, she said. What did he want to do with Johan's clothes and furniture?

Oliver thought about it for a second and decided that, for the time being, it was probably best to do nothing. He wanted to consult his mother on this as well. Maybe he would come back, visit a second time to wrap all of this up. He didn't quite expect the hug Flora gave him after he said that. Of course, he was always welcome.

She laughed while holding him close for a second longer. He laughed too, out of politeness, while gently disentangling himself from her embrace. By the way, did she know a good place for a real espresso?

Flora laughed again. "Poor baby, missing out on real coffee, are you? We can fix that. Just go to Doppio Doppio. Henri knows where to find it. Great croissants, too."

Henri dropped him off and said he had to run some errands and to call him whenever he needed transport. The entrance to Doppio Doppio was tucked away in a corridor between shops selling spare charger cables and canned vegetables. A cream-white, tiled staircase led to an open space with wood-paneled walls and large windows offering a view of the city and the mountains. A cast-iron spiral staircase led to a roof terrace with the kind of patio furniture that Oliver had always wanted for his small garden, comfortable and weather resistant. They were still wet from the rain, so he went down to the main café area on the floor below.

He found himself a bar stool at a high table in a corner by the window, ordered a medium macchiato and a croissant, and put his father's phones in front of him. He knew he had only two attempts left on the larger smartphone. He had largely run out of ideas of what PIN Dad could have used that wasn't immediately obvious. Or maybe he needed to think about the obvious—like Mom's birthday or his own. Or a combination of his birthday and his sister's. Or maybe the inverse of the ribbon code that had worked on the other phone. Oliver tried the last one first, but the only result was to whittle the number of attempts down to one. Maybe he should ask Mom for advice on this.

His coffee and croissant arrived. He smiled back at the waitress and took a sip of his macchiato. That was good, soothing, and smooth—just what he needed. He was going to have to come here for breakfast. He wasn't the only one who appreciated the good coffee. A mix of mostly young, wealthy locals and foreigners filled the place. He recognized several faces from the memorial service.

As he savored the croissant, he decided not to rush it. He would take the smartphone home with him in a couple of days and find some techie who could help him rather than take a gamble and lose. Besides, he had plenty of information to go through for the time being. He opened the flip phone and started reading. There were many attachments that the old flip phone couldn't handle, but by forwarding these to his own smartphone Oliver managed to open them, albeit with a bit of delay.

After finishing his second macchiato, he had developed a pretty good idea of what his father's professional life had been about. For the last two years, after a massacre committed by Christmas, in which a foreigner was killed, Johan had been running around setting up this program to remove weapons from Christmas' group in exchange for a vague promise of jobs and what amounted to a goodie bag for poor adults. There was a fair amount of back and forth about money and fund-raising, a big role for some guy called Zamorski, as well as a steady drip of e-mails from Bruno worrying about "our image."

Oliver could well imagine: how could you do business with a guy like Christmas and not be tainted by all the dirt?

Nothing in the e-mails pointed to Johan being involved with the gold trade that Christmas was supposed to be running. The government took part in the running of the disarmament program, but it didn't seem to take a great deal of interest in it. There were monthly minutes of an "Inclusive Implementation Management Committee" sent to about a hundred people. Oliver read a few of them, which caused him to raise his eyebrows several times. How the hell are you supposed to manage anything through a committee of bureaucrats and diplomats? Real decisions were far and few between, and most of the time, Johan seemed to get away with the "recommendations" he had outlined in the beginning of each meeting. In a side e-mail to Bruno, referring to the committee's name, Johan had remarked cynically that "one out of four ain't bad."

Things weren't going well in the weeks before Johan died. Costs were skyrocketing, and there was increasing pressure on his program to deliver more surrendered weapons, which seemed to be all that counted. Everybody seemed to be complaining. The former fighters were waiting for jobs that couldn't be found, local organizations offering to create jobs or offer education were asking for exorbitant fees, donors were clamoring for results *or else,* and there were terrible delays in the procurement of the items for the goodie bags. The local press was having some fun with the program as well, much to Bruno's dismay. One headline he quoted read, "What's worse: fighters or foreigners? GAPI, go home!"

Dad's tone in his e-mails was generally upbeat, much like Oliver expected, but toward the end, he sounded more despondent. There was an exchange that started with a confidential note to Bruno about "how to exit with our faces intact," listing various options to pull out of the program and convert it into something else, say "rural development" to manage all unmet expectations, many of which had been unrealistic or even naïve to begin with, so Johan admitted to himself.

Bruno's response was quick and brutal: "Need to keep it going, too much at stake, you got us into this mess, you keep it going."

The last bit was manifestly unfair, thought Oliver. From what he read, the whole thing was just as much driven by Bruno, fully supported by GAPI Headquarters, and happily embraced by donors. Dad had good reasons to be despondent. And Bruno was an asshole.

Oliver put down his phones and looked at his watch. He was hungry, but it was too late for lunch, too early for dinner. He called Henri to pick him up, and while he waited for him to arrive, he paid the bill and sent a text to Vashti to ask if she wanted to meet him for drinks and dinner.

The response came while Oliver was on the way to his apartment, Dad's apartment. She would love to meet him and suggested a place called the Floating Cloud. She would pick him up at 6 p.m.

# Chapter 26

## RAMBO

She didn't bother knocking. Oliver had just taken a shower and, hearing footsteps on the staircase, was able to wrap a towel around his waist just before she came in.

"Well, please come in then, and make yourself at home," he said jokingly.

"Look at you, all wet and shapely. Let me get us a drink while you put something on. Beer or scotch?"

"A beer, please."

"Your dad was strictly scotch—beer only when he could get it really cold, almost frozen, which rarely happens around here. Go on, then. I promise not to look."

Oliver realized he had stood frozen since she came in, just looking at the way she moved. He turned and went into the bathroom to change. He could hear the hiss as she opened a beer bottle, and then another.

"Don't you think, Oliver, that this whole thing—I mean the deals everyone is making with everybody else—is totally criminal? I mean, how long have you been here now, almost a week? You must have seen the bullshit here by now. Everybody deals in it, and some get disgustingly rich from the shit trade, while those who, at the end of the day, scoop up the shit for the rich guys, get nothing. Nothing. Here's your beer. Cheers."

"Cheers. I'll be just a second."

Oliver was struggling to get into his jeans. It felt good to dress relaxed, after all these official and semi-official meetings. He put on a shirt, left the two top buttons unbuttoned, and rolled up his sleeves. He looked in the mirror and saw a man tired with his day. He forced himself to smile, and somehow it stuck.

"Right, here I am. Thanks for the beer. What were you saying again?"

"Caught you by surprise, didn't I? I was talking about the many layers of bullshit people—especially the ones who are too clean, the official ones who never touch any shit anyway—are spreading on their sandwiches. And everybody takes a bite."

"I'm not sure I follow you. As far as I know, there's bullshit everywhere, no? And speaking of a bite, I'm very hungry. Last thing I ate was a croissant at Doppio Doppio, so where are you taking me again?"

"Floating Cloud. Nice view, good food, right on the water. *Everybody* goes there. Been there with Johan many times. I miss him. Surprised you haven't been there yet."

"Well, I've been to Little Tromp Tower. Had dinner with the police commissioner there."

"Snake pit. Nothing but human-rights abusers there. And don't trust the commissioner, ever. He's dirty, very dirty."

Oliver felt some regret creeping up. Maybe he shouldn't have given his new police friend any money. Done some diligence first. Too late now.

"You want to tell me about it over dinner? After we finish the beer?"

"No problem, dear."

Vashti put the bottle of Hyper Pro to her mouth and finished it in one gulp.

"Let's go, then."

Oliver followed her example, put the beer bottle down, suppressed a burp, and walked to the windows to close the blinds.

"Leave those. Who's going to look in?"

Vashti walked up to him and took his hand. She pulled him through the door and left him to lock up as she walked down the stairs. She was wearing tight black jeans and a brown T-shirt with a bright orange shawl. Oliver looked at her walking down the stairs and couldn't help wondering if his father had looked at her the same way. No matter what this woman wore, she'd look beautiful. In his head, Oliver compared her to every woman he'd ever met or seen—to Mary, to Geneva, a high-school crush, a few college flings. This one was different. He shook his head as if to deny that this was happening and followed her down the stairs into the car.

Oliver would not easily forget the drive to the restaurant. As a rule, he did not like to be driven, and he was rather anal, or so his wife told him, about focusing on the road and anticipating trouble ahead. As he found out to his terror, Vashti did not believe in applying his level of caution. She drove at breakneck speed, taking every possible risk that Oliver could identify on the road, black-smoke-belching trucks barging in from the right, angry motorcycles from the left, dreamy pedestrians crossing the road without looking, didn't matter. Vashti avoided all danger with just inches to spare, while expanding loudly on her theories about bullshit in society in a rapid-fire stream of words, occasionally interrupted by her cursing at some idiot man, woman, or child who did not immediately understand the rules of the road as she interpreted them.

It was a quite a relief to get to the Floating Cloud. Oliver could see why the place was popular with expatriates, whose logo-bedecked 4x4s crowded the parking lot. The place was both secure and comfortable— two pluses for foreigners in a land that might kill you if you didn't know where to go.

There was only one access through a door in a high wall, guarded by two mean-looking armed men in uniform. The restaurant was essentially a luxury picnic area—a tall roof over a large, steel barge anchored in the river, which at that precise point flowed over invisible shallow areas and rocks, causing white, crashing turbulence, a constant rushing sound, and a light breeze that blew through the open walls.

"Would you like to have a drink first, like there?" Vashti pointed to an empty couch on an oriental carpet at the edge of the barge. "Or maybe sit down at one of these tables and talk over dinner?"

"You decide."

Vashti had been in command since she walked into his apartment, which was fine with Oliver. A bit of a change from home, honestly, where he felt as if he had to decide everything and eternally defend his choices afterward.

"Drinks first, then."

Vashti led him to the empty couch, greeting friends and acquaintances along the way, introducing Oliver as Johan's son. Most of them already seemed to know who he was and why he was here. They all offered condolences or comments on Johan's many great qualities—so sad, he was *such* a wonderful man—a leader, a true peacemaker. We *all* looked up to him.

"Don't believe a word they say, Darling. They all envied Johan, because his program got more money and attention than theirs. Some of them, like this one," she said, turning to a skinny woman with a sharp nose in black leather pants, "tried to get her shitty little projects funded through Johan's money."

"Wait a minute." Oliver smiled, remembering seeing something in Dad's e-mails. "Didn't your outfit—*Inherent,* wasn't it?—get some money from Dad for something having to do with helping widows and victims?"

Vashti let out a deep laugh, brushed her hair aside in exaggerated soap star fashion, and looked him in the eyes in faked disbelief.

"That, my dear Oliver, is totally different, of course. Plus, and I'm not lying here, it was your father's idea. I gave him hell for doing business with a monster, and it must have made him feel guilty. But I prefer not to talk about work."

"OK, let's order some drinks then."

On Vashti's recommendation, they both ordered a local cocktail called Sylvester, a concoction made of vodka, guava juice, ginger, and crushed dry peppers on the rim, like salt on a margarita.

"Why is this called a Sylvester?" Oliver asked.

"I don't know. The guy who invented it was killed a year ago by a burglar. Can't ask him, but rumor has it that this drink will slay the dragon, like Saint Sylvester did. Or Sylvester day comes after Christmas, so the drink is supposed to make Christmas go away. Or maybe it's supposed to make you feel like Rambo."

"I drink to that—all three options. Cheers!"

Oliver raised his glass. While he started to feel good, having a drink with a beautiful woman who made him laugh, he couldn't forget why he had come to this city in the first place.

"I'm sorry, Vashti. I really need to talk about my father—what happened to him and why. Can you help? You knew him really well, didn't you?"

Vashti's expression turned sad quickly, and she didn't respond at first.

"I'm sorry, Vashti. This must be—"

"No, it's fine. I totally get it. You need to understand."

She sighed, sipped her drink, and took a deep breath. "Yes, I knew him well, and I was very fond of him. I loved him, and we were very close, but never in a romantic way. He was like an older brother to me, despite the vile gossip going around among this crowd here. Your dad was a good man, had his heart in the right place. He tried hard to make things better for the locals here. His thistle project made a world of difference to a lot of people here, even though the science behind it was completely false. And the interesting thing is that, in addition to creating jobs, it saved rhinoceros's lives, because the consumers overseas were convinced that the 'mystical' power of the thistle was better than ground rhino horn."

Vashti looked down at her drink and smiled. "Your dad could sell bullshit like the best of them, but he managed somehow to make it work for the local farmers here, who adored him. Did you know there are toddlers here named after your dad?"

Oliver shook his head.

"Anyway. He tried hard, all the time. You know about the DSP, right?"

"I do. Big lines. Trying to create jobs for fighters in the bush in exchange for their guns. Bring stability and prosperity and all that good stuff."

"Wrong."

"What do you mean, wrong? I read the basic documents, and that's what it says."

"Sure, it does. Fancy phrases, all the right buzzwords, all designed to make you feel good. And make donors reach for their checkbooks. And, *of course*, as our friend Bruno would say, GAPI is the best and only organization to handle *all* this money for the betterment of humankind, yesterday, today, and tomorrow. But that's not what's going on."

"So, what's going on?"

"See this ring?"

Vashti held out her right hand to show a gold ring with an intricate design, like a piece of Arabic calligraphy or vines around an open heart.

"Gift from an old admirer. But I made sure it wasn't made from gold mined by Christmas in those mountains over there."

She took Oliver's hand and pressed it for a moment.

"I think the DSP meant well, from the beginning. Outrage over killings, money flowing in after a foreigner was killed. I knew her, by the way. She was a friend of mine. Those days I wanted to kill Christmas myself. Johan designed a nice program, short-term and long-term goals, spoke to Christmas several times about it, and he went along because it gave him some sort of recognition he was craving, in addition to alcohol."

"I'm sorry about your friend, Vashti. I didn't know."

"How could you? Anyway, gold is what it's all about."

"That's right, I heard the same thing from the chief of police. He said the army is in collusion with Christmas."

"They are. Nobody has proof, but it makes sense. But the police aren't clean, either. They would love to take the army's place or take a share of the profits. To hell with law and order. They want to get rich too."

"OK, so where does my father come in?"

"I think he got in someone's way. Who, I don't know. I'm sorry, but I can only offer speculation at this point. And I really hate speculation. There are too many fools around here, and pretty much everywhere, who love to confuse a guess with the facts and start a rumor that then turns into one of those immortal ghosts that roam about town."

"Well, in that case, just list the options. It'd be really helpful to me."

"Well, for starters, Christmas loved the attention he got through the program, suddenly acting like a big statesman—protocol, honor guard, what have you. But when some of his better fighters started disappearing *with* their guns to get a job from Johan, he was seriously pissed off. In one blow, both his military power and his labor pool were going down.

"Second, the program brought attention not just to Christmas, but also to the army, who suddenly looked like idiots for being unable to do for years what a foreigner with a bit of cash could do in a matter of months—I mean undermining Christmas. They had a good deal with Christmas, people say. Again, this is speculation, but the army left him alone in exchange for gold. That peace and quiet went out the window when the DSP came in, with donor diplomats looking in and, thanks to me, yes me, greater attention to the victims."

She paused to take a sip of her drink and get the waiter's attention for the menu. "Which, in turn, turned up the heat on Christmas, because word got out what a monster he is. Calls for his arrest increased, which, *in turn*, put a spotlight on the government again for not doing anything about it. Bottom line, lots of people with or without guns hated what your dad was doing here. Don't get me wrong. Most people loved it. Not me, though. I think Christmas should go to jail. Or be shot. You know I'm a human-rights person, against the death penalty, for due process and all that jazz, but for Christmas I would make an exception."

"But why kill him? I mean, kill my father? The program is going on without him. GAPI isn't going away because they killed their program manager."

"Exactly, darling! It's all guesswork, anyway. People like to go for big conspiracies to explain big or even little events. Maybe it was simpler. Maybe your father had a local girlfriend with a jealous husband. Now, hold on, don't look so surprised. I don't think so. He loved your mom. This is just to make the point that there's always some other simple solution. Or maybe he had some bad debts or something."

"I doubt that."

"Yeah, me too. Enough about Johan. It makes me sad."

"Me, too."

They fell silent for a while. The waiter brought the menu and escorted them to a table in the restaurant section. The ceiling was decorated with mosquito nets hanging over steel chandeliers. The river breeze caused the filtered light to weave over the tables, much like a fireplace in an otherwise dark room.

Oliver swallowed to make the sadness go away. "Let's talk about you. How did you end up here, Vashti?"

"Oh, long story. I studied law, got into human rights work because it was about real people. Moving from contract to contract, basically I go where some organization, government or not, public or private, wants me to do human rights work. There's so much work to do here, and Inherent gave me a great contract. And a chance to hang out with Johan again. Did you know we've been stationed in at least five countries at the same time, sheer coincidence? Or maybe not, karma or fate, whatever, or just the fact that we both like, sorry, liked to work where people never go for their vacation."

"Sorry for a bourgeois question, but how come you're single? No need to answer if you don't want to, but, well, you're a very beautiful woman and—"

"Thank you, Dear. Another long story. Do you really want to know? I need a drink for that one. The wine here is imported, pretty good actually. Let's order a bottle."

The wine came with the food, standard expatriate fare, steak and fries for Oliver, grilled shrimp for Vashti, who started her story after ripping the tail off a shrimp.

"To be frank, I like being single. I get enough passion and love out of my work. I love my work; I love helping people who have nothing— no money, no justice, no power, and no way of getting any of that in a society like this, where the government doesn't give a damn. Lip service, yes, of course, human rights are important, blah, blah. None of these bozos at the top would like to be seen as an exploiter or an abuser— wouldn't go well with their designer suits and silk ties. But they don't give a shit."

Oliver looked at her as she spoke. He admired a woman like her, so free, so driven. So beautiful, too. So hard not to admire. He made a mental note to himself to not let it show. He was in mourning, after all, and married, too.

"Sure, I have lovers from time to time. Had my heart crushed too, like you, I suppose, my dear."

Oliver said nothing. Mary had been his first and only lover to date, and while there were some minor flings along the way, he'd never had his heart crushed—or even scratched. He liked it that way. Or was he missing something?

"The thing is, Oliver, I mean, look around here. Do you see any real men here?"

Oliver looked around as discreetly as he could. There was a large group near the bar of men and women, or better, boys and girls, in their twenties, maybe early thirties. They were loud and exuberant. The guys in the group were doing their best to impress the ladies. To him, they looked OK; some might even be labeled attractive. Older folks occupied other tables. He thought he recognized one of the beer bellies he saw on his first night in the hotel. A few military types—muscular, tattooed, and self-confident—were having a quiet conversation while drinking beer and glancing at the young women by the bar. They had been checking out Vashti ever since she entered the place.

"I don't know, Vashti. You tell me. I'm not an expert in this field. I can tell you what a beautiful mortgage looks like," he tried as a joke. She ignored him.

"None of them," she said. "To begin with, the young ones, they are boring, really, and basically interested in themselves only. Some of these kids—they like to wear these indigenous scarves, see?—are research students, doing a PhD study into the causes of violence or poverty or something else too big to understand. They start every sentence with 'in terms of,' and end them as if they doubt what they just said themselves. They believe they suffer, Oliver, suffer *so* much under the moral weight of their subject. They love it and flaunt it. I hate that. The fat business guys there—well, I'm not into that at all. Simple. The tattooed and muscular crowd could be fun for a night, but don't expect a good conversation over your morning coffee. Or they get attached to you big time, and you can't get rid of them. No good. The locals? Forget it. Too dangerous, and many of them treat women like property. And *of course*, you met Bruno. He's an interesting man—good-looking, athletic, married. Bit like you, but older. And smart enough to know that in his position he can't afford a local girlfriend. People would talk. Wonder why he always goes off to the neighboring capital for some R & R? Because he's got a woman there. So, I like being single. Can I change the subject?"

"Sure."

"Going back to recent events, do you know who you should really talk to?

"No idea."

"Military intelligence. They run the gold trade, and they are the ones negotiating with Christmas. Brigadier-General Grachev. He's the slippery kind, hard to catch. Knows everything, they say. Well, most of the time. Has his finger in every pie. Or there's the local intelligence guy by the name of Colonel Neptune. He's rather big; can't miss him."

"I read about him in Dad's work e-mails."

"What? You have his GAPI e-mails? Wow! You're a slippery one yourself."

Oliver frowned. "I found them on his phone. Don't ask me how. But I saw a few reports on meetings of a committee where Neptune was sitting in. He never said much."

"On his phone, huh? Nice. Maybe it's too soon, but have you thought about going to the media with these e-mails, perhaps later when everything seems stuck and you get no answers from anyone? A bit of leaking to the press can really stir things up. I've done it once or twice myself, off the record, of course, always speaking as 'a well-informed source' or something like that."

"I don't want to do that, Vashti. It feels to me like losing control. And I don't know the game. So where do I find this fellow Grachev?

"He'll find you. Word on the street is that he'll meet you only when he thinks it's in his interest. He has an office in the capital, but he's never there. He was seen here in town at the time of the massacre. Ask Ibrahim. He must have his mobile number—at least one of them."

She fell quiet, as if a dark or somber thought had taken over her head. She leaned forward and smiled. "Do you want to do small talk now?"

The rest of the dinner went by quickly. Oliver showed pictures of his children and talked about their little interests and after-school activities, which felt familiar and strangely distant at the same time. Vashti listened politely and didn't ask any questions.

They talked about her work. She took off in what sounded like a well-rehearsed speech about human rights and how they always seem to get trampled by some petty material interest or power scheme. The thing that bothered her most was that the political elite had no qualms whatsoever about making people they didn't like disappear. The last thing you'd see of them was a dark-blue SUV with tinted windows and no license plate that swallowed up dissidents and troublemakers like a big fish eating a smaller one. International protests didn't make any difference, and if you made too much trouble, the government would cancel your visa and kick you out of the country.

Oliver didn't really listen to her. He wasn't feeling well. An invisible, heavy, dark blanket was draped over him. He told Vashti that it had been a busy week; they should have dessert and go home.

They were silent on the way back to his father's apartment. The roads had emptied, but were barely lit. Dad must have driven here often, Oliver thought, as an invisible hand gripped his chest. He was hurting now. The dark blanket pushed his head down and tightened around his chest.

"I don't know how to grieve him, Vashti," he blurted out, head down and tears streaming down his face.

"Nonsense, sweetie, you're doing so well. Just let your emotions flow, come and go, and you'll be all right. What are you feeling now?"

She slowed down the vehicle and grasped his hand. She held it and put it against his chest.

"Tell me. What's in there?"

"Loss. I lost him. We all lost him. And for what? I'm so fucking angry too. Nobody seems to care. I mean, except you. They are more interested in squeezing money out of me, this stupid foreigner, than to find out what happened. But it feels like nothing would happen if I weren't here. What am I going to tell my mother?"

"You'll tell her what you feel. She's your mother, after all. Here, this is your place. Would you like me to come with you upstairs?"

"No. But thanks."

They said goodbye in the car, or rather Vashti gave him an awkward hug across the center console and a gentle kiss on the mouth. Oliver said nothing, his face wet.

# Chapter 27

## NOTHING FOR A MINUTE

Oliver found a nice spot on the rooftop of Doppio Doppio to have his breakfast after a relatively good night's sleep. He woke up in the middle of the night after hearing gunshots, but he wasn't sure if he had actually heard them or perhaps had dreamed it all.

It was quiet on the rooftop. The sun was shining through errant clouds that looked as if they had just soaked a village in the foothills. He felt so much better than last night, eager to move on. He would see Ibrahim and another colleague of Dad's for lunch. He had already packed his bags for tonight's trip back home, traveling with Dad, in a casket in the cargo hold. Flora called him early this morning to say that all the paperwork had gone through and was ready for pickup at the office, together with the tickets.

Interesting, he thought. They hadn't asked him for the form he hadn't signed, the "exoneration of guilt" one. The minor hiccup of the day was that he had to take a local flight first to the capital, since the repatriation of human remains had to go through some ministry there as well as get a stamp from his own consulate. It was a local airline that he had never heard of, and he wondered if it was safe.

Someone was coming up the spiral staircase. Oliver was looking forward to his cappuccino and fresh croissants. But the sounds of steps were not caused by the sneakers of the waitress. These were heavy shoes or boots. As he looked up to see who it was, a head with a military beret emerged from the staircase, followed by a lean body in a camouflage uniform wearing a sidearm in a holster on his thigh. The soldier said something to someone below and took a seat in the far corner of the terrace.

Another one was coming up the staircase, this one slowly and panting. A large man in uniform, bedecked with ornaments and decorations, came up the stairs. Once he made it, he pulled out a handkerchief to wipe the sweat from his face. Oliver had seen this guy somewhere before. The officer walked over to Oliver's table and sat down without asking. He looked at Oliver with cold eyes and a fixed smile.

"I hear you are leaving today, Mr. Oliver. We should have a word before you go."

"Why? Who are you?" Oliver had been looking forward to a quiet breakfast and was none too pleased with the arrival of this man who seemed to be aware of his plans for the day.

"Colonel Neptune. Military Intelligence. I worked with your father. Please accept my heartfelt condolences."

Oliver felt he didn't really mean that. He remembered him now. He was the fat guy in the hotel lobby when he was checking in. And now he was showing up unannounced where Oliver was having breakfast. He had told no one about going to Doppio Doppio this morning, except Henri. Were they watching him? Oliver felt a wave of discomfort coming over him. What had they seen or heard? Did Henri work for them? Not likely. What did this man want from him?

On the other hand, Vashti had told him to talk to Military Intelligence. Maybe this was a good opportunity to get some more information before he went home. He decided to keep an open mind, be friendly, like talking to a new customer at the bank.

"Thank you, Sir, that's very kind of you. How may I help you? Did you order coffee?"

"I'm fine, Mr. Oliver. Tell me, Mr. Oliver, did you know your father was involved in a matter of national security?

"I guess so. He was dealing with Captain Christmas."

"Right. He's a big problem for us, as you can imagine. And Johan was e-mailing him, texting him, and sometimes he went out to talk to him in the bush. Your father only shared with us what was important to that disarmament program of his, but we really would like to know a bit more. Maybe you can help us."

"I don't see how. I'm just here to pick him up and take him home."

"Not what I hear. You want to know what happened as much as anyone else. You have gone to the police and have read your father's e-mails to find out."

This was a coolly delivered statement of fact, not a question. Oliver felt blood rushing to his head and became very conscious of the bulge in his pocket where his father's phones were, fully charged overnight. He was going to read some more this morning, but now he was not so sure. He looked at Neptune, hoping his bafflement didn't show, to no avail.

"Don't look so bewildered, Mr. Oliver. What did you think? That we did not know or could not hack into anything we want? Rest assured, we have no intention of doing you any harm or stopping you from getting on that plane tonight with the casket. There is, however, a small service we require of you."

Neptune paused to catch his breath and wipe his brow, which was still sweating from the climb up the stairs. Oliver looked at him intensely but could not get a good read of the man's mind or character. Neptune's facial expression seemed constant, like a fish's.

"How can I help you, Colonel? I'm ready to assist in any way I can, but in turn, I'd have to ask for something in return, like who killed my father?"

Neptune's faced changed for the first time, and his mouth produced a small giggle in ridicule.

"Ha! Yes, yes, yes. All will be revealed in good time, dear Mr. Oliver. For now, we have little to go on, and I'm afraid I cannot share our intelligence with you, being a foreigner and all that. But here is how you can help us. We know you have your father's phones. We need them. Just for a few days or so, and then you can get them back, in the same condition as they are today."

Neptune held out his hand as if he expected an immediate response.

"I'm afraid I can't do that, Colonel."

Oliver's mind was racing to come up with answers why not. He didn't trust this man. In fact, he had met very few people here he trusted. And what would he trust him with? He didn't know what information was on the phones. Maybe it could incriminate Dad, smear his reputation. Maybe he was involved in ways that Oliver didn't want to know about.

Neptune was keeping his hand out.

"I can wait. As long as it takes. You and I are not going anywhere."

He turned to the soldier in camouflage and nodded. The soldier got up, adjusted his holster and put himself by the staircase. Oliver was trapped.

"You know, Oliver, the army is planning an operation against Christmas. This is a secret, but I'm telling you anyway. We need to end him and his network. He's an embarrassment and an eyesore. Your father's program has put a big spotlight on him and also on us, because his program made us look like we were doing nothing. Countries in the region want us to get rid of him. Your own country wants us to get rid of him. And we will. But he's hard to find. Your father's phones may have some good intelligence on them—maybe even GPS coordinates. They could help save lives."

His hand was still out.

Oliver felt cornered. Either way, he was or could be in trouble. What harm would the phones do, even if they could unlock them? Neptune was still looking at him with a cold smile.

"And we need the PIN codes as well, please. Of course."

"I have only one. The other I was unable to open," Oliver blurted out. These guys were dangerous, and lying seemed to be a bad idea. They already knew anyway, or so it seemed. He put his hand in his pocket and fished out his father's smartphone, the one with only one attempt left before it would lock itself permanently. He opened the phone and quickly typed in a random code, before Neptune reached out with surprising speed to wrest the phone from Oliver's hands. He looked at the phone's face and raised his eyebrows.

"No more left. Locked. Don't play any games now, young man. Let me have the other one."

"I expect the smartphone back. Same condition, as you said."

Next, Oliver took out the flip phone and held it behind his back. Somehow, Neptune had activated Oliver's resistance, which didn't happen very often. Oliver did not like to be told what to do, even if— or especially if—a threat was made or implied. He analyzed the situation and concluded the soldier with the gun was a bluff. He couldn't imagine they'd actually harm him or force him to surrender the remaining phone, not with all the publicity that would follow. Imagine the headlines.

"No."

"Excuse me?"

"Here's the deal. You already have the smartphone, and you'll probably be able to hack into it, which I can't. This phone here only contains work e-mails and text messages, which, I'd imagine, you've been reading all along anyway. I need it to share it with my mother. It's a keepsake. I cannot come home and tell my mother that the army took my father's phones away from me. Imagine what she might say to the newspapers."

Oliver looked Neptune in the eyes. He was bluffing too, but he felt good with the cards in his hands. Neptune shrugged and said nothing. His hands were resting on the table, palms down.

"Very well, then. Enjoy your cappuccino and croissant."

Neptune seemed to take an eternity to get out of his seat, put Johan's smartphone in a uniform pocket, and follow the soldier down the spiral staircase. Oliver let out a sigh of relief.

Later that day, at a restaurant near Oliver's old hotel, Ibrahim told him he had done well not to give in to Neptune. "Don't be fooled by these intelligence games," Ibrahim told him. "At the end of the day, they want to protect their own turf and stake in the business. This isn't about military operations or getting rid of Christmas. Neptune was right, though. Johan's program made them look bad."

"Did they kill him, then?"

Both Ibrahim and Aisha shrugged their shoulders in unison.

"It's a possibility, but somehow I don't think so," said Ibrahim. "If that were true and it would come out, as everything usually does in the end, the international ramifications would be really bad for the army. They may be ineffective and corrupt, but they're not stupid."

It was a pleasant, if somewhat emotional lunch. Oliver had felt immediately at ease with this man and with his colleague, Aisha. Ibrahim and Aisha wanted to show Oliver how much they liked and admired his father and told him stories about his work with the farmers and with former fighters. What came through most for Oliver in these stories was his father's kindness and patience with people. Johan would listen, never appear to make any judgment, and always promise to consider what people said, even if that was impossible. Oliver was making mental notes of these things. Mom would love to hear it for sure, and he himself could learn a bit from his father, albeit posthumously.

Ibrahim and Aisha had interesting stories to tell about themselves, as well. Ibrahim had been involved in some armed rebellion in the past, which ended peacefully after a decade of negotiations and occasional flare-ups of hostilities. Part of the political deal that was reached in the end was that the government would leave him alone on condition that he wouldn't take part in politics and would keep his mouth shut in public. The ten years of negotiations "with everybody, from my wife, my children, my uncle, the undertaker, the generals, diplomats, and his Excellency, the President" had left him with an unparalleled list of contacts at home and abroad, in the bush and at the capital, as well as with serious street credibility as a dealmaker.

Bruno, who was included in that list of contacts, was quick to realize the potential for GAPI and offered him a job. Ibrahim took the offer without hesitation. Working low profile for an international organization with a high profile provided him with political shelter as well as the possibility to do some good—to redeem himself for his immoral past, of which he did not want to provide any detail. He and Johan, with whom he worked the most, had become good friends, despite—or maybe because of—their different backgrounds.

Aisha, for her part, had been a farmer's wife when Johan came along with his thistle project. She spoke often and eloquently at meetings between GAPI and the farmers' groups. Oliver was surprised to hear that she was illiterate until only a few years ago. From childhood onward, she had always worked in the fields. To make the point, she opened her rough and scarred hands, masked by nail polish and gold rings. Her parents needed her to work and did not have any money to send her to school.

Johan had recognized her for the smart woman she was and gave her a job in the program, basically to teach her to read and write, which she accomplished in a matter of months. Johan was in the process of helping her get further education when he died. She and her children would be always grateful to him. "Always," she said, wiping away a tear.

Oliver could feel the warmth and affection these two had for his father, which they now also extended to him. His loss had also been their loss. At the end of their lunch, he looked at them, took their hands in his, and said nothing for a minute.

# Chapter 28

## UP YOURS, ASSHOLE

Oliver had to twist his neck to look outside the window of the plane that would take him to the capital. It was an old plane—difficult to say how old. It had markings and notices in a strange-looking alphabet, and the seats were narrow and uncomfortable. Fortunately, it wouldn't be a long flight. The plane was crowded with people who brought with them what looked like their entire life's belongings.

There was a woman who had tied a goat to the seats near the casket that held his father's remains. It was a metal case. It looked like zinc, and it had been welded shut. He had protested at first, having in his head a scene at home where his family would say goodbye to him over an open coffin, but Aisha had gently explained to him that there would be little recognizable to look at after a long cross-ocean flight. Besides, it was the law. The alternative was to have him buried here, today, away from home.

The casket didn't fit in the plane's hold, and the crew had to fold down three rows of seats to be able to put the casket in the plane, using the seatbelts to strap it down. He sat behind the casket and, reaching over the seatback, put his hand on it. He saw and felt everybody look at him, but they never looked him in the eyes. People were quiet, and some made the sign of the cross boarding the plane when they saw the casket.

Looking outside, he recognized the old plane wreck he saw when he landed. Planes come here to die too, he thought. Owners running out of money or out of spare parts. Planes unable to fly or move by themselves were simply pushed out of the way and left to the elements and to the inventive spirit of the poor, who inhabited the carcasses of dead planes like maggots in a rotting corpse, stripping away what could be sold, taking what could be used.

"Not you, Dad. I'm taking you out of here, taking you home, to Mom," Oliver whispered to the metal case.

As the plane rumbled down the runway for takeoff, Oliver felt strangely incomplete. On paper, his mission was about to be accomplished. In his heart and mind, he felt that he could've done more, understood more. There were just too many things that didn't make sense or that could make sense if some missing piece of information would suddenly pop up.

He wondered if he should come back to deal with all the unfinished business and loose ends. He closed his eyes as the plane took to the air and didn't open them until they landed at the capital.

There, a barrage of officials and paperwork was waiting to ambush him, or at least that was how he felt. Ministry officials, airport staffers, a well-dressed diplomat from his embassy—they were all eager to have his signature or explain to him what their role was, or put multiple stamps in his passport and on expatriation papers for Johan's casket.

Nearly out of patience, he thought he was done and had taken a seat in the airport lounge to relax a bit when a tall, uniformed lady came to ask if he was Mr. Oliver in an accent that reminded him of his hometown. She sat down next to him.

"I'm sorry, Sir, but there's a problem with the human remains. We need to solve it. Otherwise, it cannot board the plane back to your country."

"What? Why? Who are you, by the way?" Oliver said, while his thoughts were far less polite. Could he just go home already?

"Airline security, Sir. We run our own security checks, company policy, and the law as well. The fight against terrorism, you know. I'm afraid the local security measures don't quite meet our own stringent standards."

"My father's dead body is not a terrorist, and there's no bomb in his casket. The papers were all in order," Oliver said sarcastically.

"Indeed, yes, I'm sure you're right, but there's a slight problem. If you could please come with me?"

Oliver realized that there was no point in fighting these people. He got up warily and followed the lady to an unlabeled door that gave entry to a maze of corridors, equipment, and storage rooms. The lady opened another unlabeled door and let Oliver in.

In the middle of the room stood what looked like an extra-large version of an airport X-ray screening machine, with the metal casket of his father's remains on its conveyor belt. Two men, in the same airline uniform as the woman, were standing by the machine.

"So, what's the problem here? A pair of nail scissors?"

"Please give us a moment, Mr. Oliver. Let us explain," the lady said in a tone that left no misunderstanding that she was in charge here. "In short, there is ammunition in the casket, and we cannot allow it to board. These are the rules, I'm afraid."

Oliver was aghast. What the fuck was going on? Ammunition? Who would've put it in there, and why? When? Who knew about this?

"But that's impossible. The body was at a morgue. It's been autopsied. Yes, he was shot, but any bullets in his body must have been removed for the investigation. He's been embalmed. They put it in the casket under the supervision of his employer. This is crazy. Are you sure your machine is working right?"

"Yes, Sir," replied one of the men with a righteous tone. "From what we have seen you are right that the bullets that killed him are not there. But it looks like the ammunition in the casket went in there with the body. It's ammunition we're talking about, a single round, casing *and* bullet. Put it in a gun, and it will fire. And it can't go on the plane. Rules apply. End of story."

The lady looked at the man disapprovingly. She turned to Oliver and changed the tone.

"We know this must be difficult for you, and we offer our condolences for your loss. But rules are rules. The exact location of the round is, how shall I say, rather delicate. Sensitive. I mean people do smuggle things in there."

"Where in there? What do you mean?"

"Let me show you." The lady nodded to the other man, who pushed a few buttons and pulled a lever with a loud click. The machine started to whir, and the casket disappeared in its tunnel. A large screen to the side of the machine lit up, showing the images of the scan.

"See here. This is the outline of the body. Here is the spinal cord, the pelvis, and there you can see the round. Looks like a standard AK-47 round, right where the rectum is."

Oliver first put one hand to his mouth, then hid his face in both hands. He didn't want to be here, look at the screen, at this *thing*. There was no explanation. Or maybe there were too many. The guy at the morgue said that they had conducted an autopsy that he had *paid* for. They should have found it then. Or was it such a *clean* death—two bullets through the heart—that there was no reason to look further?

And why would anyone shove a round up his father's rectum? He felt a chill coming over him. His murderer must have done it. Add insult to injury. *Up yours, asshole.* Some sign of humiliation or warning not to fuck with them again. Christmas?

He felt a hand on his shoulder, intending to comfort and remind him that there were people on this planet who had a job to do, with rules to apply.

"So, what are my options? We can't open up the casket here, unless you know a way to weld it shut again. Isn't it effectively sealed? I mean if someone wanted to use the round in there"—Oliver pointed to the casket with a dismissive gesture without looking at it—"somehow get it out, load it in a rifle, and hijack the plane or shoot someone, he'd have to come with a blowtorch in addition to the rifle, neither of which you'd allow on board, right?"

The airline employees nodded in agreement. Sensing that he was making headway, Oliver went further. "And even then, who would want to dig a piece of metal out of a dead body? Look. I plead with you—leave my father alone. Fur humanitarian reasons and practical ones. Besides the four of us, who else knows? Why don't you check with the captain? Isn't he the one who has the last word here?"

The lady was listening intently and seemed sympathetic to that last idea. She put up her right index finger to indicate they would have to wait a bit. She pulled out a mobile phone and left the room.

Oliver closed his eyes. This round inside this casket does not exist, he said to himself. He was not going to tell anyone at home about this. It was better that way. He could not put that on Mom's shoulders. Plus, he would have no explanation to offer. He needed to talk to someone who might understand. Not his mother or sister, for sure. Not Mary, his wife. She would freak out. Vashti, or Ibrahim—yes, they'd be able to help. The more he thought about it, the clearer it became in his mind. He'd have to go back to the City by the Water.

The lady came back with an expression of relief on her face.

"The captain is aware, and he'll sign off on the manifest. One casket with human remains as documented, nothing else. It will go in the cargo hold. He'll personally check that it's properly sealed, and that's it. End of story. And he sends his condolences."

One of the men was about to speak in protest, but she raised her hand to preempt what would have been a pointless regurgitation of the rules.

Oliver let out a short sigh. Thank God for pragmatic pilots in command, he thought. He thanked the lady, nodded farewell to the men, and went back to the lounge to have a drink, his head spinning with thoughts he couldn't master, questions he couldn't finish, let alone answer.

# Chapter 29

## YOU WON

The funeral at home became a big event. Mom didn't want it to be a small and intimate family affair. She loved Johan and wanted the world to know what a great man he was and what he had done all those years abroad. She worked hard on the event, digging out old photos and videos, setting up a mini-museum dedicated to his life in the back garden, where they had put up a big white tent where his casket would stand, still sealed, but now with an elegant, cream-white, wooden coffin around it. Oliver saw that his mom, Charlotte, had gone into overdrive, which she rarely did, and guessed correctly that she didn't really want to think about Johan being gone by delving into memories and losing herself in the logistics of organizing this celebration of life and the funeral.

Oliver, who was perhaps a bit further along the road of mourning, could see it coming that Mom would suffer a crash into reality later, after the event.

As she was selecting photographs from a pile on the kitchen table, Mom was delighted to get a call from Geneva, who fondly remembered Johan from the Garden of Peace ceremony at San Francisco. Gin was heartbroken to hear that he'd been killed and offered to come to the funeral, if that would help. Mom, an avid reader of celebrity pages, was over the moon. This, if anything, would send a message to the world that Johan's life mattered.

The whole thing was a circus to Oliver. His wife, mother, and sister had been fussing intensely over what dress to wear for the paparazzi that would surely want to take pictures of the whole thing, what food to serve, what flowers to order. He couldn't care less, but he did his best to help or stay out of the way.

When Gin arrived at the front door, he didn't join the melee and chose instead to stand with Johan's coffin, he and Dad alone under the canopy of the white tent. Goodbye, Dad, he thought. I wish you and I could've been together more, for a while, at least, in the City by the Water, to see you do what you did best, what you loved to do. Forget all that shit about your murder and what they put inside of you and why. I told no one, and they will bury you with it. But you won. Look at it this way. You won, Dad. You took one last bullet away from them. I'm proud to be your son. I promise I'll go back to that place, find out what happened to you, see to it that they finish your work. They're coming. Goodbye now.

After the funeral was over—the guests had left and Geneva and her entourage had made an exit—a terrible silence set in at home, and everybody but Oliver crashed in successive squalls of emotions.

Mary was upset with him for not grieving with her as she grieved, accusing him of being hard and heartless. Oliver tried to explain that he wasn't, that he was handling this in his own way, that he had much to think about after his trip and, if she didn't want to listen to his stories, could she please not judge him or just leave him alone? In response, she did leave him alone. He went to bed hours after she fell asleep, with a drink too many and thoughts of the City by the Water in his head.

The press coverage of Johan's funeral was by and large disappointing, everybody thought. One glossy gossip magazine featured an article consisting almost entirely of photos of Geneva and her presumed "baby bump," red circles drawn around her belly, together with speculation about who the father might be. One paragraph of the article even speculated that Johan was the father: "Gin's love child born an orphan?" To Charlotte, Louise, and Mary, this was far less offensive (because it was simply impossible) than the fact that they weren't visible in any of the photographs taken at the event at their house.

The regional newspaper picked it up with the somewhat misleading headline "Local resident and martyr for peace killed by the guns he tried to take away." It was otherwise a good article, with a nice picture of Johan (personally selected by Charlotte), describing some of Johan's work for GAPI, while exaggerating his accomplishments. The article mentioned his work with dangerous warlords in the bush and speculated that his death may have been related to his disarmament work, which, according to a quote from the GAPI spokesperson, would continue "relentlessly" in honor of his memory.

# Chapter 30

# THE HAT

"Relentlessly?" Davey slammed the newspaper on the bar of his local hangout, a run-down bar near the shooting range called the Old Blind Bull. It was a bar like any other, with beer on draft and liquor on the shelf in front of a mirror, rusty old rifles brought up from the bottom of Little Tennessee River and defect fishing gear on the wall, and a sign that said, "free beer tomorrow." The owner had called it the Old Blind Bull because, in his words, anyone who came here for a drink always hit bull's-eyes on the range and had massive *cojones*. At that moment, Davey felt aptly described by that phrase.

"Relentlessly? Don't these people ever learn?" he said in a loud voice to no one in particular, hoping that some of his drinking buddies would react—or better, the hot little bartender whom he'd had a crush on since high school. God, he'd love to fuck her, to lose his virginity with Vicky Jane, yes, please, Lord. But VJ, as she was known, did not seem to notice him and kept punching in numbers at the cash register.

"What's bugging you, Davey?" his fishing buddy Frankie responded after finishing his bottle of beer, tapping the counter for another.

"Listen to this. Do you remember we were fishing not long ago, and I told you about that guy who got shot overseas? Who was taking guns away from rebel groups who were fighting for their freedom? Burning them, too! Remember that?"

"I sure do. You got pretty worked up about it."

"I'm now as well. Read here. The guy is dead, which is sad and all, they had a nice funeral too, but they'll keep going taking guns away over there, no matter what. And relentlessly too. That's what it says here."

Now Davey was getting some more attention. Several people chimed in, including a group of older guys, pretty well dressed in suits and hats, from out of town. Davey had seen them at the range earlier that afternoon. Some sort of office team-building event, they said. You should have seen the amount of ammunition they blew through—like they were practicing for the zombie apocalypse. Now they wanted to hear more of what Davey had to say.

"Taking guns away? Where is that? Tell us about it, Son."

Davey was never much of a public speaker, but there and then, with a willing audience, after a few beers, VJ's eyes on him and on a topic that he'd perhaps thought about more than anything else, except for fucking VJ perhaps, he put on quite a show. Borrowing heavily from his Uncle Bob's conspiracy theories, he explained that they should all feel threatened by those naïve do-gooders who want to take guns away from true patriots, freedom fighters, and God-fearing people overseas.

"Which is just the start," he warned everybody to heartening cheers from his audience. He paused for effect.

"This is a worldwide conspiracy. They'll soon come after your guns too. Yes, the same ones that you fine gentlemen were firing this afternoon. No more team-building at the range when these people are done, I'm telling you that. And no more guns to defend yourselves with when the black helicopters and the white-painted trucks come to establish the tyranny of a world government with the excuse of promoting stability. And that, gentlemen—'stability'—is a code word for 'tyranny,' you know. And now they admit it themselves. 'Relentlessly,' they say. Look here," he said holding up the newspaper, "this means they won't stop until they got every gun stuck in concrete as some sort of monument of, like, our stupidity."

The team of older gentlemen from out of town exploded in applause. "Wow, you go, Kid! You tell it like it is."

"Oh, Davey, shut up," VJ interrupted, obviously not impressed. "I've heard you say these things a thousand times now. But what are you going to do about it? Huh? Huh?"

"Well, I'd do something about it if I could. You guys know that. Right, Frankie?

"I'm not so sure, Davey. Sometimes, you can be so full of shit. I think you're still pissed off about that time you were arrested for 'shooting while drunk' and got your rifle taken for a week," Frankie teased Davey to the laughter of a good number of people who had heard this story a few times before.

"But all right, okay," Frankie continued, "what *would* you do then, if you could?"

Davey's felt that his honor was on the line and he couldn't let this challenge go unanswered. He made a fist, put it down on the bar, straightened his back, and explained to all who would listen.

"Well, here it goes. I'd go overseas, talk to those rebels over there, and tell them that if they give away their guns, they'll surrender their freedom and that *we're* going to be next. That's why *they* need to stand up and resist that disarmament stuff. You know I would if I only had the cash. VJ, can I have another beer?"

One of the older gentleman, likely the most senior of the group, raised his hand to command silence and spoke.

"Well said, young man. Well said, indeed. I personally feel that there are not enough fine young freedom lovers like yourself around to pick up the cause you just described so passionately. I'm with you one hundred percent, Son."

His colleagues nodded in agreement, one of them giving Davey a thumbs up and signaling to VJ that Davey's beer was on them. She understood and smiled at Davey.

"Now, as far as the money is concerned," he said, taking off his hat, "why don't we all have a little collection here and see how much we can get to let young Davy here go after this noble cause of his? I'm putting in two hundred!"

The hat went around the bar, Davey following it with his eyes, trying to look collected, glancing at VJ, who seemed surprised by the whole thing. Donations of bills were greeted with hoots and whistles, the one poor soul who put in a handful of coins with the excuse that he didn't have any cash was met with scorn and laughter.

The hat came back to its owner, who gave it to VJ to count and give them the total result. "Quiet, everybody. Let's hear from the young lady."

VJ threw back her hair, took on a pose that she hoped looked like a pretty hostess on one of those TV game shows, cleared her throat, and announced that the total amount collected came to—suspenseful pause—two thousand, three hundred, seventy-seven dollars, and sixty-six cents.

The crowd in the Old Blind Bull exploded in cheers and applause. VJ walked the hat back to the older gentleman, who took out the cash, dug a folder out of a briefcase, and gave it to Davey who, grateful for all the noise, didn't know what to say, now that his bluff had been called.

The gentleman put his hat back on and raised his hand again for silence. The noise took a while to die down, but it did eventually. As he spoke, he had a big smile on his face.

"Well, here you go, Son. Pack your bags, and bon voyage! Go after these do-gooders for us, will you? But seriously, now. What do you say, all the people here today, who gave their money for your noble cause? Let's meet here again in a month, to hear from Davey what the outcome was of his crusade for freedom."

The bar erupted once again in shouts and laughter. Everybody came to Davey to pat him on the back and wish him luck. He felt like a million bucks, even if he had no clue what he should do or what he'd be up against. The best thing was that VJ kept smiling at him, but he couldn't tell if she was encouraging or mocking him. Either way, there was no turning back now, and he was just gonna go with the flow. Tomorrow, he'd tell uncle Bob that he'd have to take care of the range by himself for a few weeks. He sure wished he could take his Q13 with him.

# Part III
# Davey

# Chapter 31

## NOT ON MISSION

Davey looked at himself in the mirror of the airplane's toilet and didn't like what he saw. His hair was too long, and he really needed to do something about a few spots of acne on his face. He also wished he had more muscle on his arms, neck, and shoulders. Didn't matter now. His focus now was on the erection he got from sitting with squeezed legs for too long, checking out the blonde flight attendant in the tight skirt who looked a lot like VJ. It had kept him awake throughout the flight and distracted from the movie that was on the tiny screen on the back of the seat in front of him. He opened his trousers and pulled out his penis, spat in his right hand for lubrication, and masturbated until he came with a grunt that he feared could be heard in the pantry over the noise of the plane. He washed his hands and wiped some semen off the bowl. He felt better now. Maybe he could watch the movie now or fall asleep.

He wasn't ready yet to think about his mission, as he started to call this thing. It didn't get off to a good start: Uncle Bob was pretty mad when he found out about the money collection and Davey's trip overseas. 'You've been had,' he had said, but Uncle Bob let him go anyway 'because you might actually learn something useful over there and broaden your mind, or something like that'.

From the corner of his eye, Oliver saw the green light come on to signal that the toilet was no longer occupied. He got out of his economy-class aisle seat and made his way to the toilet. Its previous occupant, some skinny kid with long hair, stepped aside to let Oliver cross the aisle. He needed to splash some water on his face, wipe away the cobwebs that seemed to have stuck around his head since his father had died.

Things had gotten worse at home. Mom had taken it really hard, going through the stages of grief with either silence or endless monologues. One day, she'd taken Oliver aside and asked him if he was sure that the body in the casket was really Johan's. Could there have been any mistake? Maybe Johan was away on some secret mission or had found a reason to hide. She didn't know why, but still she couldn't help herself wondering if perhaps there was a chance that he was alive somewhere, somehow. Oliver had to admit to himself that he wasn't one hundred percent sure. He hadn't witnessed the actual sealing of the casket with Dad inside, but he knew for sure that Dad was dead, and there was no point in giving Mom any false hopes. So, yes, he was sure, he told Mom.

Oliver's decision to go back was not well understood by his family. Mary was very upset. "Why do you have to get back there? I need you here. You have a job, a family. Why can't you let GAPI or FedEx take care of Johan's furniture and stuff? The bank can wire the money. You don't need to go there." She'd been telling him all this in a sharp voice since the day he announced he was going back, after he had fixed the dryer.

Oliver never seemed to be able to explain himself to her. In his own head, he was clear that he needed to go back—not for the furniture, but for himself. He had made investments in the City by the Water, so to speak, literally and figuratively. There were things he needed to find out about his father first and foremost, but also about himself. There was something in his chest—a bizarre longing for randomness that he had avoided all his life, a desire to be with these real people who had received him with such warmth, which had taken him by surprise. Flora, Ibrahim, Aisha, Henri, and yes, Vashti too. He loved his wife and kids, and he was sure that they would understand him later in life. For now, this was something he just had to do. He would explain it to them once he found the words himself.

The arrival at the airport of the City by the Water was chaotic. Without the benefit of GAPI support, Oliver and Davey had to stand in line for an hour before a grumpy immigration and customs officer heard them. Oliver got through relatively easy. His visa—courtesy of GAPI's good offices—was still valid. The immigration officer entered his name on a computer as well as in an old-fashioned ledger as a backup. The officer raised her eyebrows after the screen flashed some information, but said nothing as she gave Oliver his passport back. Oliver wondered how fast Colonel Neptune would hear about his return. He made his way outside and climbed onto a moto with his backpack that he had brought to avoid the hassle with luggage he remembered from the last time. He'd call Vashti from his Dad's apartment.

Davey had considerably less luck. He was told that his visa was the wrong type and didn't have the right stamps and seals. After some back and forth, he agreed that he was actually a tourist, not "on mission," as he had put on the form by mistake and could not justify through some sort of official letter they wanted from him, because he didn't have one. He could get into the country, but he had to wait for an hour to pay an administrative fee in cash at the office near the back of the arrivals hall.

Cursing these damn foreigners under his breath, he pulled out a few hundred from a pouch hidden under his camo jacket, took his passport back in an angry gesture, and stepped toward the exit. Good thing he had only cabin luggage, he thought, looking at the crowd around the baggage belt that hadn't moved in the last hour. He stepped outside with his duffel bag to look for a taxi, but he needn't have bothered; they found him.

Half a dozen drivers came up and started to pull on the strap of his bag to take it to their car. Davey held on tight and picked the smallest of the cabbies competing for his business. In case the driver was going to rob him, he should be able to handle him. He got into the old car, holding on to his bag, his hand on the pouch under his jacket. He had found a good and cheap hotel online, and he was going to check that out first. Then he would have a look around and think about his first steps. It seemed to him these people here actually had no problem with guns. He saw them everywhere. Soldiers, guards, policemen—they all had rifles, nice AK-47s, but some of them looked like they could do with a good cleaning and oiling, he thought.

Davey's hotel was indeed cheap but otherwise a disappointment. Sheets and towels you could see through, blankets made of some synthetic material that created static electricity with every move. And the bathroom at the end of the corridor was filthy. Artificial light was provided by a single neon tube on the ceiling that flickered a good two minutes before turning on. The one good thing about it, though, was the lock and several deadbolts on the door, as well as a metal grate in front of the window. A prison, he thought, designed to keep the bad guys out. That and the overwhelming smell of mold, barely masked by the floral sweet perfume of cheap soap, would do the trick. But hey, he wasn't on vacation, and Uncle Bob had told him he would be spending other people's money, so better be frugal, nothing too fancy. Tomorrow he'd go and find out about that disarmament thing. And he could be relentless too, like GAPI with their stupid disarmament job. They'd soon find out, he said to himself while he fell on the bed for a quick nap.

Oliver opened the door to his father's apartment, or maybe now this was *his* apartment until the lease ran out. He sniffed the air and asked himself if it was good to be back here. He looked at the view outside; the mountains in the distance seemed to welcome him home. It was good to be back here, with a sense of purpose that he had not felt before—a new determination to be relevant, to find out what had happened to Johan.

The thought of his father clawed at his chest, but he fought off the gloominess by going to the fridge and getting himself a cold Hyper Pro. Wait a minute. When he left, there were five beers, and the bottles had been lying down. Now there were three, and they were standing up. Oliver took one, closed the fridge door, and looked around the apartment again. It didn't feel right. Henri's nephew, Joseph, had been coming here to clean up, but he didn't drink beer. Nor was he a very good cleaner. He didn't put piles of papers neatly lined up with the nearest edge at straight angles. Oliver hadn't had a chance to remind him how he liked his stuff put away.

The intensely neat appearance of the apartment felt out of place. Somebody had gone through his father's belongings again, but had not wanted to leave a trace. He walked over to Dad's desk and immediately saw a key difference. Johan's notebooks were still there, but neatly closed with the cover down. The last time Oliver had looked at them, he had put them away, opened to a random page of notes. They, whoever they were, must have taken photos, cleaned up, and left, with a beer as well, to reward themselves. Not quite one hundred percent professional, but nothing anyone could do about it. He should ask Neptune about it. The apartment didn't feel quite as welcoming anymore.

# Chapter 32

## CLEAN SHOES

"Oliver, you're back! I knew you'd come back. Come here," Flora cried with her arms wide open, reaching for his neck then planting four loud kisses, two per cheek. Oliver reciprocated and pulled her a bit closer than the last time they hugged. It was nice to see her again, smiling and exuding a human warmth that was rare in this world. She wanted to know everything about the funeral, about Geneva, how his family was doing, how he was doing. He obliged by giving her the same story he had given to so many others—college friends who reached out by phone, colleagues at the office, neighbors on the street walking their dogs. Of course, she had seen the magazine photos.

"Such nonsense, Oliver. These people write no matter what. Surprising they didn't make a big deal out of the whole bullet thing."

"What? What are you talking about?" Oliver thought this was a small secret, held by himself, a few airline officials, and a responsible pilot who had no links to anyone here.

"You were there, Oliver! When they found it—I mean the bullet in Johan's body. I heard about it from someone in the military. He said it was a story that went around in the capital. Oh dear…" She stopped talking and raised her hand to her mouth, "Isn't it true? You are *not* hearing this for the first time? I'm so sorry."

"Don't be. Be sorry, I mean. It's true, and I was there when they found it. I thought it would go no further than the airline people."

"What did you think? This country is at war. Grachev, Neptune—these people need to know what goes in and out of the country. I bet you they're all over the airport."

"Makes sense, Flora, but why leak it here?" But as he said it the answer came to him immediately: to send a message, to let people know that this had happened to Dad, and that it could happen to anyone who had done whatever it was he had done wrong.

"I need to talk to Bruno."

"Sure, sweetheart. I'll let him know you're here."

"Flora, I don't have time for him. I'm very busy," Bruno said in an irritated tone. Bruno didn't look Flora in the eyes. Instead, he stared intently at some important information on the screen.

"He's come here on his own. Maybe just ten minutes? Or shall I tell him to come back?"

Shit, Bruno thought, if he's come all the way here on his own account, he'll come back and ask whatever he has on his mind, until he has his answer. Better to preempt this and set the narrative, or maybe even get him off my back. All right, then. He got up and walked to the door to welcome his guest.

"Oliver! How good to see you! How have you been? The family? We heard all about the funeral, of course. Have a seat."

Oliver sat down in the same seat he had occupied the last time he was here, but it felt stranger now. As Bruno sat down, Oliver noticed his impeccable brown suede shoes that did not have a speck of dust or mud on them. Did Bruno ever go out in the field, like Johan did? Oliver remembered the look of his father's shoes in the closet back at the apartment. They were all dirty, with caked mud stuck to the soles. Bruno flicked an invisible or imaginary insect off his white, starched shirt and looked at Oliver with concern.

"I've come back, Bruno, because there are too many loose ends, and I want answers."

"But of course, my friend. Don't we all? Don't we all? I wish had answers for you, dear Oliver, but we're pretty much in the dark ourselves. My headquarters is putting a lot of pressure on us to get to the bottom of this and see to it that whoever did this is behind bars. And soon, too, of course. But we can't replace the local police. They're in charge, so we really have no choice but to wait for them. It's bad for business too, you know. Donors are withholding money, and we're having a hard time recruiting people for the program. But we must go on, of course. So how can we help you, my friend? Of course, we can't give you any official support this time, you understand."

Oliver moved to the edge of his seat with increasing irritation. He wasn't Bruno's friend, *of course*, and he couldn't believe that Bruno didn't somehow have more information.

"I couldn't care less about your headquarters or your donors. Or your support. What the fuck happened to Johan? Did he get between Christmas and the army or someone? It was a clean kill, not a robbery or a ghost. Someone aimed and pulled a trigger. Who, Bruno? And why?"

Bruno raised his eyebrows in feigned indignation and crossed his legs. He took the crease of his trouser at his knee between his thumb and index finger and pulled it straight toward his belt.

"Now, Oliver, please. No need to be so direct. I can assure you that we're *fully* committed to finding the culprit in *full* cooperation with the local authorities. As far as I know, we're dealing with a tragic crime, a senseless killing, and I'm not aware of any type of relationship between Johan and Christmas and the army that could not stand the light of day. Everything he did was completely aboveboard, *fully* in accordance with GAPI's *highest* standards of integrity and professionalism. This is what I tell the government, the press, the police, the donors, and it's what I'm telling you as well."

Bruno smiled and looked at his wrist to check his watch, which looked large and expensive.

"Well, that's good to know, Bruno. Thank you for your time."

Oliver got up and left. He didn't shake hands or look Bruno in the eyes. This arrogant dandy was *full* of shit and more interested in protecting his ass and keeping dirt off his shoes rather than finding out who killed his most successful program manager. Oliver realized that he wouldn't be getting any help from Bruno or GAPI. Too bad. He could have used Henri's driving services again.

He walked straight outside to go look for a moto taxi. It was warm and humid. The gravel creaked under his shoes with a dull, wet sound that was strangely soothing. He had never before been this irritated or direct, which was really another word for rude, and he couldn't really say why. But it felt good. Without regret, he left for his apartment, determined to go and find Christmas.

Whatever had happened, Christmas was involved, one way or another. Time to get his shoes dirty. As the bike pulled onto the street and into the dust, he could have sworn he saw the skinny kid from the plane step off a moto.

# Chapter 33

## SNOWFLAKE

Davey followed the girl to a set of chairs and a table set up in the shade on the balcony to the side of the GAPI building. She was kind of hot, but not really his type—a bit of a hippie with sandals, big, wide eyes, and some artsy shawl over a wide cotton dress with a flower pattern. A large fan was whirring in the corner, blowing the hot and humid air over the table without providing any cooling whatsoever. How come these guys can't meet me in the building? There were air conditioners humming everywhere around the building.

"I'm sorry for this arrangement. Davey, it was, right? I just got here, and don't have an office yet. By the way, my name is Tamiko, or call me Tammy, if you like. I'm the junior public information and liaison officer for GAPI and would like to answer any questions you may have. Please have a seat."

"Well, I'd really like to talk to someone a bit higher up, you know. I got some real important questions to ask."

"Well, maybe you can make an appointment later. But I would love to tell you about the important work GAPI is doing here, and around the world, by the way."

"I have a question about the guns. Why you are taking them away from these guys?"

"What guys? Are you perhaps talking about our Disarmament and Stabilization Program, the DSP?"

Without waiting for a response from Davey, who had started fidgeting with a loose strand of cotton from the sleeve of his T-shirt, Tamiko launched into her pitch to make GAPI and the DSP look like the best thing to ever happen to that corner of the world, if not the whole world itself.

"DSP is GAPI's answer to the real threats to peace and development around here. You know, peace and development is what we're all about and, by the way, is the reason I so wanted to join this organization. Anyway, back to the DSP, *we* are not really taking weapons away. That isn't really the objective. What *we* are about is providing livelihood opportunities to fragile communities to allow the men, women, and children in those communities to reach their full potential. So, you could say that we're not taking guns away, but giving away jobs, education, and healthcare for the people who need it most."

Davey had pulled off the strand of cotton, rolled it into a ball, and put it into his pocket. He didn't give a shit about fucking fragile communities and their fucking potential.

"Hold on a minute. Why can't you give all that stuff like healthcare to the people and let them keep their guns? Why would they trade their gun for a job? I don't see the link here. I mean, this is a pretty rough neighborhood, and you're gonna need a weapon just to stay safe, not to mention defend your freedom, you know."

Tamiko studied her guest with a puzzled look. This wasn't quite the audience she expected to deal with when she joined GAPI. But she wasn't going to give up.

"The DSP is our flagship program. Every major ambassador and high-level government official says so, and they must know what they're talking about. They all say that the weapons have to go, because they're a threat to stability.

They've been used for crime and murder, and that has to stop."

Davey heard it again. Stability was their excuse to control people. This chick, her bosses, the ambassadors—they were all in it, even if they didn't really understand what was going on, like this hippie snowflake flower girl.

"So, what does that mean, Tammy, *stability*?"

"I'm glad you're asking this question. Stability, as *we* understand it—you can read it in our brochures and on our website—is *the* essential precondition for peace and development, and for the establishment of institutions for governance, like police and courts and city councils."

"And you guys do this all over the world?"

"We have offices and programs in over a hundred places, so yes. It's such wonderful work we're doing."

Davey felt a rush of excitement and truth going through him. She said it. She actually admitted it. They took guns away to establish stability. That code word kept coming back again and again, and then they'd install their courts and deploy their police. And they were doing it across the world! He had to talk to Uncle Bob about this. He was on the right track. Had been all the time. Wow. These people needed to be stopped, right here, right now. He had heard enough.

"I should be going now, Tammy. Thanks for your information."

"But wait. Don't you want some of our booklets and video material? I could send you some, if you like. You have e-mail?"

"Nope. Gotta go."

He got up and left for the street where his moto driver was waiting for him. He got on the backseat, tucked his hair behind his ears, and after repeating "hotel" three times to the driver, they took off. He needed to get away from this place, into the bush, and talk to his brothers in arms, literally. He needed to get to this Christmas dude, and quickly too, wherever he was, before his money ran out.

# Chapter 34

## REAL MONEY

Rivers do not have a horizon, Oliver realized after half an hour on the VVVIP Express. Every turn on the wide and fast-flowing river revealed a mountainside, or a beach with stacks of firewood, or dried fish, or some village where boats and canoes feathered into the river, tied to an invisible dock or to one another. But never just the sky above the water. He actually loved this trip, despite the destination—the rush of the water under the boat, the soft bouncing on the waves of the river, and the air on his skin.

His wife didn't like the water, unfortunately; otherwise, he would have bought a boat himself long ago. He knew his father had made the same trip many times, and the captain, who carried the strange name of Boutique, confirmed this. Apparently, he was a friend of Ibrahim, who had been as effective as he had been kind upon hearing that Oliver was back in town and needed some help to get to Christmas. Ibrahim said it was going to be a quick meeting at an agreed-upon point on shore, about a mile inland on a small tributary to the big river. Christmas had been pleasantly surprised that Oliver had wanted to see him and reacted immediately and positively—actually a bit too positively for Ibrahim's liking.

He urged Oliver to be careful and not say too much too early. Let Christmas do the talking, and don't let him distract you.

About half an hour after passing a large town, the speedboat headed for the left shore without slowing down. Oliver couldn't see any inlet or opening in the mountainside and was worried that Boutique had lost control of his vessel. About two boat lengths away from the shore, the boat slowed suddenly and veered to the right, underneath the canopy of a large tree with intricate roots protruding from its base, some of which were anchored under water. Right before them, under the tree, was a narrow stream with water that was crystal clear—at least compared to the brown-blue tint of the big river that carried silt from thousands of square miles of land and mountains upstream.

"Mountain spring," said Boutique, as if he could read Oliver's mind.

The stream meandered in tight turns and was covered by tree branches from both shores, woven into a tunnel of green above them. The engine had been silenced to a gentle burble, and Oliver could hear a cacophony of birds' songs and the cries of other animals. Beneath the boat, he could clearly see the grass waving in the current. A snake made its way to shore ahead of the bow wave, its head barely above water. There was no evidence of any human activity anywhere.

Oliver felt some anguish coming over him. While the big river had no horizon, this stream seemed to have no sky. Oliver had lost his bearings and didn't know what direction he was traveling. He should see Christmas soon.

They came upon a large tree that had fallen across the water not too long ago. Its branches were still carrying green leaves. A man with a rifle appeared from the bush and stepped gingerly to the middle of the fallen tree, using his weapon to point the boat to a small, V-shaped opening in the shoreline. Boutique revved the engine for a second to run the boat aground at that spot and then switched off the ignition.

The birds' chatter and song had now become deafening, and Oliver wondered if they perhaps knew something he didn't.

A canoe appeared from under the fallen tree without making a sound and came alongside the speedboat. Two men climbed on board, the older one needing some help from Boutique, who pulled him over the side and sat him down in the faded leather seats that had once held a dictator's son. The man looked around the vessel, as if he was taking in its history and looked at Boutique first, who responded with a nod, and then turned his bloodshot eyes to Oliver.

"Oliver, son of Johan, I'm honored to meet you. I am Captain Christmas. This is my lieutenant, Mirage." Christmas extended his hand in a greeting and offered a twisted smile.

"It's a pleasure to meet you too, Captain Christmas." Oliver regretted the courtesy, a habit of his profession, as soon as the words left his lips.

It couldn't really be a pleasure, meeting this man who had killed many an innocent soul and possibly his father as well. Nevertheless, he took the hand and shook it, trying to look as serious as possible.

"Oliver, do you know why I agreed to meet you at such short notice? I'm a busy man. I lead a great movement and have many concerns to deal with."

"Frankly, no idea, other than perhaps out of respect for my father's memory?"

"Yes, indeed. Would you like a drink?" Christmas waved a few loose fingers at Mirage, who produced a bottle holding a creamy liquid. Christmas put it to his mouth and took a swig, wiped his lips clean with his sleeve, and offered the bottle to Oliver, who refused politely.

"Indeed. Indeed. Your father was a great man, and I regret his passing every day. I heard about the funeral. My deep condolences to you and your family. Tell me, are these tits real? You hear so much about plastic surgery on all these movie stars, and Geneva's breasts did not look real to me on the photo."

Oliver's eyebrows went up an inch or two. Christmas giggled and put his hand on Oliver's knee.

"I know, son of Johan. I know you haven't come here to talk about boobies. I like boobies. But you want to know if I killed your father, right? Well, I didn't, nor did Mirage, did you, now?"

Mirage shook his head, expressionless.

"Nor anyone else under my command. Let me get that out of the way. I mean, why would they? Johan was bringing us help, gave us some attention and exposure, not to mention money and jobs. Well, at least a promise of jobs, but that's better than nothing. Speaking of which, I want my money back."

"Excuse me?" Oliver was not sure if he had heard correctly.

"Your father, God rest his soul, has my money. I gave it to him, all in cash, of course. I would like it back, since it belongs to my people."

Christmas still had his hand on Oliver's knee and had begun to squeeze his leg.

"I have no idea what you're talking about." He was about to end his phrase by saying "sir" but managed to swallow it just in time. He wished he could make Christmas stop squeezing his legs.

"Well, you must have figured out by now that there is official money and real money. Your dad had lots of official money but no real money, and without real money, nothing moves. You know that, but it's probably not the same where you come from."

"No, it is not. Not like here. We move everything above the table."

Oliver was getting nervous at the thought that his dad hadn't played by the rules of accountability, despite all the resolutions and guidelines littering Bruno's office.

"So, what are you talking about?"

"Simple, son. Everybody here is corrupt because the system is corrupt. The government is corrupt. The army is corrupt, the police, the banks, the businessmen, the pilots, the priests—even God-fearing freedom fighters like us—we *all* have to be corrupt. You get nothing done otherwise. Simple."

Christmas helped himself to the bottle and cleared his throat. He had stopped squeezing Oliver's knee and held out his hand.

"I gave your dad cash so he could use it as real money to get us the official money from the donors. Pay the officials, the merchants, and the customs people, all of them. But I don't think he spent it all, so I would like it back. It was a good deal actually, worked out well."

Mirage nodded his head, smiled at Oliver and looked back at Christmas, who continued his story.

"So, why don't you go back and get me my money? Should be about eighty thousand or so. We've been looking for it but could not find anything. But you're the son, so you inherited your father's debt, to me. You know, I was so happy when I heard you had come back. We can do business together. Like father, like son, heh?"

Christmas slapped Oliver on the knee and laughed out loud. "You'll take care of that, and then maybe I'll tell you a few more stories about your daddy. But killing him? Me? Never!"

Christmas started to laugh again, which almost immediately turned into a nasty cough. He took a deep breath and spit some mucus overboard into the stream, then had another drink from the bottle.

Oliver was searching for words and ways to say them. He needed to think about this. He knew the money in his father's bank account had to have come from somewhere. There had been a lot of cash moving in and out, so Christmas could be right. Or Christmas could be trying his luck, bluffing this young foreigner into giving him money. Or maybe Dad was not as clean as he thought. Did Bruno know about this? He needed to stall.

"This is all new to me, Captain Christmas. I'm going to have to investigate this. I'm not aware of any money lying around that would belong to you. As far as I'm concerned, my father or I owe you nothing."

"Very well. Go back and investigate. Go. But make sure you come back with my money, my people's money. I keep them poor most of the time because it keeps them desperate, so they obey and fight better. But I am *Christmas* and need to provide my people with gifts, so they are grateful and obey me and fight for me better. Like everybody else, I need real money, and I'm willing to do anything for my people's money. Anything. You must know what that means by now. So, goodbye for now it is, Oliver, son of Johan. We'll meet again soon."

Christmas finished his bottle and threw it in the clear water of the stream, leaving a milky trail on its way to the bottom. Mirage helped him over the gunwale into the canoe, and they disappeared without a sound, the birds overhead serenading them as they paddled out of sight. The armed man on the tree gestured again with his rifle at the same time Boutique started his engine.

The trip back to the City by the Water seemed to be a lot shorter to Oliver. He barely looked at the passing landscape or at the glow of the sunset, mulling over the information and the not-so-implicit threat he had just received from Christmas. Just before nightfall, they reached the city and docked near the large, unwieldy ferryboat that was getting ready to depart to take the same trip upstream.

On the deck of the ferry stood a skinny kid with long hair, who looked at the speedboat that had just docked beside the ferry. Davey saw the big red letters on the cabin of the speedboat spelling "VVVIP Express." Dammit, he thought, that's one big motherfucking outboard, not like the old two-stroke he and his buddy Frankie used to go fishing with back home.

He wished he had known about this speedboat before. Now he'd paid a good amount for passage on this ugly ferry that looked like a concrete building on its side and that probably moved just as slow. He cursed again and went to explore the vessel a bit, to see if he could grab something to eat, maybe have a beer. This was going to be a long trip, and he wasn't really comfortable around the poor crowd on the ferry, who all seemed to look at him as if he were an unwelcome visitor—or a target for pickpocketing.

# Chapter 35

## SPINACH, TOOTHPASTE AND DIRTY HANDS

As the ferry got under way, blowing vast quantities of black diesel smoke into the air without moving forward for several minutes, Oliver was waving off several moto drivers vying for his services. He held up his index finger to ask for one minute more. He flipped out his cell phone and called the number he had been eager to call since he had landed.

"Vashti? Is that you?"

"Yes, it is, my dear. I knew you were in town. Why didn't you call earlier? Frankly, it's been a bit boring without you here stirring up trouble. Wanna meet?"

"Yeah. Tonight?"

"Great. I tell you what. I have a lot of food in the house, so let me bring some over to your place in about twenty minutes and cook dinner for the two of us."

Oliver was happy to agree. He hung up the phone and hopped on the nearest moto.

Vashti hadn't yet arrived when he got to the apartment. He walked up the stairs and tried to recall what she looked like, how she drank beer, and what she had told him about her love life at the restaurant. It all came back to him with surprising clarity, as well as with a feeling he hadn't felt in a long time: a nervous longing to be with her.

Maybe this wasn't such a good idea. Maybe he couldn't afford the distraction to take him away from his home, his family, his job—his life. He fumbled with the keys to open the door just as he heard the echo of steps on the stairway on the ground floor. She climbed the stairs quickly and effortlessly, like an athlete, while singing some rhythmic tune he didn't recognize.

Oliver stepped inside the apartment and left the door open. He felt the need to wash his hands, quickly, before she made it to his floor. He went to the sink in the kitchen and opened the faucet to wet his hands just as Vashti made her appearance. She looked radiant and beautiful as she put two plastic shopping bags on the kitchen table and moved toward him with her arms open. He turned the faucet off.

"I love wet hands. Come hug me now."

Oliver turned around and embraced her. The water on his hands touched the silk blouse she was wearing and caused it to stick to the skin on her back.

"Ooh, that's cold. But nice. It's so good to see you." She kissed him twice on each cheek and once on the mouth. "You look tired, my dear. A beer should fix that. You have some cold ones? If not, I brought some. Tell me, how have you been?"

Vashti took two beers from the fridge, gave one to Oliver and started to unpack her groceries, while Oliver started to explain what had happened since they last met. It felt like an eternity, and so much had happened: the flight back, the story with the bullet inside Johan, the funeral with Geneva, the fights with his wife, and today's trip to see Christmas.

Vashti listened intently, occasionally raising an eyebrow or touching Oliver's hand when he recounted some of his emotions. It was easy with her, talking about how he felt, not in any way constrained or afraid of doubts. He told her how he had said goodbye to Dad, alone in the garden, telling him how he had won in the end, something he hadn't told his wife or sister or mother.

Tears started to come quietly, and Oliver was happy to let Vashti wipe them away with her thumb. Then she hugged him and held him close, now kissing away his tears.

Oliver shuddered involuntarily and stepped back.

"Enough sadness, Vashti. Let's talk about you and what happened here."

He moved to the apartment's sitting area, sank down in one of the deep armchairs, and invited Vashti to do the same.

"That's right, enough with the sadness. Now, on with the absurd!" She laughed her generous laugh and sat down to start talking about life in the City by the Water.

It had been much of the same, she said, except for the fact that Bruno had been conspicuously invisible, as if he was trying to keep a low profile. He was avoiding meetings and most definitely had stopped talking about Johan, she said, nodding to the picture of him and Charlotte.

Then there had been some interesting rumors around town about the army gearing up for an offensive against Christmas for the umpteenth time, except now they were saying it was really serious, and it was really going to happen. The other rumor was that— and this one she knew to be true—donors to the DSP were thinking of pulling their money out, and some were thinking of giving it to her, that is, to Inherent, for some human rights work. Which was pretty exciting, of course.

"Otherwise, same old, same old. Boring, really. I missed you."

"What, me?"

That last part had taken Oliver by surprise. He took a swig of his beer, hiding as much as possible behind the beer bottle, since he wasn't sure what his facial expression would reveal. He had missed her, too. She'd been a voice of comfort and sanity throughout this whole episode. And damn, she was so terribly attractive.

"Yeah, you. There's no one else here. Unless, of course, military intelligence is listening."

She waved at an imaginary microphone somewhere in the ceiling, then looked him in the eye.

"But seriously, you're fun to be around. You're attractive, and you're so normal. It's really hard to find a normal man around here. Didn't I tell you that?"

"You may have. I mean, I'm flattered. But I missed you too, you know, especially at the funeral back home. It was a zoo, and I had the feeling that no one there really knew Johan or what had happened to him. You should've been there. Are they really listening, by the way, the military?"

'I know, I wanted to be there. Now, let me tend to the food. Come join me in the kitchen. And no, I don't think they're listening."

She put on an apron and started to cut vegetables, all the while chatting about her work, about the street dog she had just adopted, a real ugly mix of breeds, but with an independent streak, which she really loved. The dog was a bit like her, she thought. Sometimes, it would go out and come back with a dead lizard, snake, or rat.

"What, is that like you too?" Oliver laughed. "Am I the lizard you're going to kill and take home?"

Vashti laughed and turned around to face him, chopping knife in her hand. He was standing with his back against the wall.

"Hmm, the night is still young. Who knows? But I think I have other plans for you."

She put the knife down and embraced him with her elbows. "Dirty hands, sorry," she said and kissed him tenderly on the lips.

Oliver felt he had no choice but to put his arms around her, return the kiss, and let the feelings come over him. The first wave left him staggering and speechless. The feeling of falling or floating in water or space, or whatever it was that surrounded him, was overwhelming and physical, something he had never felt before, not even with Mary. He took his arms back from the embrace and spread his fingers against the wall for support.

Vashti had turned around matter-of-factly and continued to prepare their meal. "Tell me about your meeting with Christmas today, Handsome. By the way, that was a nice kiss. So normal. So, what happened? Is he still on the booze?"

Oliver, grateful for the distraction, found his composure and started to explain what had happened—the trip upriver, the clear stream, meeting Christmas by the fallen tree. When he came to the point where Christmas was asking for his "real" money back, Vashti almost dropped the knife on her feet.

"Shit. We almost had skewered toe for dinner. No way. You're kidding me, right?"

"I'm afraid not. And by the way, what's so good about normal?" Oliver was intrigued by her references to him being so normal.

"I'll tell you later. This money thing explains a lot."

"Like what?"

"GAPI had been under a lot of pressure to show results with their disarmament program, and they had issues with the procurement of the goodies they'd promised Christmas in exchange for the guns. But lately, stuff started to move, ahead of schedule, which *never* happens here. So, I think Johan cut some corners, broke the rules, and borrowed money from Christmas to do it."

She threw her arms in the air and looked up to the ceiling. "Jesus Christ, Johan, how could you? Make a deal with that monster? Fuck! I can't stand him, from any distance."

Oliver could not help himself but agree with that last thought, as he watched her pour out her indignation in angry, flowing moves of her hips. He knew he could make love to her, but not now, not yet, maybe not at all.

The wine she brought was great, but the meal was rather tasteless, thought Oliver. A mix of sautéed and raw vegetables, with a few mushrooms and bits of cheese thrown in for protein. Not his type of dinner. He was more a meat-and-potatoes kind of guy, and so he told her.

"I know, my dear, so normal. Very cute. Just eat your carrots now. Meanwhile, I think that Bruno knew about the money. Which is *why* he's being *so* quiet. I bet Christmas has asked him too for his money back. What do you think?"

"Possible, I don't know. Meanwhile, the money, real or official, is mine, sitting in a bank account here, and I think it should go to Mom. She needs it more than Christmas."

"I agree. Take the money and run. Fuck Christmas. And Bruno too."

"Tempting. But what about you?"

"Darling, you can fuck me too."

She put down her fork and gently caressed his arm, while she quickly but not convincingly downplayed the suggestion she had just made.

"Now, I didn't mean that. Or maybe I did. Some more wine?"

Never before in his life had Oliver been seduced by anyone. With Mary, his wife, there had been no seduction that he could remember. Everything had been mutually convenient and pleasant. Logical, even. Here, tonight, there was no logic or convenience. It was all feeling, all heart, all emotion, and yes, lust. Oliver could feel the stirrings of an impending erection and decided he needed to distract himself before his feelings became too obvious.

"Yes, please. Now, why do you keep saying I'm normal and that you like that?"

"Yes, I do happen to like that. Do I *have* to justify myself?"

"No."

"Well, then, drink up your wine, and take me to bed."

Oliver didn't waste any time finishing his glass of wine. He put down the glass and looked up at Vashti, who had stood up from the table and now towered over him, her breasts hovering over his head, her pelvis thrust against his chest. She smiled at him while she started to unbutton her blouse, but the smile was spoiled by a piece of spinach stuck between her teeth.

"There's a piece of spinach or maybe parsley between your teeth. Sorry to spoil the moment."

"You're not just saying that to stop me from doing what I'm doing, right?"

"No, as you said, I'm normal."

"Don't move."

She turned and danced to the bathroom to inspect the errant piece of vegetable. "You're right. Can I use your toothbrush and toothpaste?"

"It is—was—my dad's, but go ahead."

While she brushed her teeth, Oliver took a deep breath and asked himself what the fuck he was doing with this gorgeous and bewitching woman. He, normal person, was *married*, for God's sake. But the rules of normality didn't seem to apply here, whether it was money, business, or sex.

Vashti wasn't normal, either—a passionate human-rights advocate in the body of the Playmate of the Month. Or maybe he was just her playmate of the month, a passerby who would leave again and wouldn't stick around to distract or annoy her, so she could get on with the love of her life—her work. But whatever Oliver was thinking while he listened to the sound of Vashti brushing her teeth, he was helpless against the forces of nature, which manifested themselves in a hard and longing erection that would not be denied. Fuck it, he thought, let's live a little.

He got up and moved to the bed, where he sat with his hands by his side. Vashti appeared from the bathroom and walked slowly toward him while unbuttoning her blouse.

"Now, where were we?"

She knelt down by the bed and started to take his clothes off. He took off her blouse in a dance of arms, reaching for buttons, hooks, and zippers, while their mouths and tongues reached for each other. She pushed him down onto the bed, stripped off his trousers, and admonished him to stay where he was and not move. She bent down and took his erection into her mouth and hands, moving slowly up and down. At first, Oliver felt a surge of desire rushing through his body, but then he realized something wasn't quite right. There was a tingling feeling around the tip of his penis—something electrical, almost painful.

"Vashti."

No response. The tingling feeling had now become plain unpleasant, a distraction that would no doubt cause him to lose his erection. He could feel it.

"Vashti, stop. It hurts."

"What? What hurts?"

"What you're doing. I mean, I love oral sex, but this is tingling a bit—and painful."

Oliver could feel his erection go down as he spoke about it.

"I don't understand. Oh, wait a minute, I think I know." She laughed as she put her hand to her mouth.

"It must be Johan's toothpaste. 'Extra strong whitening power,' it said on the tube. Oh gosh, I'm sorry. I guess Johan doesn't want us to have sex on his bed."

He had to laugh as well, despite the awkwardness of it all, and decided to take control, since his desire hadn't quite gone yet.

"Come here. Lie down on the bed."

They moved their bodies close and kissed. He pinned her arms down and kissed his way down, across her breasts, over her belly, down to where her legs met. She groaned with pleasure as he moved his tongue over her clitoris. He put his mouth over his right index and middle finger to wet them and then slowly moved them inside her, listening for any sound or breathing that would tell him this was right. Vashti's breathing had stopped. Oliver took that to be a good sign and continued doing what he was doing. She stiffened and stretched her legs.

"Stop."

Vashti put her hands around his head and pulled him up toward her face. She looked at him with sad eyes. Oliver was confused.

"Did you wash your hands when you got back?"

"Not since this morning. Things went really fast since you came here. I had just wet my hands when you came in. Why?"

"You shook hands with Christmas. He has blood on his hands. I didn't see you wash your hands. Not with soap. You could have blood on your hands."

She pushed him away and put her fingers in her hair. "I feel dirty now. I'm going to take a shower. It's not your fault, Oliver. I should've told you."

With those words, she got up and left for the bathroom, leaving a naked and confused Oliver behind. He looked at his hands and couldn't see anything evil about them. They were *his* hands. He got up, wrapped a towel around his diminishing dick, and went to have a beer in front of the balcony doors. Maybe it wasn't meant to be, he thought, looking at the mountains in the distance.

He wondered how Vashti was feeling under the shower. He felt bad for her as well as for himself. He guessed there was a lesson learned today: always wash your hands, with soap, after meeting a mass murderer. He wondered again what the fuck was he doing here, promising young banker with a mortgage, suburban normal, married with kids, now learning lessons like this one, and in this way, too. He got up, shook his head, and walked to the kitchen.

# Chapter 36

## THE SYSTEM

The river ferry didn't get to the town upstream until the following day. Davey had spent the night in a corner on the top deck as far away from the other passengers as possible. He managed to buy a few lukewarm beers from a fellow passenger as well as a plastic bag of green peanuts, which served as breakfast, lunch, and dinner. There was a little air flowing over the vessel to keep him cool and the insects off. There was not much to see on the water or ashore, so he tried to sleep a bit but couldn't get comfortable against the moist and rusty railing.

The disembarkation process was brutal. Everybody tried to get off the boat as soon as possible, pushing and elbowing forward, with their luggage or merchandise in bags or in large plastic bales. Davey held on to his backpack as tightly as possible. All his money, his clothes, and his passport were in it, and these folks down here had no appreciation of giving a guy some personal space. Anyone could rob him, and he wouldn't even notice. He was determined not to let that happen.

He looked out over the crowd to meet his guide, some dude who would take him to see the leader of the outfit whose fighters were supposed to hand in their weapons, so they could be "stabilized." He was going to be sure to ask him why he called himself Christmas, which was a bit offensive to good people, Uncle Bob had said.

He could see a tall guy on the quay, scanning the crowd, maybe for him. They made eye contact, and some sort of recognition took place. Davey reckoned that not many people around here would wear a trucker's hat with an old blind bull on it.

"Good morning, Sir," the tall guy said with a lazy intonation, as if the words were too heavy to pass through his lips.

"Yeah, good morning, how are you doing? What's your name?"

"My name is Prosper. I will take you to Christmas. Where is the money?"

"OK, OK, half now, half when we get back. That was the deal, right?"

"Yes Sir. Follow me. You pay me half now. Plus, some extra. The weather has been bad, the roads are muddy, we need more fuel. And first, we eat."

Davey was about to protest, but he realized that he'd be stuck here without Prosper. He paid the money, 750 plus 50 extra, and followed Prosper to a stall on the side of the road where Prosper ordered two sandwiches and two coffees from a bored-looking woman, who stared at Davey with a puzzled look. They sat down on the low plastic stools and ate, in silence at first. Davey felt that he needed to hear some local perspectives about guns and stuff—and about Christmas and GAPI.

"So, Prosper, do you have a gun? I got a Q13. It's old, but it shoots straight as a laser beam."

"Guns cost money, not much, but the people here are poor. But I do have a gun," Prosper said. He lifted his shirt, showing a pistol with spots of rust on the barrel.

"So, would you give it away in exchange for money?"

"Depends. How much?"

"How about in exchange for stability?"

"Huh?"

"You know, stability, like having good courts and police and stuff."

"Depends. How good?"

"I'd never give up my gun for anything, you know. You have to defend your freedom at the end of the day."

"Easy for you to say. You come from a rich country with good police. Is your freedom under attack?"

Prosper looked over Davey's shoulder and scanned the road. Not seeing what he was hoping to see, he turned to Davey with a serious look and rather sad eyes.

"You are not tired, Mr. Davey. Your people are not tired. People here are tired. Tired of bad police who charge you money just for crossing the road. Tired of struggling for food every day. Tired of killing, of war, of thieves who will shoot you to take your car. People who are tired and who can afford it will have guns. Not because they want freedom, but because they will live a little longer. Or they use their guns the same way you use a credit card, to get stuff, but without paying."

At that point, the woman who ran the stall interrupted Prosper and started a monologue in a local dialect. Prosper was looking at the woman and made deep grunting noises as if he agreed or understood the points she was making. When she was done, the woman pointed at Davey, as if it was his turn to understand what she had been saying.

Prosper scoffed and looked up at the woman, who kept pointing at Davey, who was beginning to feel uncomfortable.

"What's up, dude?"

Prosper turned to him and also pointed at him. "You will call me Prosper. That's my name."

"OK, sorry, Prosper. What'd she say?"

"She wants to know if you are one of these people who come here with big promises and big cars and big millions, but who never change anything. She says the same thing I did. She's tired of this place. Nothing ever gets better, except for the rich, who are already rich."

"Well, you can tell her that I'm not one of them people with big cars. And I'm not rich."

"So why are you here? None of my business, really, but the lady here would like to know. She's wondering if you know what Christmas has done."

Davey sat up straight and hoped that he sounded convincing enough, like when he spoke to the businessman with the hat in the Old Blind Bull.

"Well, I've read about this program that an outfit called GAPI is running here, where people have to give up their guns in exchange for some goods, some money, and a job, so GAPI can stabilize the country. But that's plain wrong. Some folks back home where I come from, including myself, tend to think about it that way. See, your gun *is* stability, a guarantee that your government can't come into your house and tell you what to do or think. So, I really came here because I want to talk to this Christmas fellow and talk him out of this program, which I think is damn dangerous for your country and the world too, if they're successful here. So, yes, my freedom could be under threat."

Davey was rather proud of himself. He hadn't thought of that line before—the bit where he said that guns are stability.

It would sound so good back home. But he wasn't so sure it was much of a success with Prosper, who looked at him with droopy eyes, shaking his head slowly.

"Let me tell you something, young man. Everybody here would give up their guns in a heartbeat if that meant they could have a life like yours, in a country like yours. Yes, they would. Here, guns are as cheap as lives are. People use them not to defend their freedom, but to take away other people's money, or their homes, or their daughters, or just shoot them because they're in the way."

Prosper jabbed his index finger into Davey's chest as he continued in a mildly angry voice that seemed to come from deep inside his chest.

"You know, this nice lady here has been robbed at gunpoint three times now and raped once, and the police are doing nothing. She's the lucky one, mind you. And if they can, the bad people will use knives instead. It's cheaper. Christmas does that all the time. It's not about the guns, *dude*, it's about the system, get it? About the politicians and the bosses in charge and the little poor people they feed on and don't give a shit about. About being deprived by those vultures in suits of what you need to feel human. And some use a gun to get what they need, but they lose their soul in the process."

Davey didn't follow him. "But don't you need guns to fight against those things, or for freedom or justice or something?"

"Some people have taken up the gun to fight. I have too, long time ago. Sometimes, you need to feel the weight of a gun in your hands, just to feel bigger than you really are. But it does not change anything. The system in this country always wins."

"I don't know what you mean, Prosper. What system?"

Prosper looked over Davey's shoulder again and got up. "Let's go. Our transport is here. You wouldn't understand, my young friend, even though I'm guessing that you're a little deprived person yourself, where you come from."

Two motorcycles stopped at the curb by the stall. The drivers wore aviation-style sunglasses under their helmets and looked from Prosper to Davey and said nothing, waiting, revving their engines.

"You take that one. Hurry up. First, we need to buy booze."

Davey finished his coffee and sandwich as quickly as he could and got on the motorcycle to begin his trip to where the guns were. He didn't believe that he was a little deprived person, or whatever it was Prosper had said. He was on an important mission and would blow this thing sky high.

# Chapter 37

## TREAT A GUEST

"So, what does this guy want from me?" Christmas asked a tired and aching Prosper, who had come to the commander's hut after dropping off his charge at the camp's entrance.

"He said he wants to talk to you about guns and why you shouldn't give them up to GAPI. I don't know why, Captain. He seems a confused kid."

"All these foreigners are confused, Prosper. You have brought me quite a few. And this one may actually make sense. Did he pay?"

"A little more than the usual, plus a few gifts, as usual."

"All right then, have him talk to V-6 first, and then maybe I'll see him. I like it. Not giving up my guns. Says a foreigner. Impeccable timing, too. Speaking of which, you should try to get back as soon as you can. The army, you know."

Prosper nodded and left to look for a bed to lie on for a few hours. One day, this trip through the hills and the forest would break his back. At the same time, the money was good, and he had been able to keep his nose clean between his clients, the army, and Christmas.

Recently, the police had spoken to him a few times. They were insistent to hear what he knew about the whole gold trade, and they had roughed him up a bit. He had said nothing, though. He was a professional. Maybe he should call Ibrahim when he got back. He would be interested to find out what this kid wanted to do about GAPI's gun program and see what it was worth to him.

After Prosper had dropped him inside the rebels' camp, Davey followed a young rebel to a cabin where they searched him and his backpack, against his impotent protest. It was hard to see inside the hut. There was no lamp and no direct sunlight coming through the opening and the few holes in the walls. There was some sort of bed made of branches and rope, and he decided he might as well lie down to get some rest, even though it smelled like garbage in there. He had just made himself comfortable using his backpack as a pillow, when the inside of the cabin became even darker. A large man, armed with an AK-47, stood in the opening.

"You Davey, right?"

"Yes, I am Davey."

"And what do you want from our leader?" V-6 said with a fair amount of aggression and suspicion in his voice and expression, or so Davey assumed, because he couldn't see the man's face in the darkness of the hut.

"Hey, take it easy, man. I'm on your side here. I wanna see your boss to explain it'd be a really bad idea to give your guns to those GAPI people, because they'll take over your government next."

V-6 snickered. This one, he hadn't heard before. At least it was simple and direct, and there was none of that sanctimonious shit the other foreigners came here to tell them. He had much less patience for that stuff than the boss.

"Sounds good. Explain that to me."

"You know how GAPI has these gavels and plowshares in their logo? You see them everywhere here on signs by the road and on cars, you know. They want to take your guns, turn you all into farmers, and establish a government here under their gavel. Which is another word for 'hammer,' really, and you all are going to be nails. And I am telling you, man, if they can do it here, they can do it at my place too. And then the whole world. And that's just wrong. You gotta keep your guns."

V-6 was not a stranger to conspiracy theories. In fact, he lived one himself. But this one was just too good to be true. Captain Christmas spearheading the fight against world government, and this kid was showing the way. Perhaps a waste of the boss's time, but the boss might have other plans for this kid.

"Very well. Stay here. I'll come get you when the boss can meet you. Good story, by the way."

So far, so good, thought Davey after V-6 left. He stretched out on the bed once more. If the folks back home could see him now. Especially Vicky Jane. He should be out of here soon and going back home. Prosper had said that the army was getting closer and that they needed to move sooner rather than later. Fine with him. This place stank.

Davey was getting impatient now. It had been over an hour since he saw the tall guy with the AK-47. He had tried to take a few steps outside the hut to go for a walkabout, but he was stopped by a young rebel, no more than fourteen, who waved a machete to make him go back into the cabin. Davey was upset. This was no way to treat a guest, especially one that was on your side, after all. At the same time, he imagined this was like a military camp, where it made sense to stop strangers from snooping around. Not that there was much to see around here anyway—a bunch of cabins and huts spread out under the canopy of tall trees. The soil was muddy and dirty with leaves and plastic bags moving in a slow wind. And there were only a few guys with guns in sight.

Davey had to wait another hour before he was brought to Christmas, who turned out to more welcoming than he expected after the treatment he had endured earlier.

"Well, Mr. Davey, welcome to our movement. You are our guest! Please join me for a drink."

Davey was offered a seat under the shade of a tree next to Christmas, who occupied a chair on a platform, so Davey had to look up to him. He didn't look at all like Davey had imagined him. Instead of an athletic hulk carrying at least a few weapons, he saw an old man who didn't look too good, with yellow, bloodstained eyes and skinny hands that were shaking as he extended them to greet Davey.

"First things first. I have asked Prosper to return without you. No, don't worry. I took care of his money. Because you will be staying with us for a few days as our guest. Yes. I'm so interested to hear what you have to say and how things are over at your end of the planet. I'm afraid that it will take more than just one meeting to go over all of this. So, welcome!"

"Why...thank you, sir. I wasn't counting on that, but I guess I don't have much of a choice, now that Prosper is gone. When is he coming back?"

"Not for a while. But don't you worry. We will take good care of you. As much food and booze as you want. Here, have a drink. Ubamolak—you'll like it."

The young girl that had been standing behind and to the side of Christmas stepped up with two glasses. She was rather pretty, thought Davey, who looked her up and down and returned her smile with a grin.

"You like her, Mr. Davey?"

"Oh yes, Sir, very pretty." She was. And in any event, Davey didn't want to offend his host so early on.

"Excellent. She will sleep with you tonight. You will have an excellent stay here with us. She's my niece, you know. Now, tell me about your views."

Davey took a sip of his drink and swallowed hard to make the thought of the girl go away. He needed to focus on his mission now. He cleared his throat and began his story in the most complete way possible—how he had spoken up in the bar and how he got here, together with his very best version of his theory to date, encouraged by Christmas' nods and signs of approval. When Davey was done, he finished his drink and was immediately offered another one. So, this was it. He'd said his piece. Now he was anxiously looking at Christmas for the result. Christmas kept nodding for half a minute.

"This is extraordinary! Could not have said it better myself. My friend, I totally agree with you. Isn't that interesting? We're worlds apart, and we end up with the same ideas. Of course, we will never give up our guns. Never. They are our freedom, indeed. Let me tell you something, a secret that everybody knows. The guns we have given them so far are worthless. Cannot shoot—no boom, no bullets. And these people gave us money in return. Not a bad deal, heh?"

Christmas' laugh quickly turned into a mucus-heavy cough, which he drowned in alcohol.

"No, Sir." Davey laughed too, relieved, his mission a great success. He looked at the girl again and liked what he saw. He was going to get lucky, finally, and even better, anonymously. No one back home would be able to tease him afterward, or start some nasty gossip about him and some girl.

# Chapter 38

## GHOST STORIES

The numbers didn't make any sense to Oliver. He had woken up, early and unsettled, in the bed of his dead father. He was trying to do the math, accounting for the money found and spent, to find comfort in the neutrality of numbers, but it did nothing to clear the feeling of being lost that he had felt since Vashti had left the apartment last night after dinner. She had kissed him goodbye, apologizing and saying that it was perhaps better that way. Still friends, she affirmed, with her head tilted to one side. See you soon? Definitely, as far as he was concerned, and, yes, he was sorry, too.

He needed to find some new information today, if not for his own sanity, then to defend his father's memory. He was going to follow the money, for a start, and see what it had bought. He left the apartment and took a moto to police headquarters. Maybe they had found something, or hadn't spent it all.

As he drove up to the gate, the policeman on duty was about to stop him but let him through after he seemed to recognize him. He was shown to a waiting room with the assurance that he would meet the chief momentarily, and what a surprise to see you, Mr. Oliver, Sir.

This time, Frank Eugene came from behind his desk to greet Oliver as he stepped into the office. "Did *not* expect you back so *soon*! How are you? We saw the photographs of the funeral, you know. Quite the affair. So, what can we do for you? Come, sit down. Tea? Coffee?"

The chief of police led his visitor to a sofa and chairs in a room off the main room. He sat down in the taller chair, took his holster off, and placed his handgun on the coffee table before them.

"No, thanks, Frank Eugene, but if I can skip the small talk, how is the investigation going? Did you put my money to good use?"

"Of course. I was going to give you a full briefing. For starters, putting the reward out there was very successful. Of course, every crackpot and nutcase on the street came forward with some very important information, they all said. The usual conspiracy theories involving the local ghosts, the head of state, even the Pope. Many folks say they saw Christmas in town on the night of the murder, but that's not really credible since very few people actually know what Christmas looks like. There was one woman, however, who said she saw the shooting, or at least the muzzle flashes in her rear-view mirror as she was driving by that night, but we have been unable to find her after she came to the station. Maybe scared. In any event, no need to fork out the reward money at this point."

"What about any forensic evidence, chief? That's what I paid you good money for."

Frank Eugene reached for his pistol, flicked a speck of dust off the grip, and put it down again at a different angle, the barrel now pointing at Oliver. Frank Eugene looked up at the painting on the wall, probably, Oliver assumed, of one of his predecessors in full paraphernalia.

"Extensive, very broad research, expensive tests, but nothing to go on. We're very grateful—still—for all your support. You know, at the end of the day, justice is all that matters."

"I agree. Can I see the reports then?"

"Ah, you see, very unusual to share with a civilian, confidential, et cetera. You must take my word for it, I'm afraid." Frank Eugene explained with his hands spread out, as if he was weighing a large balloon.

"Your word? That's all?"

"Afraid so, but you know you can trust me."

Oliver was not sure about that anymore. The short sentences, the play with the gun, the way he avoided looking at him by staring at the painting—it didn't feel very truthful. The joviality of the first meetings had gone. He'd been *had* and knew it, right there and then. He tapped his knees for a moment while the both of them looked up at the painting of the former chief of police. Oliver believed that he was looking down upon them with an authority that was weighed down by the sadness of what he had to observe.

"Trust you? I have no choice. So, what *do* you have?"

"Well, I'm sorry to say, but it looks like your father—may God rest his soul—got into some trouble that may have gotten him killed."

"What kind of trouble?"

"There is really only one kind of trouble here. Money. Mr. Johan was taking *and* handing out bribes left and right to keep his program going. He also got into bed with the army. I don't know what they had cooked up between them, but they were awfully cozy. My bet is he helped them with the gold business."

"Are you sure about that?"

"Most certainly. I spoke to him about it once, but he did not want to talk about it to me, and that was proof enough to me. The army was keeping him safe, he said. He did not trust the police, including myself. Your father was actually quite rude, not like you at all. Turned me down cold."

Frank Eugene looked at his gun again and let out a deep sigh.

"Look. We're doing our best too, you know. The police are here for you. We were there for your father and for GAPI too—always been there. I'm asking you, was it so unreasonable to ask for our fair share?"

Oliver could not imagine his father being rude and so direct. He must have had good reasons to keep Frank Eugene at arm's length. He wasn't dreaming. The local chief of police had just told him he had asked his father for a piece of the pie, whatever pie there might've been, and Dad must have turned him down. He felt the blood rising to his head. He needed to get out of here and tried to get out of his seat, but Frank Eugene held his arm in a strong grip.

"Not so fast, my friend. I'll tell you one more thing. Christmas has a lieutenant. Big guy, very athletic. They call him V-6. Runs on all cylinders, people say. Personally, I think he runs on booze and drugs. Never mind that. Does everything Christmas asks of him. He was seen in town the night of the murder. We got at least three tips about that, all anonymous. People are afraid of him, you know. He *is* a killer."

He let go of Oliver's arm.

"There. That's what your money bought you. V-6. Christmas must have given him the order, and he came into town to do it. Wouldn't be the first time. Just ask yourself, did Captain Christmas have any reason to want your father dead. Money? Politics? You tell me, my friend."

Oliver tried hard to keep his cool while he could feel a

throbbing pain coming up behind his eyes. He needed to get out of here. Now! He got up and shook hands, immediately wondering—he couldn't help himself—where he could go to wash his hands.

# Chapter 39

## PERCENTAGES

Ibrahim had agreed to meet Oliver over a coffee at Doppio Doppio. Oliver simply had too much in his head, and he needed some sort of counsel, or at least someone to talk to who might understand what was going on. Absent his father, he felt that Ibrahim might be the best person to ask what to make of all this—of the corruption, of the police, the army, Johan somewhere in the middle with Christmas' cash in a local bank account, that his son now controlled, for fuck's sake. Vashti had said it. She thought that Johan had gotten himself in the middle of something or in somebody's way.

Speaking of Vashti, Oliver wasn't sure of himself anymore. Did he want to finish what was interrupted or stay away, ban her from his thoughts, concentrate on who he was— Mary's husband—rather than on what he was about to change into? Did he miss Vashti enough to pursue her again? He cared for her, but was that enough? He wished he could do something to help her deal with her anguish, her almost allergic reaction to Christmas.

On the rooftop, in the shade of a tan umbrella, Ibrahim told him that things had taken a turn for the worse.

"Not good, Oliver, not good. Since you left with your father's remains, my phones have not stopped buzzing and ringing with calls and text messages. Some bizarre e-mails too."

Ibrahim had laid out his four phones in front of him and tapped each one of them in sequence to see if anything else had come up.

"Clear. For now. All right, then. You need to know that your father's death, this whole thing with the bullet at the airport and also you coming back, has caused a whole twirling, song-and-dance show of conspiracies across town. Everybody is taking part. Haven't you noticed anything? People looking at you on the street? The waitress just now was looking at me with question marks in her eyes after she saw you."

"No, I haven't seen anything—been a bit absorbed with my own thoughts, you know."

"OK. Here are the main stories that you can ignore, but some people take them seriously. One, you have come back to kill Christmas. Two, you are taking over your father's old job. Three, he was killed by a ghost using a magic bullet or by Christmas using some other magic trick. And four—"

"Enough with the crazies, Ibrahim. Sorry to interrupt. What do you know about V-6 being in town the night of the murder? And what about some funny-money business going on between my father and Christmas?"

"Both true. I know. I was there when V-6 met your father that day. V-6 was always the one bringing the money. It was dirty but necessary. Please understand, Oliver, your dad could not move a thing without the cash lubricating the deals for the kits and the hospital. I couldn't tell you earlier."

"It wasn't clean, Ibrahim, and therefore wrong. Doing business with a murderer, making deals off the books. What if the donors found out?"

"That's the thing. Bruno is pissing in his pants, scared that they will find out. He knew about it and did not disapprove. This was his flagship program, and he needed it to be moving or at least to be seen as moving. If this comes out..."

Ibrahim pulled his index finger across his throat and then tapped it on the phone to his left, as if that contained the information he was about to divulge.

"The other thing—and I got it from military intelligence itself—is that the army is getting more assertive. Christmas' gold is not enough to keep the top brass quiet. The DSP made them look stupid and powerless. They resented that, and now the government is slowly but surely ratcheting up its rhetoric. They want to be rid of him. So, look for army trucks moving out to the mountains. People say there could be an offensive anytime."

Oliver had the words in his mouth before his thoughts had fully formed. This was a rare moment, so unlike him, but it felt right.

"I was thinking of going out to see Christmas again. Somehow, he's at the center of it all. It all leads back to him, the money, V-6, the army. If he didn't have my father killed, then he must know—or at least have a good idea—about who killed him. The police here are useless."

"Did you speak to them?"

"The chief himself, who was very friendly and helpful the first time, but not so now. He was talking about how he wanted a piece of the pie. He sounded bitter, called my father rude, said that Dad didn't trust him."

"Nobody trusts the police. They are nasty, Oliver, looking for money in all places—big business, small shops, folks on the street. Nothing like what you are used to back home—not your friendly neighborhood cop. They beat you up or come to your house to take stuff away to sell on the market. If you don't play along, they find an excuse to put you in jail for as long as it takes for you to scrape your bail together. They take your cell phone and charge you money to make a call."

Ibrahim shivered involuntarily, scratched his elbow, and paused for a few seconds. He blinked and continued.

"Occasionally, someone disappears in a dark blue SUV, never to be found again, or if they are found, because they want to set an example, you need to pay the morgue, who will then pay Frank Eugene. The mafia is wearing uniforms here, my friend. Beware. Frank is a dangerous customer. But no matter what, I wouldn't go see Christmas, if I were you. Much too dangerous now."

"Look, I have some leverage over him, which is more than others can say. Remember, I have his money. Although I spent some of it, he doesn't know that. And he wants it back. Money matters, and if there is one thing I know, it's how to make money work. I want to finish what my father started and somehow, I don't know how yet, use the money to make Christmas talk or, even better, get him out of the bush so someone can take care of this bastard. And I want to do it now."

"You are talking about playing a game that you don't understand, my friend."

Oliver didn't hear what Ibrahim was saying. He was taken by surprise at the clarity of his conclusions and how they came to him. In the end, it was a numbers game, he thought—a game of percentages, really. His father was a hundred percent dead, but his work only forty percent or so finished, his reputation not a hundred percent clean. If he had only a twenty percent chance to make those numbers move to his favor by making a minor investment, putting his father's money in play, at some risk to himself in the single digits, to somehow get rid of Christmas, then it would be worth it. He could tell Vashti that his hands were clean. Dad would be clean. Then he could go home having made a difference.

"I'm going, Ibrahim. I see no other way."

"You should leave now. Leave this place. Go back to your wife and kids. Take or leave the money, but go."

"No."

Ibrahim shook his head.

"You're crazy. I will help you, against my better judgment, for the sake of Johan's memory, but this is the last time. Bruno will have me fired if he finds out. After this, you are on your own. I'll call you as soon as possible with the arrangements. Make sure you have the cash for the trip. One more thing: if you get to Christmas, I've heard that there is a young compatriot of yours staying at the camp. I don't know who or why he is there. Tell him to get out of there, fast. It's not safe."

Oliver took Ibrahim's hands in his to thank him, after which they said goodbye. Oliver left to get back to the apartment. He wanted to be ready when Ibrahim called, and he also wanted some time to look at his father's notes again, which had been useless so far, a lot of bureaucratic scribbles and meeting notes.

Ibrahim stayed for a while to make calls from the rooftop, since the signal there was really strong. He used his red phone for a text message to Colonel Neptune, then called Boutique and Prosper on another phone, the black one, to fix the trip upstream. They protested but agreed after Ibrahim promised that Oliver would pay double. Once that was squared away, he made two more calls. The first call was to Flora, whom he asked to warn Bruno. The last call was to Christmas' satellite phone.

# Chapter 40

## PARTY TIME

He had done it, Davey said to himself as soon as he woke up. The girl had left sometime in the middle of the night, but he could still feel her skin against his, her young breasts in his hand. She had been very quiet and did not want to kiss him at all. For Davey, this didn't matter. He wasn't going to propose to her today or anytime at all. It had been good, really good, second time better than the first, which came too damn quick. Now he knew what it meant when folks said that there was only one thing better than firing your weapon, and that was firing your gun. He reached down to touch it. It felt a bit sticky. Maybe he should take a shower. He smelled his hand. Yes, this was a good smell. Hard to describe—bit of sweet, bit of salt, bit of sour, bit of bitter. He wondered if it would smell different with different girls, if VJ would smell different.

He sat up and realized his stomach was empty. Yesterday's dinner had been pretty awful. Some sort of corn in a mild sauce with little meat. Goat it was, they said, but more bone than meat. At least there had been enough booze.

He strolled outside the hut to see where he could get some food and maybe a shower. There was a guy outside, about his own age, who got up from the ground and asked Davey what he wanted. He took Davey to the center of the camp and told him to sit down and wait in the shade of a tree. As he was waiting, he saw it. A Q13, just like his, but not in as good a shape. He waved at the man wearing it, all smiles. The man came over, looking suspicious.

"Man, I really love your rifle. I got one just like it at home."

The man did not seem to understand him, so he tried gestures and, when that did not work, he drew stick figures wearing rifles in the dirt.

"This is me. My place. This is you, right here. See? Same gun."

He had to repeat it several times before the man understood. He gave Davey a narrow smile and held out the weapon for Davey to touch after he removed the magazine.

"Yeah, same. Same good old Q13. Shoots straight, doesn't it?"

Davey was really curious to find out where the hell this guy had found this weapon. It must have made a really long trip to end up here. He patted the weapon and gave the man a thumbs up as he was moving along. Davey sat down again and waited until someone came with a piece of bread and a bowl of water.

Later that day, he tried to find the big guy—the one with the name of a car engine—to find out if they could reach this Prosper fellow so he could go back home because he was done here. He was really getting bored. Not yet, someone told him. V-6 was real busy at the moment.

The camp had turned real quiet. There were only a few women around and some kids, mostly toddlers. Maybe all the rebels had gone out on patrol or were on some sort of drill in the forest to prepare for when these GAPI people came to take their guns away. He was keeping his ears out for any gunfire in the distance. He really missed his weapon now. Wait. That was it. A volley of gunfire in the distance. Hard to say where it was coming from as the cracks echoed off the trees and hills.

It lasted about ten minutes—all different calibers—and then it stopped as abruptly as it started.

End of target practice, he concluded.

After a while, some of the fighters trickled back into the camp, armed with rifles, pistols, and machetes. They looked sweaty and self-confident. They came to attention in formation, while Davey was looking on. V-6 came into view, with Christmas and two bodyguards beside him. On command, the fighters raised their fists with their necks bent sideways and gave out a shout that must have met with Christmas' approval, judging from his expression. Christmas gave a little speech, after which the fighters disbanded into the huts to meet with their families, Davey supposed. He saw his opportunity and walked toward Christmas, but he was stopped by one of the bodyguards.

"Hey, Captain Christmas, sorry to bother you, but I'd like to go home now," Davey shouted.

Christmas did not look up, but he must have heard it, since he said something to V-6, who came to Davey to explain what the deal was.

"Not today, Mr. Davey. It's already too late. But we have another guest coming soon to keep you company. He is from the same country as you. Maybe you can leave together. Tomorrow!"

Davey went back to his hut to take a nap, but found that he couldn't sleep on the uncomfortable bed. He replayed the memories of his recent sexual adventure in his head and was wondering if perhaps he could get some more of that. Maybe, if Christmas was in a good mood, he could ask him.

The sun had begun to set when a young fighter stepped into the hut to fetch him. "You. Come now. Party time."

"All right, party time!" Davey got up, adjusted his clothes, and straightened out his hair. He could really do with a shower now. He stepped out of the hut and walked toward the center of the camp, where most of the camp seemed to have assembled, armed fighters to the front, women, children, and old men to the back.

He saw Christmas sitting on his throne under a tarp that had been strung from the trees. Next to him, to his left, sat a foreigner, who looked vaguely familiar. It was a guy Davey had seen on the plane, but he looked very tired and serious. Christmas gestured Davey to come forward and sit down to his right. In front of Christmas stood a table with glasses and bottles of scotch, vodka, and that creamy drink that Davey had the night before. Christmas stood up and raised both his arms to the sky.

"God has blessed us. Today is a great day!"

The camp erupted in cheers and hollers. Christmas let his arms fall to his side, paused, and raised his arms again. The camp turned quiet.

"We have scored a victory over the army of those who want to deny us our rightful place in history. Hail to our brave fighters!"

Cheers came again, this time led by the fighters, who started to stamp their feet in a pounding rhythm. Davey realized now that what he had heard was no target practice. This had been for real. These guys had used their guns to defend their freedom, as they should.

Christmas asked for silence again, this time with a single swipe of his hand. Davey was impressed. This was a true leader the likes of which he had never seen. Not even his old football coach came close to displaying such authority. He'd have some stories to tell when he got back home.

"We're also blessed to have among our midst two distinguished guests. First, Mr. Davey, who has been our guest for a while now and who has come all the way from abroad to support us in our struggle to keep our guns and our freedom!"

Christmas pointed at Davey, who got up, made a few awkward nods of his head, and pumped his fist in the air.

"There you go, young man. And here to my left is Mr. Oliver. Maybe you can see something familiar about him. He is the son of Mr. Johan, whom we all remember fondly, don't we?"

An approving murmur went through the crowd. Davey wondered where he had heard that name before; it sounded familiar and somehow important.

Christmas continued. "Mr. Oliver is an important banker. And like his father before him, Mr. Oliver has come to bring us money. Welcome, Mr. Oliver."

Davey took a closer look at his compatriot. He didn't seem happy at all and was looking nervously around the crowd, which had started to applaud him. He had refused his drink, while Davey had helped himself to a large glass of scotch, since the Ubamolak gave him heartburn.

"So tonight, we celebrate. We have found some goats and vegetables from villages nearby. There is food; there is plenty of drink. Let us celebrate our good fortune and praise the Lord."

The crowd answered immediately—men, women, and children. Davey shuddered. The passion with which they all recited their prayer startled him.

"Praise the Lord, and may he protect our leader and savior Christmas as he leads us to the promised land. Amen."

The launch of the party was over, and people started to line up for the food that had been prepared for all. Christmas stepped off his throne and asked Oliver and Davey to stand up with him. He put his arms around the both of them and smiled.

"Historic moment. Calls for a picture, don't you think?"

"Not really," Oliver said. Davey was more enthusiastic, since he needed proof of where he had been and what he had done. He put on his best smile for the camera.

"Come on, Mr. Oliver. You cannot refuse me this honor, if you really want my help."

Oliver reluctantly moved as close to Christmas as he could stomach. Mirage stepped forward and took a few pictures with his cell phone of the three of them, with Christmas' bodyguards in the background. Outside of Davey's view, they had pulled out their pistols.

"Excellent. You know what to do, Mirage."

"Yes, leader."

Mirage walked behind the bodyguards to type in a few lines on his cell phone. He looked at it for a final inspection and gave it to a waiting motorcycle driver, who nodded, pointed to a distant hill, and took off.

The party was on. People had eaten and enjoyed a few drinks. A few teenagers appeared with drums and set them up in front of Christmas. They started a strong beat with unexpected rhythmic variations, bringing out a group of women who started a dance that seemed well rehearsed, since they all knew what to do. Davey had never seen anything like this. Old and young had joined in the dance, while the boys and men looked on approvingly.

Christmas took Davey's arm and explained that they had been dancing this dance since they left the homeland. It represented their recent history. The first part symbolized the exodus with rapid feet movements and jerking movement of the head to look for any pursuers. Then came the time of suffering, he said, and the dancers started a slow movement of the shoulders and hips, moving closer to the ground, their hands swatting away invisible enemies. The drums went silent except for a small, high-pitched drum whose beat went slower and slower until the women had reached the ground, kneeling in a semicircle facing Christmas with their faces touching the dirt. One woman got up and pointed at Christmas, then the others followed and waved with their hands and, so it seemed, with every part of their body.

"What does this mean?" Davey asked.

"I became their leader with the blessing of God, and now everything is going to be all right. We will return to our homes. Look how determined and happy they dance. Big moment."

Davey could see a lot of determination and sweat, but not so much happiness. He'd been looking for the girl he had slept with the night before, but she was nowhere to be seen. The dancers were leaving the circle, sipping from plastic bottles of water.

"Now I have something for you, Mr. Davey. They tell me you are a real good shot with the Q13, right?"

"Yes, Sir, you bet!"

Christmas turned to his rear and made a gesture to one of his bodyguards, who produced the Q13 that Davey had seen earlier. He put it in Davey's hands and put his hand in his pocket to take out a shiny single round of ammunition. Christmas looked from Davey to Oliver, who looked away uncomfortably. Davey didn't know this Oliver guy, but he sure wasn't going to let him spoil his fun tonight.

"A single round? What's the target?"

"Wait a second, my eager friend. So, you tell me that we should never give up our guns, right?

"Yes, Sir."

"What would you say if someone had tried to break ranks and give this beautiful weapon to GAPI—to the friends of Oliver's father?"

"That would be a shame, Sir." Davey was too focused on the Q13 to have heard and understood the connection between Oliver and GAPI and, thus, himself.

"Exactly. Don't you think we ought to make our mistaken friend change his ways and set the right example?"

"Yes, I do."

Davey looked around and saw that the festive mood in the camp had gone. No one was smiling or dancing, and they were all looking at him. He was looking for something that would be an obvious target, like a mango on a stick or something, but he couldn't see anything like it. The crowd parted, and a handcuffed young man, about Davey's age, was pushed to the middle and made to kneel.

"Here is your target, Mr. Davey. He tried to run off last night with his girlfriend, who had just spent the night with you. And worse, with a good weapon that we need in our struggle, against my orders. This is a crime, you understand."

Christmas gave Davey the round.

"I thought that I would give you the honor of killing him, since you came all the way here to support our cause. Shoot him anywhere you like. Just one round. Then maybe his girlfriend will sleep with you again!"

Davey's eyes and mouth were wide open. This was not the deal. He couldn't kill anyone. He looked at Oliver, who was looking back at him urgently, almost imperceptibly shaking his head. But if he didn't shoot him, some of the others would do so anyway. He had often fantasized about being in a war, a hero who would kill the enemy with his trusted rifle in defense of his country and his freedom, but never did he look his imagined enemies in the eyes, like this young man on the ground, who was now staring at him. There was no emotion visible on the victim's face, yet it deeply disturbed Davey to see his intended target breathing and looking straight at him. He could not do this.

"Sir, I can't do this," he stammered. He gave the round back to Christmas. "I'm sorry."

"Sorry? You're full of empty promises, young man, just like the rest of you. Come here with a big mouth, to my camp, eat my food, drink my booze, sleep with our women, tell me we should never give up our guns and our freedom, but you're too much of a coward to do what is needed. Now, watch! And remember, I gave you the choice to shoot him any place you wanted and kill him quickly."

Christmas looked around and called out for volunteers. All the fighters raised their hands. Christmas selected one of the younger ones.

"With a knife. We need the bullet, which I'll keep as a souvenir of a foreigner's cowardice. Remember, he is our enemy now, no longer your brother. Impress me, and you can have his rifle."

Davey saw the blood drip from the first cut and looked away. The victim began to scream, and Davey looked up to see the younger fighter cut off his victim's ears, nose, dick and balls, then move the knife across the belly, drive and twist it in four different spots, careful to avoid the heart. Davey's stomach reacted quickly, and he threw up his food and drink in a violent spasm. Christmas looked at him with disgust and ordered him taken back to his hut and to make sure that he would stay there.

Oliver could not look away, because he felt responsible. Please die quickly, brother, please die. He was praying for the young man who was going to die because of his father's program, because he had a good weapon, because this stupid, skinny kid had slept with his girlfriend, because Christmas wanted to be a good host, because Christmas was a pig. He was going to die because he was born in this tribe.

How could people turn so evil, so nonchalant about human life? Life was nothing more than a tool to Christmas—

a tool to enforce what he wanted, to set an example, to push his crazy beliefs to empower himself. Oliver studied the crowd for answers. Christmas' followers looked on, most without any show of emotion whatsoever. Had they seen this before? Oliver wondered. Seen this before so often that any human reflex had abandoned them? Or were they afraid that it would happen to them? Probably both.

Oliver noticed some people were not looking at the execution, but at V-6, some with puzzled looks on their faces. V-6 stood still with his arms crossed, nervously flexing his biceps, looking down at the earth with gritted teeth, as if he was angry at the pebbles in the dust. Oliver didn't know the man at all, but this posture seemed to be a bit out of character for V-6.

The kid was no longer moving. In fact, Oliver thought, it was no longer a kid, or even a human being. A clump of disorganized molecules without purpose or hope, like the bodies in the morgue, like his dad. How foolish he had been, how naïve, to think that he could come here with his utterly useless banking skills and make Christmas see things differently. Instead, he would see what he just saw for the rest of his life; every time he closed his eyes, he'd be here again. Tears of anger and frustration streamed down his face. He had to leave—leave quickly, get out of here, fuck them all, take the money and run. He got up and looked around to see if there was a gap in the crowd or some opening between the huts that could serve as an escape.

"Forget it, Oliver. You are staying here," He heard Christmas say, just as someone behind him twisted his arms in a tight grip.

"Lock him up with the other fool. And have someone clean up the mess. I'll have another drink now."

# Chapter 41

## FIRE AND SMOKE

One of Ibrahim's phones was buzzing. He pulled out the phone and opened its screen. About nine hundred yards away from Ibrahim in the City by the Water, Colonel Neptune was having dinner at a restaurant that had just been opened when his aide-de-camp handed him a buzzing cell phone. He clicked to see what message had come in. Ibrahim and Neptune saw the same message and its attachment at the same time. It was a photo of Christmas smiling and embracing two foreigners, one of whom they recognized as an unhappy Oliver. The message read: *"If the army comes any closer to our camp, I'll kill them both. Do the necessary. Merry Christmas!"*

Unaware of their new status, Oliver was escorted away from the execution site to join Davey. He found him very upset, pacing the ten-foot length and width of the hut that served as their prison cell in all directions, clasping his hands and pretending to pull a trigger.

"Why the fuck did he have to do that for? What the fuck...what the fuck...I mean, should I have shot the guy? I didn't come here to kill anyone. Or see someone being cut up like that. What did he have to do that for? Please..."

Oliver felt sorry for the young man and less so for himself. He felt more guilty and stupid because he should've known. Davey must have come in here innocently. Yet nobody can ever be prepared for this.

"It's not your fault, Davey. He would have killed the man anyway. He was trying to put you on the spot. You did well, Davey, really well. There's no shame in what you did."

Davey looked up at Oliver with wide-open eyes, his shaking hands still clasped as if he was holding a gun.

"I could have fired the round. Should I have fired the round? It was awful what they did to the guy. And I fucked his girlfriend. Is she dead too?"

"Look, Davey, you're a good kid as far as I know. Maybe you should have kept your dick in your pants last night, but you're not a murderer. I don't know about the girl, but I do know this. Listen to me; look me in the eye. Christmas is as evil as they come. If you had killed the boy, some of that evil would have rubbed off on you. And you didn't. They would have killed him anyway. Your hands are clean."

Davey sat on the bed and started sobbing. Oliver sat next to him and put his arm around him.

"Tell you what. We need to get out of here. Together, as soon as we can."

"Yeah, right."

"Listen. We ate, we drank. All we need is sleep now. Once we're ready, we'll start looking for an opportunity. The army isn't far from here. I know. I passed some of their patrols on my way in here. But they're still a way off, and they're really taking their time. Let's figure out what direction they are, and then we go. What do you say?"

"Whatever you say, man."

Davey felt tired and lay down. He really wanted to sleep, but he couldn't chase away the images of the night, mixed with those of the night before, from his mind.

Knowing that sleep wouldn't come to him, either, Oliver sat on the mud floor, listening to Davey breathing. He had begun to fear for his life now and started to review the scenarios whereby this could happen. Christmas could kill him on a whim; he could fall off the motorbike down a ravine, get shot by the army as collateral damage, or drown in the river.

He felt a mosquito bite him on the ankle and thought, well, add malaria to the list too. But he could not die. Not now, not here. He was too young. He wanted to be a father to his kids. He needed to survive for them, for Mary. He looked around the hut and checked the walls to the back. They looked flimsy, and he bet that, with a good kick, he could open up a hole to escape through. But what then? Better wait until morning and do a recon first.

After a short and uncomfortable sleep, Davey woke up because of the noise outside. He looked out and saw everybody running around with weapons, food, and bottles of water. He stepped outside to find their guard nervous, nostrils flared. He waved his pistol, said something that must have meant go back inside, and pushed Davey to make sure he understood. Davey went back inside and wondered if he should wake up Oliver, who had been really nice to him the night before after that thing, that terrible thing. Maybe he could make sense of what was going on outside. It looked like something big was about to happen.

"Yo, Oliver. Wake up, man."

"Huh?"

Oliver was stiff from sleeping on the floor. His neck hurt, and it took him a while to get his bearings. Once he realized where he was, he was sharp and focused.

"What's going on?"

"Don't know, man. The guard wouldn't let me go outside."

Oliver tried to step outside as well. He tried to charm the guard with a smile and open hands, pretending he needed to get a drink, go for a piss, you know, between guys. It didn't work. The guard pushed him back, so Oliver tried an old trick that worked at his bank: insist on talking to the manager. His expression changed to one of authoritative anger, and he demanded to see Christmas, or V-6, or Mirage—anyone in rank above this simple foot soldier, who had probably been told not to let the hostages out, or else.

It caused a minor commotion, which was noticed by an old gentleman in a three-piece suit, who was packing up his goods at a hut nearby. The old man came up to the guard, and they talked for a bit. Oliver interrupted them.

"I'm sorry, sir, but I really need to go to the toilet and have something to drink. And so does my friend here."

"We will give you a bucket and a bottle of water. You stay here."

"What's going on? Are you leaving the camp?"

"Getting ready. Christmas gave the order to prepare for our move. It's the seventh one since the exodus. He said God told him so, in the forest, last night. We'll make it to our homes, hopefully before I die."

"Why leave? What's wrong with this spot?"

"Army is getting close. They may find us soon. Now, get back into your hut. For your own safety."

Oliver and Davey stepped back into the shade of the hut, but not before Oliver made a quick scan of the surroundings. He counted the guards, then spotted a pile of leaves, plastic bags, and cardboard boxes to his right, near the edge of the clearing. Back inside the hut, Davey was getting nervous.

"The army? What's going to happen? Are we—?"

At that point, there was a series of sharp cracks in the distance, closer than those Davey had heard the day before, much closer. He ducked involuntarily.

"Fuck, man, that was close. I recognize the AK-47s. That must be the army."

He looked around at the walls of the hut.

"We're not safe here. No cover. Bullets will go right through this shithole. We have to get out of here."

"Take it easy, Davey. How far away do you think they are?"

"I dunno. Maybe a mile or so east of here. Hard to say. Could be a day's travel in this jungle." He remembered that last bit from a copy of *Survival Magazine* that was on the table at the shooting range.

The shooting stopped. Instead, they heard a few shouts and anguished cries, which soon died down. All became quiet. People in the camp started to move more slowly. One woman started a smokeless charcoal fire and prepared to cook a meal.

The two men sat on the bed and decided that they couldn't really do anything for now. Without drawing attention to himself, Oliver slowly made holes in the walls of the hut in every quadrant of the compass so he could peek out at what was happening all around, but for now he could see little of consequence, except for the fact that it was going to be a sixty-yard dash from the back of the hut to the cover of the forest. Oliver looked at the sun and concluded that they needed to travel with the sun at their back if they were to make it to the army lines through the forest—at least if that was where the firing had really come from. They were going to need water, and maybe a machete as well.

The bucket came, and so did a few bottles of water and some food. The day passed without further commotion. A trickle of fighters came into camp to eat, then went back into the forest and the hills after they were done. Christmas was nowhere to be seen. Oliver looked at the bucket. It was a sturdy plastic that would hold a gallon of anything. And it was the only tool they had. He kept staring at it, trying to think of some way to use it to their advantage. Looking outside the hut again, it came to him. There was barely any wind, so any smoke would rise vertically to indicate to anyone looking for where they were—where Christmas was.

"Davey?"

"Yeah?"

"Look outside. See the woman cooking to the left? Now, look right. There's a pile of garbage. Don't you think it looks dry enough to catch fire and send up a whole lot of smoke, so the army can see where we are?"

"You crazy or something? They'll shoot you," Davey replied, scared at this point for his own life.

"Not if nobody is around with a gun. The only permanent armed guy is our guard, and he's pretty small. So, here's the plan: at the right time, I'll go outside and use my weight and height to knock down the guard and pin him down. You take the bucket, go to the charcoal fire, scoop up as much hot charcoal as you can, and throw it on the pile of garbage. Move quick, or the bucket will melt. What do you think?"

"Then what? Make a run for it?"

"Good thinking, but no. Once I let go of the guard, he'll sound the alarm, and then they'll shoot us for sure. If not, we'll probably get lost in the bush or shot by the army. So, I say, just come back to the hut. My bet is that the guard will be terrified to admit he let this happen, and for sure he can't shoot us because we're back in the hut and still worth something to Christmas."

"That's a big gamble, man."

"Yes, I know, but life is a gamble." Oliver surprised himself saying that. "So, look out for fighters. As soon as there are no fighters other than the little guy outside, we execute. Can you handle this, Davey?"

Davey was looking away from Oliver, looking outside for clues. He was scared shitless, but wasn't about to admit it.

"Sure, sure."

It didn't take long for the opportune moment to arrive. There was no fighter in sight other than the guard, and the woman abandoned her pot to fetch something in her hut. Oliver stepped outside and pretended he had to stretch. He smiled at the guard who had come halfway up from his stool, decided Oliver posed no immediate danger, and looked back down at his stool, aiming to sit down again. At that point, Oliver crashed into him, using his weight to pin down the guard and his pistol to the ground, and put his hand over the unsuspecting guard's mouth.

Oliver strengthened his grip, while Davey made a run for the charcoal, scooped up as much as he could, and ran to the garbage pile. He poured out the burning charcoal on a concentrated spot in the middle of the pile and ran back into the hut.

"Well done, Davey," Oliver said calmly. He looked down at the young guard underneath him, whose eyes were wide open, his nostrils flaring with fear and anger, and struggling to breathe.

"Shhh. Stay cool, man. I'm going to let you go now. Nobody saw what happened, and we'll be back in the hut, like good prisoners. If asked, we'll say we've been in our hut all the time, didn't see anything. It was not your fault. We didn't escape, so you did your job. Understand? Nod at me if you understand. Nod at me!"

The guard nodded.

# Chapter 42

## IN ONE PIECE

The fire burned fast for about three minutes—enough to send up a thick, smelly cloud. The camp went into a panic, with the guard playing the role of discovering hero, directing the women who fought the fire with buckets of water and dust. After the fire was out, the guard returned to duty, but decided to stand a bit further away from the door now, his hand on his weapon at all times, casting furtive glances at his prisoners.

After the fire, Davey felt a bit better, now that he had done something real to help himself and got away with it. But after a while, he began to pace the hut again, clasping his hand and pulling an imaginary trigger. "What the fuck," seemed to be the only words that he could find to adequately describe how he felt.

Nobody told him it was going to be like this. What was he going to tell his buddies, the folks that put up the cash, when he got back to the Old Blind Bull? *If* he made it back? That he saw some dude get cut up, because the guy had left with his gun and his girlfriend, after some drunk, lunatic leader gave her to him for sex? That he should have killed him maybe, or not?

This was all local stuff, he realized, no big international conspiracy to take everybody's guns away. Right now, he wished that there were such a conspiracy. As far as he was concerned, *let* them take Christmas' guns and knives too, so they could walk out of here and go home. Go home to Vicky Jane, to his Winnebago.

Davey looked out the opening. Still nothing going on. Every five minutes, he shuddered a bit, like a wet dog, hoping to shake off the weight of his unwanted memories. Like this Oliver dude, he should focus on getting out of there.

Throughout the day, they had talked a little, and it hadn't dawned on him until late in the conversation that *this* was the son of the man whose funeral he had read about, who had organized this Garden of Peace thing with the hot movie star. The guy, in fact, who had been the whole reason for him being here in the first place. Oliver had told him a few things about his father's life and death.

Turns out this wasn't a bad guy after all. Davey had thought that all these do-gooders were misguided folks, who were serving some crazy master plan, but the dad, Johan, from what his son had told him, seemed to have had his feet on the ground. Like helping farmers make money. That was the kind of stuff that they could use back home as well. They shared a laugh when Oliver explained the whole thistle story and how Johan had helped set up an industry around a totally useless product by playing on the despair of vain old men who would try anything to grow hair. Still, Davey wasn't entirely convinced that these GAPI folks didn't have another sinister and hidden motive, but so far, he hadn't seen any real evidence of that.

"Aren't they trying to establish some sort of world order, like what they call *stability* and set up their own courts and stuff?" Davey demanded.

"You serious? I'd say that even big and powerful governments can't keep things stable in their own backyard.

And an outfit like GAPI needs money from those governments to do the stuff they do *on behalf* of these governments. Hell, if they don't like what GAPI is doing, they simply stop giving them money, close the tap, and then they're dead in the water. I'm a banker, you know, and in my experience, if you want to find out what's happening you should follow the money."

"So, you tell me then, Oliver—where is the money going to?"

"Down the drain, in this case. Hold on. You hear that?"

"Shit, something is going on," Davey whispered after he heard the sounds of vehicles and people shouting.

Davey looked out the window to see more while Oliver checked the holes in the walls. A procession of official-looking men, some uniformed, some in civilian clothes, were entering the camp under escort from Christmas' fighters. They were walking toward the center of the camp where the night before Christmas had staged his macabre celebration.

"I know some of them, Davey."

Davey looked at Oliver with some surprise.

"One of them, the fat guy, is Colonel Neptune. He's military intelligence. The tall man walking in front of him behaves like his boss. Maybe it's Brigadier Grachev himself."

Oliver searched his memory for a clue to where he had seen this man before—a man with a fixed smile, who seemed to despise everything and everybody he saw. It would come to him.

"The guy in the white shirt and polished boots is Bruno. He was my father's boss. He runs the GAPI office back in the City by the Water, and with him is a guy I don't know. See him, the military type? And there you have Ibrahim, a friend of mine. Was a friend of my dad's too. Jesus, it's quite the delegation. They need to see me. Now."

Oliver got up and walked outside, ignoring the push by the angry guard. Davey followed in his wake.

"Hey, Ibrahim, we're here!"

Oliver waved and managed to get everybody's attention. They seemed relieved, rather than surprised, to see him, except for V-6, who emerged from the group of fighters with his weapon angrily pointed at Oliver.

He walked toward the hut, cocked his weapon, and issued a simple instruction in a low voice. "Get inside, stay, or I'll shoot you now."

Oliver and Davey thought it better not to argue with V-6 and went inside.

"You see? This was good. I bet you anything that we're at least part of the reason these people are here, and now they know we're alive and nearby. Do you think they saw the smoke?"

Oliver looked outside and saw Neptune's boss give instructions to Christmas' fighters. This was a man who was used to being in command and whose command should not be doubted. Through the murmur of the fighters setting chairs near Christmas' throne, Oliver could make out the word "excellency" a few times. Where was the last time he heard someone addressed by that title? The airport, when he arrived the first time. Yes, that was him, Grachev. He'd shared a flight with him. What was he doing here?

Christmas arrived at the meeting and took his throne. Oliver and Davey couldn't hear what was being discussed. Grachev did most of the talking. Bruno was sitting on the edge of his seat, clearly wanting to speak, but every time he started a sentence, Grachev raised his hand and cut him off.

When he was finally allowed to speak, he must've made a good point, because everybody but Christmas was nodding in approval. Bruno tapped the thigh of the military type next to him, who got up and walked toward the prisoner's hut.

"How are you two gentlemen doing? Healthy? In one piece?"

"We're good, thank you. Who are you?" Oliver asked of the man who eyed them up and down with a look that mixed concern with amusement. Oliver and Davey saw nothing to be amused about.

"Tom Jenkins. I handle security for GAPI. I knew your dad well, Oliver. He was a good guy. And what's your name, kid?"

"Davey."

"Well, Davey and Oliver, I don't know what the fuck you think you were doing here, but we're going to get you out sooner rather than later."

"What do you mean?" Davey asked anxiously. "I have this dude Prosper, who was coming to take me back. Are you now taking us back?"

"Yeah, Davey, but not right away. You're in the middle of a big game that was really none of your business, but now you're in the middle of it as Christmas' hostages—or guests, if that's what you prefer. You two ladies are what are stopping the army from coming in here and killing everybody. Christmas sent us a postcard, nice picture with the two of you and him in the middle, plus the message that he would kill you both if the army got any closer."

"Shit," Davey concluded.

"Deep shit," Tom countered. "So, you two stay here and behave. Don't make any more fires, if that was indeed you."

Davey and Oliver nodded in unison, trying to smile modestly.

"That was bloody helpful, by the way. Really pissed Christmas off too. So, I'm going to go back and confirm that you're OK, although I frankly believe that you are both fucking crazy. Oh, yes, and Oliver, Vashti says hello."

Oliver bowed his head and said nothing. Hearing Vashti's name somehow didn't make him feel better. It made him nauseous with a guilt and shame that he couldn't explain to himself. Tom was right, of course. He had been a fucking idiot. He hoped nobody had told his family about his predicament. Maybe he could get out of here before this came out and made everybody back home worry, perhaps over nothing.

"Oliver, you think we'll get of here? What do they want from us?"

"I think it's our lives in exchange for Christmas' freedom. That's what they want. His whole murderous outfit will disappear into the jungle once again, and we'll live happily ever after. Clever man, Christmas."

"How come?"

"My bet is that if he had just told the *army* he had taken us hostage, they would have come in anyway and killed everybody. And if there happened to be two foreigners as collateral damage, well, they could say that they didn't know and that we shouldn't have been here in the first place—our own bloody fault for walking in here like we did."

"So why didn't they do that? Just kill us with the rest?"

"Because he made it international by copying GAPI on the picture. These GAPI guys have a reputation to protect and, in a way, I'm here because of them. Long story, Dave, but I told you some of it, about my father. But the bottom line is that *now* the army knows full well that we're here and, at least in my case, knows *why* I'm here as well. And they know that GAPI knows I'm here. Killing me, and you, would cause all sorts of exposure and trouble that they don't want, mainly because it's bad for business. In a way, Christmas saved our lives and maybe his own by taking us hostage—you realize that?"

"I don't understand. What business you talking about?"

"You don't want to know, kid. Look, Tom is coming back. They're breaking up the meeting, it seems."

Tom walked up to, but stayed outside, the tent. "Why don't you two gentlemen come outside and stretch your legs a bit? They've called for a break, so I thought I'd keep you company for a bit."

This was a welcome offer, and both of them stepped outside. Oliver did a few stretching exercises—not that he felt that he needed it, but just to do something normal, something he would have done at home.

As he was doing his stretching, he asked Tom who the man in charge was.

"Grachev, real heavyweight. He runs half the country and most of its money. Military intelligence chief."

"Thought so. I heard about him. I can see Grachev talking to Christmas, just the two of them under the tree. Is that a good thing?"

"Could be. Ultimately, it's these two who decide, anyway. Bruno has nothing to say in this matter, but he came along because his headquarters told him to 'do his utmost to secure your release.' Not sure if he gives a fuck, though. He's really pissed off about the whole thing—first your father, now you."

"So, what do they want? What's the deal they're talking about?" Davey asked, while he scratched his arms.

"Simple. You walk, Christmas walks, and the army walks. Everybody walks. They're just haggling over how much luggage they'll take on the trip. Speaking of which..."

"Looks like it's heavy. What's in it—ammunition or something?" Davey was commenting on a small bag, like the kind used as cabin luggage, being brought up by a fighter to the two men talking under the tree.

"That would be gold, my young friend. About half a million, I'd say, from the way that guy is dragging the bag around. Price Christmas has to pay to be left alone and live. Grachev's personal fee," Tom said in a cynical tone. "Bastard. He always gets away like this," Tom concluded while looking at the ground, kicking an imaginary rock.

Grachev summoned a motorbike and had the bag fixed on the rear seat. He shook hands with Christmas and patted him on the shoulder. The meeting was over. Grachev turned away from Christmas and walked toward the three men in the hut, followed by Neptune, who had a hard time keeping up. Grachev stopped in front of the two foreigners and looked at them harshly.

"You are free. Now, go with Bruno, and never come back to this country again. Is that understood?"

"Yes, Sir," Davey stammered.

Oliver didn't respond. He couldn't promise he would never come back, not now.

Grachev looked him in the eyes and repeated himself.

"Is that understood, Oliver? I do not like repeating myself."

"Neither do I, Sir, but I will anyway. Who killed my father?"

"You have some balls talking to me like that."

"People tell me that if there's anyone who might know, it would be you, and I might not see you again after today. I had to ask. With all due respect, Sir."

"Forget it, son. I can't tell you, because I don't know. It's better if you let it go. Now get your stuff. We're leaving. We have a helicopter half an hour's drive from here. By the time it takes off, this camp will be gone."

Grachev turned around to a panting Neptune.

"Neptune," Grachev ordered. "Give the man his phone back, as promised, in the same state as before."

Neptune pulled Johan's smartphone out of a breast pocket. It was wet with perspiration but otherwise looked unscathed. He handed it to Oliver and explained that its battery was flat.

"You'll see it's working fine once you charge it. In fact, it was really helpful in pinning down Christmas' location and finding you guys. Couldn't have come here without the information on this thing. And then there was the smoke, of course."

Grachev looked at Neptune impatiently, turned around and walked toward a group of waiting motos, Neptune waddling behind him. The camp had turned into an ants' nest where everybody was collecting goods, clothes, pots and pans, weapons, and ammunition. They were lining up at the dark side of the village where the forest canopy hung over the dirt.

Davey could see some of the fighters cutting a path in the undergrowth. Christmas had disappeared from the scene altogether. Davey heard the motos revving their engines and hurried to take the rear seat of the nearest bike, so he would be sure of his place. He really needed to leave and never visit this shithole again.

Tom and Oliver walked together to the waiting motos. Oliver kept shaking his head.

"That was gutsy, Oliver," Tom said, putting his hand on Oliver's shoulder.

"It's all too fucking surreal, don't you think?" Oliver said emphatically. "I shouldn't be here; neither should you. We shouldn't be having this conversation. I should never have met Christmas or Grachev or poor Davey."

"Well, not sure if it's any consolation, brother, but I used to have this drill sergeant called Duck Bill, who had all these crazy expressions. He used to say that 'If it ain't surreal, it isn't happening,' and as far as I'm concerned, this applies right here, right now."

"That doesn't make any sense at all," Oliver said under his breath while he climbed on the bike.

It hit him later in the day, as he looked out through the open door of the helicopter and watched the shadow of the helicopter dance and jump over the hills and the trees a thousand feet below, that Duck Bill's paradox actually was dead on. He had been scared—still was, in this flying piece of junk. He had been horrified and excited and felt *relevant*—for a moment, at least. Or was that all in his head? He was loving taking the risks, even if his own life was at stake. All of that *was* happening—all at the same time in these crazy surreal places that he had never been to and would never be in again.

But he had never felt more alive.

# Part IV
# Christmas

# Chapter 43

# PHONECALLS

Bruno could not for the life of him believe that the journalist had been able to get all of this information. Everything had been kept under control. The whole hostage episode had not been made public or discussed since. The two foreigners had visited and then left Christmas on their own account, was the narrative, if anyone asked. Oliver had left the country—good riddance. The DSP had continued with greater emphasis on victim support, while still open to any former fighters who wished to come forward—in reality, a trickle of sick kids and old folks. With Christmas gone, everybody was now talking about arresting him and putting him away in some international prison. There were rumors that he was still around and would emerge one day in another bloody massacre. But for now, everything had begun to settle into the old rhythm of the times before Johan died. The headache had faded, he thought, and now this. Somebody had leaked this stuff.

He put the magazine down on his desk and swiveled his leather chair to look at his computer screen. No nasty e-mails yet, but they would come, likely with the offending article attached and the most egregious passages quoted, like this one:

*We wrote earlier in this magazine how GAPI was more interested in buying itself fancy cars than in solving the crisis caused by Christmas' massacres. Even though the latter threat seems to have abated after the personal intervention of senior military intelligence officers, it has now emerged that GAPI had, in fact, handed over the management of its flagship program to Christmas himself, through an ingenious scheme designed to dodge GAPI's own anticorruption rules. The scheme had been concocted by the recently murdered program manager of the famous Disarmament and Stabilization Program, who received cash from Christmas and used it to bribe officials and merchants to provide Christmas with benefits that were ultimately paid for by the international community. According to a credible source, senior leadership of GAPI in the City by the Water was fully aware of this practice and did nothing to stop it, and Mr. Bruno may even have encouraged it to revive a flagging program...*

Mentioned by name. He might as well be packing his bag now and start looking for vacancy announcements. Flora knocked on the door with a telephone in her hand.

"Bruno, it's Ambassador Zamorski. He says it's urgent."

Bruno took the call, to face the music, no doubt. Zamorski was telling him, with his utmost regret, that his country and several others were pulling their funds out of the program. We will, *of course*, remain fully committed to GAPI's objectives, but in the circumstances, it was hard to justify the expense to our taxpayers, you understand.

Bruno understood very well.

"Bruno, it's headquarters on the line. They say it's urgent."

Bruno could almost predict what they were going to say. *So* sorry to let you know at this delicate time, but you are being recalled to headquarters until further notice. The internal auditors were on their way, because you know, the donors want to have nothing to do with this business. Also, we're pulling the plug on the program, but we will declare it a moral victory since, in a way, it did help to get rid of

Christmas. Looking forward to seeing you over a coffee in San Francisco.

Bruno was not far off his guess. The only difference was that they didn't say anything about having a coffee. He hung up the phone when the next call came.

"Bruno, it's your wife on the line. She wants to talk to you."

Of course, she does, Bruno sighed. She always liked the glamour of having a husband who did *such* important and noble work overseas. She was going to have to come up with a different narrative.

"Tell her I'm in a meeting. Will call her back later, sorry."

# Chapter 44

## FIREBRANDS

Brigadier General Grachev looked out the windows of his spacious, wood-paneled office. For the moment, he didn't want to look at the maps on the opposing wall that showed the positions and movements of his enemies and assets. Nor did he want to look at the text of the article on his desk about GAPI's nefarious dealings with Christmas. He needed to think, and it helped him to look at the leaves on the trees outside slowly turning in the soft wind.

It was clear to him that Christmas was finished. The old man was very sick and would soon die. Grachev was no physician, but he had been around long enough to see what damage a life in the bush can do. Liver cirrhosis, hepatitis, HIV-AIDS, malaria—any combination, left untreated, would do him in. Economically, Christmas was dying too. The yield of the gold mine he had been operating was declining and would have been exhausted soon, leaving Christmas with no option but to move again or to survive through murder and pillage. Not acceptable, nor was what Christmas wanted, like rank, amnesty, uniform, health insurance, what have you. What was he thinking, this little sick man?

Grachev looked at his watch, his first gift to himself some five years ago. He smiled as he remembered the time when he bought it. It would have paid for food for a year for the entire village of his birth. Maybe it was time to get out of this business, go back to the village, be a chief and grandfather, do some farming, maybe.

Not yet, he said out loud to himself. He needed time to cover his tracks so he could retire peacefully, without having to look over his back. Like the whole Christmas thing. It had been profitable at first, but now he had to think of a transition. A controlled transition.

These two stupid foreigners had actually done him a favor, causing a mini-crisis that enabled him to make a deal that would get rid of Christmas and his followers without putting his own soldiers in harm's way. Good thing too, because his own soldiers had more to lose than Christmas' boys. Anyway, it wouldn't have been enough to kill Christmas, or worse, imprison him.

The problem was these young teenagers, born in the bush, had grown up with nothing but the violence and hateful ideology of their parents, seriously believing that Christmas spoke to God and that God was actually on their side. He had tried to talk to them directly once, but they wouldn't even look at him, while Christmas was standing in the background with a smug I-told-you-they-would-not-listen smile on his face. Their mothers were the same, if not worse. One of them had spit at him when he tried to explain that maybe they were not doing the right thing for their sons and daughters.

So, suppose you killed Christmas in combat. These kid fighters would go crazy under some crackpot new firebrand leader to honor the memory of their martyred leader and continue to spill innocent blood. The DSP had not worked to get these hard-core fighters out of the bush and into a job. Pity. Seemed like a good idea at first, until Mr. Johan started making side deals with Christmas. Maybe, Grachev thought, he should have dealt with Mr. Johan sooner. Control was everything. As far as the madman in the bush was concerned,

Christmas needed to go, but he would need his myth intact to be able to deal with the firebrands, so he could pick them up (or off) one by one later.

He turned toward the maps and spotted the marker where Christmas and his people were located, according to the latest intelligence. It was time. He adjusted the wristband of his watch and called his aide-de-camp.

"Lieutenant, get me V-6 on his satellite phone."

Grachev made a mental note to talk to his personnel officer. If V-6 played his cards right, he would be out of the bush and into a nice house with a car and a respectable uniform to wear. Mirage, too.

# Chapter 45

## EVERY DAY

The Old Blind Bull was packed. It was exactly one month after the memorable evening where Davey was sent off with a load of cash to go save the world from do-gooders. Not everyone of the original group of businessmen who did most of the fundraising had come back, but about half of them were there, including the boss, who was wearing the same hat that had held all the money they had collected. The man was actually quite pleased. Not a bad result for a practical joke, he thought, never could have imagined the kid would come this far. He had read on the web that the program that Davey had been sent out to stop had indeed been canceled, that the country director had been fired, sort of, and that the rebel movement with the crazy-name leader had kept its guns and moved on.

Not many other details were available, so they would have to hear it from Davey himself.

Davey himself dreaded the moment where he'd have to speak up and explain what he had done with the money. The buzz around town was that he was some sort of a hero, stopping a global conspiracy in its tracks. They said some journalists were going to show up at the bar as well. He would be famous, with his photo in *Survival Magazine*. But if it were up to him, he would just hide here or get out of town—go camping or something.

Uncle Bob had already done enough bragging to really raise people's expectations sky high. He'd been really proud of him, he said, and had told his mom and dad too. They both said, independently, that they would make an exception to their vow never to see each other again. They too would be at the Old Blind Bull, sitting at opposite ends of the bar, probably, with Uncle Bob somewhere in the middle to make sure they didn't kill each other.

Uncle Bob had welcomed him with an extra box of ammo, guessing that he'd want to make up for lost time at the range with his Q13, but Davey ignored it. He hadn't picked up his weapon or even looked at it since he got back. He couldn't sleep at night and then slept late every day, barely did any work, and drank way too much without talking to anyone.

He couldn't come up with any story that would help him today. On the plane back, between flashbacks of the horror he had witnessed, he thought about it long and hard, but if he had to be honest with himself, he couldn't show any proof that there had been some evil plot to take his or Uncle Bob's guns away. He remembered what Oliver had told him about following the money. Turned out that Oliver was right. That disarmament program fell apart after the big funders pulled out. So that was where the real money and the power was, beyond anyone's reach, Davey concluded, knowing that he might have guessed that from the start.

He also remembered what this old Prosper dude had told him about deprived people and, even if he did not quite understand what Prosper meant, he had the feeling that these folks over there could really use some stability, if that meant they could live like him in this country right here, with good cops and stuff. As for the guns, if anything, they should've taken Christmas' knives and machetes away as well, he realized with a shudder.

Davey had hoped that the memory of the execution he had been asked to perform and then watch would fade away with distance and time, but the opposite was true. The less his surroundings resembled anything he saw while he was away in the jungle, the more he had to think about it. Nothing made sense to him anymore. He thought about calling Oliver to talk, but wasn't sure what to say to him, either, if he could find his number to begin with.

VJ had been rather nice to him and tried to start a conversation when he got back, but he had ignored her too, since he didn't know what to say.

She had the feeling he was far away, like he had physically crossed the ocean to come back home, but had left his mind behind over there. Some jokers in town were saying that Davey never actually went over there, but instead spent a week at an exclusive resort, getting drunk on the beach every day and *that* was why he wasn't saying anything.

"Is he coming or what?" the businessman with the hat said out loud to no one in particular after several rounds of drinks had come and gone. "Somebody go get him, please."

Nobody moved. VJ looked at Uncle Bob, then at Davey's dad and mom, but they were too busy talking to notice anything—all big smiles, gulps of beer, and loud laughs.

"I'll go. Be just a minute."

She took off her apron, much to the bar owner's displeasure, because this was prime moneymaking time, and he needed every pair of hands on deck. She threw the apron at him and left the bar to walk the few hundred yards to Davey's RV. She had to step over a dozen empty beer cans and bottles of liquor before she could knock on the door.

"Davey, Honey, you there?"

She was well aware of Davey's feelings for her, at least from before he left, and she thought adding a touch of endearment might help him get out the door.

"It's Vicky Jane. It's time for your big meeting."

"Go away. Tell them to fuck off," came an angry shout from inside the RV.

"You can't do that, Davey. They're all waiting. The businessmen, the whole town—even your folks have come. They all think you did a great job over there."

"What the fuck do they know?"

VJ pushed against the door. It was unlocked, and she stepped inside. Davey was lying on the bed, with bare feet, clasping his hands as if he were holding a weapon, pointing it at VJ. His gun trophies were laying on the floor of the kitchenette, one dented from the impact on some sharp corner.

"What the fuck do they know?" he sputtered once again through gritted teeth.

"They don't, Sweetie. You need to come and tell them; that's why. You're just being nervous, aren't you?"

She sat next to him on the bed and put her hand on his knee. "It's OK now. Let's go together; what do you say?"

Maybe, he thought, he should just go tell them how his own bragging and their stupid joke took him to that hellhole and back. He knew they were waiting and that he owed these folks. It was their money. But this was *his* fucking life. Maybe he should tell them everything and then get the fuck out of this town. He took a deep breath and wiped away a tear.

"I should come, right?"

"Yeah, Baby, you really should. Shall we go, then? Go put some boots on."

The walk from his RV to the Old Blind Bull seemed long. He kept saying to himself that he was going to keep it together, tell them what a great thing he did, while in reality he had done nothing except fuck a girl, watch an execution, and be taken hostage. He'd lie about it, keep it together, and leave as soon as he could. You can do it, Baby, VJ kept telling him. If she thinks I can, then maybe I can and will keep it together. Here we go, he thought, as he opened the door.

The bar exploded in a roar of hollers, cheers, and applause. Davey walked on with a fixed grin on his face, receiving pats on the shoulder, punches to his forearm, and hands rubbing his hair. Beers were extended to him from all directions.

"Here he is, the man of the hour, Daveeeeeeyyyyyyy!" the man in the hat shouted when the roar had died down, bringing a new round of noise and applause.

"Now, let's hear it from the man himself. Davey, tell us what you did over there to stop this *in-ter-na-tion-al con-spi-ra-cy* to take our guns away, dead in its tracks? Without firing a shot too! Be quiet, everybody! Davey, come stand up on this chair here."

Davey stood up on the chair and looked around.

"Hi, Mom. Hi, Pop."

They waved back at him.

He saw a few strangers holding out what looked like a thick cell phone. Must be those journalists. Fuck.

"Hi, everybody. Well, it's good to be back." He looked around to see nothing but expectant faces. The next sentence didn't come to him, so he looked around some more.

"What was it like over there, Davey?"

"Well, slow traffic and terrible food, that much I can say for sure," he replied. The laughter quickly died out to make way for an awkward silence and a cloud of anticipation. Do it, Davey, he said to himself. Do it.

"To be honest, guys, it wasn't me who brought down the disarmament program. They did it themselves. They were taking money from the bad guys, and it came out, so the money stopped. I had nothing to do with it. It was the money."

"Well, you must have done something over there? Don't be modest, Davey!"

"I did go to see the folks who were running that program, called GAPI, and they were fucking clueless."

Applause. "Damn right they are," somebody yelled.

"What I mean is that they are as clueless as you folks here are."

Silence and puzzled looks. Davey dug deep and managed to find the courage and the words to continue.

"Look, at first I thought there was a conspiracy and that 'stability' was really a code word for 'world government' and some stupid  foreigners telling us what to do. But these people were just trying to solve a local problem that nobody, nobody here would understand, *nobody*, to get rid of a really bad guy who was using his fighters to..."

Davey stopped talking. He felt his stomach rising to his throat and tears welling behind his eyes.

"He..."

People were now looking at him, staring at him, some with concern, others puzzled. Davey could not stop himself. He got down from the chair, sat down alone, put his hands to his face, and cried. He cried like he promised himself he would never cry again after every time, every day, he had cried since he got back from the bush. The man in the hat walked up to him and put his hand on his shoulder.

"It's OK, son. It must have been a wild trip for you. Take your time, take your time." He looked over his shoulders to his buddies and shook his head.

His mother and VJ were making their way to see him through the crowd, which had started buzzing again slowly.

VJ knelt on the floor and hugged him tight. "Poor baby. Let it go, Baby."

Davey's mother bent over to stroke his hair. "What happened, Darling? Are you OK?"

"I want to get out of this place and never come back."

# Chapter 46

## BIG BAD MONKEY

Oliver leaned back and took in the narrow landscape of his desk at the bank. The forms in his desk organizer were still in the same place. Evenly sharpened pencils stuck out of a metal cylinder with the bank's logo on it. Everything was laid out at straight angles—his business cards, his pens, his cell phone—like a Mondrian painting, except for the bright colors. His supervisor kept looking at him, as if to make sure that he wouldn't do anything unpredictable again, like taking off on a very long vacation to a distant country and coming back with a load of cash for which he had no real explanation. He needn't worry, Oliver thought. He had enjoyed the quiet and predictability that helped him get over the hangover from his adventures in the bush. He had learned nothing about the murder, since everybody and nobody could be a suspect. He knew a little more about Dad than before, not all of it good, and he had decided to keep it to himself. If Dad had not considered it necessary to tell Mom, why should he?

He had learned something about himself too. For example, how much he had *liked* it—the absurdity, the unpredictability, the depth of truth—or rather, the layers of bullshit everybody was spreading over the truth. This place here, this bank, was all too clean, too *proper*. It seemed to him to be superficial and so vulnerable at the same time. Tomorrow, the police could barge in and arrest his boss or himself for whatever reason, could they not? One wrong transaction, one wrong word to the wrong person at the right time, and lawsuits would start flying, if not bullets. He looked at the portrait of his family on the corner of his desk. His kids had been very affectionate upon his return and asked him if he would go away again soon. No, he wouldn't.

Mary was not that easily answered. She had been nervous and passive, looking at him with question marks in her eyes. She must have somehow sensed that something had happened, that something had changed. They had made love the first night, but it was awkward and more comforting, at least to him, than passionate. He had no idea how she felt about it. Maybe she was waiting for him to start talking, but he might never do that. Maybe, over time the tedious comfort of suburban life would slowly cocoon the secret knot in his heart.

He opened his e-mail. He needed to catch up on his work. There was a raft of new policies, new procedures, interest rates, oversight mechanisms, promotions, and colleagues going on retirement. He got halfway and took a deep breath. He looked at his phone to see if there was anything on his private e-mail, which he couldn't get through the bank's network.

There was an e-mail from Vashti, sent a few hours earlier. He hesitated before opening it. He looked around to see what his colleagues were up to, but they were all too busy to notice him look at his phone.

To:      Oliver@mail.com
From:    Vashti@Inherent.org
Subject: Things over here

Hello my dear,

Things got really boring since you left here in a rush.

I don't know if your mere presence was enough to stir things up, but once you were gone, everything came apart. The DSP was cancelled, including my own very successful program for victims. Bruno basically got fired. He left kicking and screaming, which I did not know he was capable of, blaming your father and my good friend Johan for everything, of course. Nobody has clean hands around here, as you well know, my darling banker, but to blame Johan for everything is going too far.

Donors have pulled out, expatriates are leaving, the Floating Cloud is about to go bankrupt, and there is absolutely no one left to flirt with. Maybe it's my punishment for talking to that journalist. On the other hand, the police on the street are getting more obnoxious and downright dangerous. So, I'm leaving. More about that later.

I sold whatever I could from your Dad's apartment, as you asked, but it was kind of hard, like I was selling parts of him, you know what I mean? I would like to wire you the money from the sales. Can you let me know where to send it? The rest of the stuff I gave to Henri and his nephew, Joseph. I think that's what Johan would have wanted, but it wasn't much. They are good people.

It's bizarre, isn't it? We set out to get rid of Christmas, and it happened, but I guess not through our well-intentioned work. His group has all but disappeared. There are occasional sightings, but otherwise nothing. The army is claiming all the credit, but I'm not sure this bunch of perennial drunks had much to do with it.

The thing is, I miss your father. I miss my brother in arms. We have been together in so many missions, disagreed so pleasantly about so many things. I think he got a little off the rails this time because he was getting to a point where it was a promotion or being stuck forever in this place. The DSP looked like his ticket out of here, big money, big visibility. GAPI likes those kinds of things.

Never mind that, I wanted to ask you something. Come with me. I'm setting up a new shop in a country of war and famine, lots of work, good donor money, everybody wants to be there, and I could really use a moneyman with balls, which I know you have. What do you say?

Affectionately yours,

V.

Oliver read it twice and put away his phone. Vashti was being very self-centered, he supposed, not giving a shit whether he had a wife, kids, a house, and a mortgage. He inhaled through his nose as if to catch any whiff of her perfume that might have traveled with that message. He closed his eyes and without much of an effort could see the tiny hairs on the skin of her arms. Tantalizing, but no.

No.

He would have to write her back when he got home. Wait for Mary to give the kids a bath, so he could type a quick response. For one thing, he didn't want to substitute for Dad.

That evening, once the kids were in their bath and enjoying it, judging from the splashing noises that came from upstairs, he opened his laptop and started typing his reply.

To:        Vashti@Inherent.org
From:    Oliver@mail.com
Subject:  Re: Things over here

Hi Vashti,

Thanks for your message. Let me first wish you luck in your new endeavor. You will do well, and those people over there could really use a compassionate person like you. I won't join you, though, although I appreciate the offer. Sorry, but that would be a life too remote from where I am.

Thanks for selling the stuff, really appreciate it. Keep the money or, better, put it to work for the best cause. You will know how.

Yes, I miss him too, and it will take time to let him go and let whatever may have happened to him go. Maybe I never will.

Warmest regards,

Oliver

A nice response, but cold enough to make sure she understood she couldn't count on him. He looked at it again, changed "Warmest regards" to "All the best," then hit *send*, closed his laptop, and ran upstairs in his best gorilla imitation, making as much noise as possible, banging the walls and sniffing loudly. The kids heard him coming and squealed in anxious delight, since Daddy hadn't put on that little jungle routine in such a long time. He stood up on the landing, beat his chest, and growled:

"Who's afraid of the big bad monkey?"

"I am," Mary said, crying.

# Chapter 47

## JOHN CABRERO

V-6 looked down at his boss lying on the bed. As usual, Christmas had retired to his hut after telling everyone that he was going to pray and speak to God. V-6 knew that this might have been true in the past, but now it was a lie to mask the fact that the boss was very sick and just needed to rest. He looked to see if the door was closed and whether the guard outside was listening. He had given orders not to be disturbed.

"You know you are not going to live much longer, Boss?"

Christmas opened his eyes and spoke slowly, his breathing raspy, but his tone defiant.

"Nonsense. I'll continue the struggle I was called to lead! It's my mission, and I will fulfill it."

"Isn't it time, Boss—time to stop hiding and killing? We have suffered long enough. We're killing our own sons and daughters. Everybody is sick."

"Enough."

"Look at yourself. You are dying. What if you are dead, then what? You think your people, our people, will be better off than before?"

"When we get to our land, they will!"

"You are a fool, John Cabrero."

"What?"

"An idiot and a damn fool."

Christmas struggled to sit up straight. He was uncomfortable looking up at V-6's muscular chest. He needed to look him in the eye, especially after those treasonous words.

"You call me an idiot and a fool? How dare you call me by my real name? I'm your leader!"

"Leading us to what? Malaria? Leprosy? Prison?"

"To the land that God promised us. I was *chosen* to lead us there, lead *you* there too. You will be my vice-president, remember?"

"You are a fool. You have always been a fool. I'll tell you what happens if we get to our land tomorrow. You and I and Mirage will be thrown in jail for sure, maybe shot, and our people will have nothing. Our kids cannot read and write. We will have no land to farm, nothing. For our people, the best thing would have been to do Johan's thing—to get jobs, get some dignity here, in this land, where we are, give up our guns, remember what he said. But you were only concerned with your own dignity, weren't you, John? Your own status and wealth."

"Where does this come from, my supposedly loyal follower? Who have you been talking to?"

"Not important. What matters is what I believe."

"I tell you what matters. What matters is what these people outside believe, and they believe in *me*."

"And they will continue believing in you, trust me. But tell me, I need to know, is there absolutely no way you will indeed lead us out of here, not to the promised land, but to some land where our sons and daughters will have some future, out of the bush, a real future?"

"What are you talking about? No, of course not. I may die before I get there, but lead us to our land I will. Now, go away, I need to pray and rest before our weekly sermon. And you better think about what you believe, or I will have you shot."

Christmas lay down again and closed his eyes.

"It's time then," V-6 said.

He took out a pair of surgical gloves from his vest and put them on. He reached for the single round of Q13 ammunition that was standing up straight among the other souvenirs and tokens on the shelf against the wall. It was the same round Cabrero had offered the young foreigner that day to kill V-6's younger brother.

He clamped Cabrero's jaw in his left hand and forced his mouth to open. Before Cabrero could make any noise, he jammed the round into the open, red, inflamed throat, which looked like a rotting wound already, pushing it deeper with his thumb. He closed the mouth and nostrils and watched his boss die. His bulging yellow eyes looked up at V-6 in despair, agony, and surprise.

V-6 let his arms drop to his side. He felt nothing. He had lived in awe of Christmas for all his life, but now, as he was looking down on a dead man who had been a corpse long before he was dead, V-6 wondered what that awe was really based on. It wasn't strength or courage. The boss always let others do the risky work because he was too important to the tribe. Fear, yes. They all feared him, because he could reward you or kill you with the same arrogant ease. That was finished now. Done. John Cabrero was dead. But Christmas had to bring his people one more gift. He had to live a little longer.

V-6 closed John's eyes and mouth, took off his gloves and sat down next to the corpse, which seemed to have shrunk after its heart stopped beating. He felt tired now, but there was still more to be done. It would be time soon for the weekly sermon, and he had to rehearse what he was going to say. It had better work, or they would all rise against him. He didn't have a way with words like Cabrero, who had been a schoolteacher, after all.

When the time came, he opened the door and asked the guard to sound the signal for the weekly sermon and asked to be told when all had gathered. The crowd looked at V-6 with apprehension when it was him, not Christmas, who stepped up to speak to them. Mirage tried to catch his attention, throwing him question marks with his eyes. V-6 had decided against bringing Mirage in, on Grachev's advice. It was too big a risk, so he ignored his calls for attention.

"Let us pray," V-6 began. "Let us pray for our own souls and for the soul of Captain Christmas."

He clasped his hands and looked down at the ground and immediately went into his prayer, ignoring the gasps and murmurs that erupted from the crowd.

"Dear Lord, please be our guide in the journey we're about to undertake, a journey that will lead us to a better life, in our land or this land. Help our kids grow up, tell our sons to be farmers, let our daughters find happiness, and we will give our thanks to you. Amen."

"Christmas is dead," V-6 shouted over the whispered "amens" of the crowd. "He asked me to give you his last message to his people."

He paused. A woman let out a wail, and a toddler started to cry. But most members of the tribe just looked at V-6 in disbelief.

"John Cabrero is dead," he said softly. "He died just now in his hut after he prayed and spoke to me. He called me to tell me what he had seen in his last prayer. He had seen his own death come, today. Listen to me. He said a magic bullet would kill him, since no ordinary bullet or disease could. He spoke to me, and then he died, quietly and suddenly, I don't know how. May God rest his soul."

V-6 looked at Mirage, who hadn't moved and who was staring at him with an empty gaze.

"I don't believe it. I don't believe it," cried one of the younger fighters. "It isn't true. Where is he? Is that his real name?"

"You, you, you, and you. Go over to his hut, and bring him here, on his bed."

The stunned silence of the first minutes had made way for an anguished whispering while the tribe waited for the return of the four fighters with the body of their leader, waited to see if it was true—if indeed the engine of their lives had been taken from them.

It was true, of course. The four fighters struggled to move the bed with the body to the middle of the crowd, but others jumped up to help. Soon, everybody seemed to be pulled in by the magnetism of their leader's corpse. The whispering had now turned into cries and wailing, shouts of anger and denial. One woman who had been sharing his bed recently wrestled her way to the body and took his head in her hands and kissed him on the pale mouth in a tender embrace. The mouth fell open, and the woman fell back from the bed into the weight of bodies behind her, scrambling to put distance between herself and the death bed.

She pointed at the open mouth and started to scream hysterically. Others looked into the mouth to see what she had seen, and they too fell back. V-6 stepped in front of the bed and summoned all to sit down and be quiet. They obeyed him for the first part, but those who had seen what the woman saw were accosted by those who had not seen it to know what had happened. The words moved throughout the gathering like a glass jar of marbles breaking on a hard marble floor, but ultimately, some quiet returned.

Mirage had moved in next to V-6. He looked into Christmas' mouth and raised his arms.

"A bullet, a magic bullet. It's true. What enemy has such powers to kill our leader without firing a shot?"

V-6 looked at Mirage, his brother in arms, for any signs on his face that might give away his state of mind, but couldn't see any. He turned to the crowd again.

"I fear that such bullets may also find *us* soon, unless we do what our leader, our dead leader—and yes, his real name is John Cabrero—has asked us to do, as he told me after his last prayer. This is a sign we must obey."

"So, what did he say? What was it? What?" shouted several people at the same time.

V-6 put up his hands and continued. "John said that after he died his body should be burned with the magical bullet that killed him. He asked me that he wanted to be remembered as John, as a simple man with a plan for his people that did not work. God told him that he had other plans for his people, that they would no longer be his people, but God's children. He told me that you should all leave here and a find a piece of land of your own, anywhere, and live in peace. Go. That's what he said. Take your weapons, or leave them here. But go. He said that after him there should be no leader, because the magic bullets would kill that leader too. I refused to believe him at first, but he was very convincing. I have always obeyed him, and I will do so now. We should burn his body now and prepare to leave."

One young soldier stood up and raised his weapon. "I will fight to the death for our land and our leader."

Several others got up too and shouted approval. Women started shaking their heads; some mothers picked up their young children and went back to their huts. A few of the older men started to raise their hands, asking to be heard, looking to be recognized by either V6 or Mirage.

Mirage pulled out his pistol and looked at it, thinking about firing in the air, but decided against it. It did help, however, to quiet the crowd.

"I don't know. Maybe we should listen to our elders," he said, pointing at the oldest among them. The old man pushed himself up and spoke, looking directly at the young fighters.

"You young men want to fight to the death? Look at yourselves. All young and eager, but let me tell you something. You are already dead, because you have not lived. I remember how it was before Cabrero became Christmas, and it was better. I can say that now. It was better. We had a life, and we lived. A little house, my wife—she died long ago—a bit of land, a job, some money. We had fun, and we lived. It was a little life, but we lived. What have you done to live? Kill and kill again in the name of Christmas? I say V-6 is right. It's time to stop. I'm tired."

He sat down, and everybody started to talk at once. The discipline that had once characterized these meetings had gone completely. Heated discussions sprung up between old and young, men and women, the tired and the agitated. V-6 and Mirage looked at each other, and both decided that there was really nothing to be said. There was a job to be done. They went out to the edge of the camp and collected sticks and branches. They took firewood from underneath the waiting cooking pots and got help from a few who realized what they were doing.

They went back to the death bed and put the firewood underneath. Mirage went into one the nearby huts and came back with a can of cooking oil, one of the items in the DSP citizen kit that Johan had struggled so hard to put together, emptied the can over the pyre and over Cabrero's body. V-6 brought a box of matches and set the whole thing on fire. The faint whoosh and crackle of the flames brought everyone to silence. Some just watched it burn. Others brought more wood. The fire started to roar and the heat caused everybody to step back. After a while, the round in Cabrero's throat went off with a muffled crack, as if to kill him again after he was dead, just to make sure. The sound served as an exclamation mark, a clear and definitive sign that this journey was over.

Mirage stepped back from the fire and made his way to Cabrero's hut unseen. He found the former leader's satellite phone that had been off limits to everybody but Christmas and dialed the programmed number, as agreed.

"General Grachev? It's done, Sir."

## THE END

## ABOUT THE AUTHOR:

Adriaan Verheul worked as an academic with the Dutch navy, as a United Nations human rights officer and peacekeeper, World Bank official, and independent foreign affairs consultant. His work took him to conflict and disaster zones on four continents. Somehow, he ended up in the business of demobilizing rebels and soldiers after civil war. He lives in Northern Virginia.

www.ingramcontent.com/pod-product-compliance
Lightning Source LLC
Chambersburg PA
CBHW072106020726
47501CB00003B/735